W...
puppi...   ...as?

Three Christmas romances with
cute, adorable canines!

A Puppy
FOR
Christmas

Carole MORTIMER

Myrna Mackenzie   *Nikki* Logan

Charming, heartwarming stories for
the holidays by bestselling and beloved authors

CAROLE MORTIMER

was born in England, the youngest of three children. She began writing in 1978, and has now written more than one hundred and fifty books for Harlequin. Carole has six sons: Matthew, Joshua, Timothy, Michael, David and Peter. She says, "I'm happily married to Peter senior; we're best friends, as well as lovers, which is probably the best recipe for a successful relationship. We live in a lovely part of England."

MYRNA MACKENZIE

grew up not having a clue what she wanted to be (she hadn't been born a princess, the one job she thought she might like because of the steady flow of pretty dresses and crowns), but she knew that she loved stories and happy endings, so falling into life as a romance writer was pretty much inevitable. An award-winning author, with over thirty-five novels written, Myrna was born in a small town in Missouri, grew up just outside Chicago and now divides her time between two lakes in Chicago and Wisconsin, both very different and both very beautiful. She adores the internet, loves coffee, hiking, attempting gardening (without much success), cooking and knitting.

Readers can visit Myrna online at www.myrnamackenzie.com, or write to her at P.O. Box 225, La Grange, IL 60525, USA.

NIKKI LOGAN

lives next to a string of protected wetlands in Western Australia, with her partner and a menagerie of furred, feathered and scaly mates. She studied film and theater at university, and worked for years in advertising and film distribution before finally settling down in the wildlife industry. Her romance with nature goes way back, and she considers her life charmed, given she works with wildlife by day and writes fiction by night—the perfect way to combine her two loves. Nikki believes that the passion and risk of falling in love are perfectly mirrored in the danger and beauty of wild places. Visit her online at www.nikkilogan.com.

Carole MORTIMER

Myrna Mackenzie   *Nikki* Logan

A Puppy
FOR
Christmas

HARLEQUIN® ANTHOLOGY

ISBN-13: 978-0-373-83780-9

A PUPPY FOR CHRISTMAS

Copyright © 2013 by Harlequin Books S.A.

Recycling programs for this product may not exist in your area.

The publisher acknowledges the copyright holders of the individual works as follows:

ON THE SECRETARY'S CHRISTMAS LIST
Copyright © 2012 by Carole Mortimer

THE SOLDIER, THE PUPPY AND ME
Copyright © 2012 by Myrna Topol

THE PATTER OF PAWS AT CHRISTMAS
Copyright © 2012 by Nikki Logan

Printed in U.S.A.

TM www.Harlequin.com

CONTENTS

To everyone who loves Christmas—
and puppies—as much as I do!

ON THE SECRETARY'S CHRISTMAS LIST

Carole Mortimer

Dear Reader,

It's that time of year again!

And what better way to celebrate the love of the season than a love story between a heroine who has been deeply hurt by the past and a hero who realizes she's the only present he wants under his Christmas tree? Throw a gorgeously endearing little boy and an endearing puppy into the mix, and you have the recipe for a perfect Christmas.

A happy and perfect Christmas to you all!

Carole Mortimer

CHAPTER ONE

'OUR APPOINTMENT WAS for this afternoon, Roger. Not tomorrow, not next week, but today!'

Bree looked up in alarm the moment her employer entered her office, growling into his mobile phone. Wincing, she realised he had to be talking to his two o'clock appointment today, Roger Tyler, a rock star who had become a legend in his own lifetime.

'I don't give a—'

Jerome Jackson Beaumont broke off mid-sentence, checking himself as he realised Bree was an unwilling listener.

'I don't give a—a flying monkey what's "come up", Roger. You asked—no, *begged* me to do the photo shoot for your next album, so you either get yourself over here this afternoon or forget the whole damn thing!' He listened to the other man's response for about two seconds before interrupting him. 'You have five minutes, Roger, to cancel your date this afternoon with whatever bimbo has caught your attention this time, before ringing me back to say you'll be here at two this afternoon after all!'

He flipped the mobile phone across the desk to Bree who, after almost a year of practice, caught it neatly in the palm of her hand, checking that Jackson had indeed ended the call—something he had a habit of forgetting to do, often exposing the unfortunate caller to the expletive-filled aftermath, before giving him a re-proving glance.

She remembered when she'd first met him. 'Just call me Jackson,' he had ordered Bree when she'd come to work for him a year ago. 'Not Jerome, never, ever Beau or Mr Beaumont, but Jackson.'

'I really wish you would let me deal with all the in-coming calls.' She had unfortunately missed this partic-ular call because of a two-minute visit to the bathroom!

Jackson gave an unrepentant grin as he leaned against the side of her desk. 'I can't imagine why!'

And really neither could Bree; this man seemed to be able to insult people, be rude to them, even totally ignore them and still they came back for more!

Because he was Jerome Jackson Beaumont, world-renowned photographer, whose work hung on the walls of royal palaces as well as in galleries all over the world. What was a little rudeness, the odd insult, a snub or two, when in the end you could own an original Jerome Jackson Beaumont?

The way he looked didn't do him any harm either—especially where women were concerned. Six feet two inches of lean, tanned muscle, emphasised by the fit-ted T-shirts and denims he habitually wore—a blue T-shirt today, and black jeans—with eyes as clear and blue as the sky on a cloudless summer's day, strong, high cheekbones, a sharp blade of a nose, and a mouth that was so wickedly sensual it should have a warning label attached to it.

As if that wasn't enough Jackson had long silky hair that reached almost to his shoulders in a raggedly wind-swept style, and it was the colour of golden honey and molasses—neither gold nor brown but somewhere in between—the same burnt-sugar colour that women paid hundreds of pounds to achieve in exclusive salons all around the world!

Within minutes of meeting Jackson for the first time Bree had realised he was exactly as everyone described. Unique. A perfectionist. And utterly brilliant. He was also, she had registered in those same few minutes, totally and utterly impossible!

She had heard the rumours, of course—who *hadn't* read about the eccentricities of Jerome Jackson Beaumont in the gossip columns of every newspaper? The employment agency had warned her too, telling her of the three other assistants they had sent to him in the previous month, two of whom had returned as gibbering emotional wrecks, and the third of whom had not come back at all.

Bree had taken those warnings in her stride. The job not only paid well, but also offered immediate rent-free occupation of the self-contained basement flat beneath the London mansion where Jerome Jackson Beaumont lived and worked. For Bree, who had been homeless at the time, the apartment had provided her with more than enough incentive to make up her own mind about her notorious new boss.

Yes, Bree had very quickly discovered Jerome Jackson Beaumont to be every bit as arrogant and impossible to work with as people had warned. With one exception.

His six-year-old son, Daniel.

Considering Jackson had never been married, Danny's mother remained something of a mystery. A mystery Jackson had repeatedly refused to shed light on when questioned by members of the press about the one-year-old son he had brought to live with him five years ago.

As the woman was obviously no longer present in either Jackson's or Danny's life, her identity didn't affect Bree on a day-to-day basis. That didn't mean Bree didn't feel a certain curiosity about her—mainly because Bree wondered how any woman could have just handed her son over to his father like that. Especially when that father was the charismatic Jerome Jackson Beaumont!

Danny was tall for his age, with hair of corn-gold, eyes the same clear blue as his father's, and a sweetly mischievous disposition. And he was, without a doubt, his father's one saving grace.

Bree had fallen in love with him on the very first day she'd come to work at Beaumont House.

The son, not the father.

She had already paid—and paid dearly—for loving the wrong man, and had no intention of repeating that painful experience!

This had turned out to be a wise decision, considering there had been legions of women flitting in and then quickly out of Jackson's life over the past year. Redheads, blondes, brunettes, and every shade in between—all of them tall and beautiful.

Bree knew there was no danger of Jackson ever seeing her as anything more than his capable assistant: she was only a little over five feet tall, passably pretty rather than beautiful, and had a slender figure that men found all too easy to dismiss—something Bree knew only too well after her engagement had come to a traumatic end just over a year ago.

Just over a year ago…?

Oh, God! What was the date? Surely it couldn't be—?

It was, Bree realised heavily, the colour draining from her cheeks.

'You aren't really concerned about my conversation with Roger Tyler, are you?' Jackson frowned down at his assistant as he noticed her face growing paler.

Bree blinked before looking up at him.

'Not if you aren't, no,' she dismissed in her usual brisk, no-nonsense tone.

Jackson was always taken by surprise by Bree's long dark lashes and smoky-grey eyes: remarkable eyes in an otherwise unremarkable face. Bree had a smooth brow, with a smattering of freckles on her cheeks and over the bridge of her nose, and a mouth that was usually thinned in disapproval above a small but determined chin. Her hair was the rich blue-black of ebony, but as it was always scraped back and secured with a clasp on the crown of her head even after a year Jackson had no idea as to its length.

He didn't want to know either. Jackson had made a point of never taking a personal interest in any of the women who had been his assistants over the years— much to the annoyance of some, he acknowledged ruefully.

But not Bree. At twenty-six years of age, Sabrina Jones was cool, calm and totally unflappable. From the beginning she had made it absolutely clear that she had no personal interest in him either. Which was probably the reason they had lived and worked together so harmoniously for almost a year now. Put just one little spark of sexual intent or innuendo into that mix and the whole thing would fall apart. And as Bree was the best personal assistant Jackson had ever had, as well as being only too happy to sit with Danny in the evenings if Jackson wanted to go out, he had no intention of stepping over that line. Even if that steady calmness of hers did occasionally tempt him to do something to shake her out of her cool complacency!

'I wouldn't waste my time worrying about a man like Tyler,' Jackson replied drily, standing up to snag his leather jacket from the peg on the wall on his way to the door.

'Where are you going?' Bree demanded as he shrugged into the jacket.

Jackson straightened. 'Out.'

'What about your appointment with Mr Tyler?'

He raised a mocking brow. 'What about it?'

'He's due at the studio in just over an hour,' she pointed out impatiently.

Jackson gave an indifferent shrug. 'When he phones back in a couple of minutes, reschedule him for some time after Christmas.'

'But you just told him to cancel his other engagement so that he could make this afternoon's appointment with you,' Bree pressed.

Jackson grinned unabashedly. 'Sometimes greatness needs reminding that not everyone is here to jump at its beck and call.'

Bree breathed deeply. 'I believe that statement could just as easily apply to you!'

He gave it some thought. 'You're right, it could.' He finally nodded in agreement.

'And?'

'And I'm flattered that you think I'm great, Bree,' he drawled mockingly.

Bree's eyes narrowed. 'Is it my imagination, or are you actually more impossible than usual this morning?'

Jackson grimaced. 'I probably am,' he admitted ruefully. 'Danny and I called on my mother last night to deliver her Christmas presents before she leaves for her Caribbean cruise later today.'

'Oh.' Bree's brow cleared as understanding dawned on her: Jackson and his widowed mother, Clarissa Beaumont, had a way of rubbing each other up the wrong way.

Tall, blonde-haired and blue-eyed, Clarissa was a classical beauty who'd had cosmetic surgery in the past, and now received regular Botox injections. As a consequence Clarissa looked no older now than she had when the photographs in Jackson's study had been taken— when he and his sister, Jocelyn, were small children. Jocelyn had died several years before Bree came to work for Jackson, so she had never met her, but if Jocelyn were still alive she and her mother could probably have passed for sisters!

'Exactly.' Jackson grimaced. 'For some reason Danny's present wasn't ready last night, so she's calling round with it on her way to the airport in...' he looked down at the slim gold watch around his wrist '...oh, half an hour or so.'

'Which is precisely the reason you've decided to go out,' Bree concluded drily.

'Which is *definitely* the reason I'm going out.' Jackson looked completely unperturbed by her astuteness. 'Seeing my delightful mother twice in as many days is asking too much of any man! Especially as she'll have the latest pretty-boy hanger-on with her today,' he added scathingly. 'Although I do believe this one may be marginally older than me!'

Bree's expression lightened as she resisted the urge to smile at Jackson's look of total disgust. Clarissa Beaumont had been left a very wealthy widow when Jackson's father had died twenty years ago, allowing her to flit around the world from one social engagement to the next, usually with a handsome young man half her age in tow. In the past year Bree had seen the older woman accompanied by at least half a dozen or so such young men.

Much to Jackson's obvious disgust.

'Just stick the present under the tree with all the others when it arrives,' Jackson told her dismissively. 'I'll be back in a couple of hours.'

'You really are—' Bree broke off her accusation as the mobile on her desk began to ring.

'That'll be Tyler,' Jackson predicted, grinning. 'So you'll have to save any more compliments for me until later!'

'As if!' Bree snorted as she picked up the mobile, ready to take the call. 'Make sure you don't forget to collect Danny from school at three-thirty.'

'Yes, ma'am!' Jackson straightened to give her a salute. 'And good luck with my mother,' he added tauntingly as he disappeared through the door.

Bree sighed in exasperation before taking the call, with an apology for Jackson's unpredictable behaviour at the ready. As usual.

CHAPTER TWO

'WHAT THE HELL is that?'

Bree glanced up at an astounded Jackson, standing in the doorway of the main sitting room at Beaumont House. He was staring across at her in horrified disbelief.

'Well, correct me if I'm wrong,' she quipped, 'but it looks like a puppy to me.'

'Very funny.' The scowl on Jackson's brow deepened as he stepped into the room, where Bree sat in front of the log fire, playing with a small dark grey and white bundle of fur and a ball of wool. 'What I want to know is what it's doing here? I'm sure I told you I didn't allow pets when you first came to work for me!'

'You did, yes,' she confirmed nonchalantly.

'Well?' Jackson prompted impatiently.

Bree smiled, raising a rueful eyebrow. 'You obviously forgot to mention that particular house rule to your mother.'

'My mother? What the hell does she—' Jackson stared down in horror at the mischievous puppy. 'No… She wouldn't. She didn't!'

'Oh, I think you'll find she would and she did,' Bree retorted, picking up the puppy as she rose to her feet. 'Come and meet Danny's Christmas present.'

Jackson made no effort to go anywhere near the puppy Bree held in her arms.

'Has my mother gone completely insane? I can't have a puppy here, chewing up the furniture and causing mayhem amongst my photographic equipment!'

'I think your protest may be a little too late, given that he's here already,' Bree teased.

'No! No way am I having a dog.' Jackson gave a determined shake of his head. 'It will have to go back to wherever it came from,' he announced firmly. 'And before I collect Danny from school,' he added with grim finality.

'I have no idea which breeder your mother purchased the puppy from, and as she's currently on her way to the Caribbean to join her cruise ship I don't see how we're going to find out, either.'

Bree held the puppy protectively against her chest. She had already grown fond of the fluffy little thing in the hour since Clarissa Beaumont had breezed in, deposited it into Bree's arms and breezed out again with a casual 'Merry Christmas' once informed that her son wasn't at home. The latest 'pretty-boy hanger-on' had deposited all the paraphernalia a young puppy would need in the entrance hall before quickly following her.

'Of all the irresponsible—! I'll call her on her mobile,' Jackson reasoned evenly as he formulated the plan in his head. 'Then while I'm collecting Danny from school you can drive the puppy back to the breeder—'

'Oh, I couldn't do that!' Bree interrupted in protest, gazing down adoringly at the puppy. 'Why don't you just hold him for a moment, Jackson?'

'No!' He backed away, hands raised defensively as she held the puppy out to him.

'But he's so cute!'

'All puppies are cute, Bree,' Jackson said briskly. 'It's what they grow up into that's the worrying part. And from the look of those paws he's going to be big!'

'Your mother said he's a Bearded Collie,' Bree mentioned absently as she stroked the puppy's ears.

'Big,' Jackson announced disgustedly as he pictured the fully grown dog. 'And not only big, but I believe the breed is slightly insane too. Nope, he's going back. And the sooner the better!'

Bree gave him an aggrieved look. 'Danny would love to have a puppy to play with.' She used the 'D' word unashamedly, knowing that although Jackson could be impossibly arrogant and selfish he had absolutely no defences against anything that might bring pleasure to his motherless son.

As expected, the statement made him pause for thought—if only briefly.

'No,' Jackson stated finally. 'I draw the line at a puppy.'

'But—'

'Bree, it's going to need taking out to the garden to pee.' He glared at her exasperatedly. 'Constantly, if I don't want little puddles all over the house! And feeding. And numerous trips to the vet for its vaccination shots. And—'

'Your mother said he's completely house-trained and up-to-date on his vaccinations,' she put in quickly. 'And I'll do all those other things if you don't want to do them.'

'I don't want a puppy!' he repeated emphatically. 'Besides which, who's going to be answering the phone and all those other numerous jobs you do for me every

day while you're outside in the garden or at the vet's? Who's going to look after it all day while Danny is at school?'

'He breaks up for the Christmas holidays tomorrow—'

'I'm talking about after the holidays.'

'We can put the puppy's basket in here with me during the day. It'll make it easier for taking him outside anyway.'

'Bree, I really don't think you're hearing a word I'm saying! *I do not want a puppy!*'

Her eyes widened. 'There's no need to shout.'

'There's every need to shout when you clearly aren't listening to me,' he snapped impatiently, running an exasperated hand through his long hair.

Hair that, annoyingly, sprang back into the same tousled style that even Bree could see would make a woman ache to run her own fingers through it. Other women. Not Bree.

At this precise moment Bree was too annoyed with Jackson to feel even remotely appreciative of his wickedly handsome good looks. In fact right now Bree could cheerfully have punched him on his perfectly straight nose!

She had been feeling slightly out of sorts all day, since realising that it was the anniversary of her wedding that never was—although cuddles with the puppy had certainly gone a long way towards healing the breach that the memory had made in her defences.

Bree softened her tone persuasively. 'Look, Jackson, I realise this is a bit of a surprise for you...'

'Make that a shock!'

Bree eyed him warily. 'Okay, so it was a shock to

return home and find your mother has given Danny a puppy for Christmas—something I decided probably shouldn't go under the tree with the other presents as you suggested earlier, by the way!' She tried to add a little lightness to the subject—only to receive a scowl for her trouble. 'But try looking a little further than that, hmm?' she cajoled. 'Danny is an only child—'

'And likely to remain so,' Jackson assured her coldly.

Bree winced at his vehemence. 'He's an only child,' she repeated firmly. 'He has no other children close by to play with. It must get a little lonely for Danny here in the evenings and at weekends, what with only you, me and your housekeeper for company.'

'Thanks!' Jackson grimaced.

'I did include myself in that number,' she pointed out wryly.

'So you did.' Jackson gazed down at the puppy Bree still held in her arms. There was no doubt it was a cute little thing: grey-blue eyes, a black button nose, and that soft, curly grey, black and white fur...

'No, it's impossible.' Jackson straightened determinedly away from the lure of all that cuteness. 'I'll go and call my mother—and if you won't do it I'll have to make other arrangements to take the puppy back to the breeder.'

'How can you be so cruel?' Bree glared up at him.

'Sometimes you have to be cruel to be kind.' He sighed as she continued to glare. 'Dogs are a tie, Bree. A serious complication when it comes to going away on holiday—or even out for the day. And what about Danny's reaction when it eventually dies? A breed like that will live—what?—ten, twelve years at most? By which time Danny will be—'

'Sixteen or eighteen years old, and perfectly capable of understanding and accepting that death is merely a part of life,' she assured him firmly. 'Especially when he's enjoyed ten or twelve years of companionship and unconditional love!'

Unconditional love, Jackson mused. Now, *there* was a concept not too many adults understood. Well, not the adults Jackson came into contact with anyway.

Over the years he had found that everyone had their own agenda. Wealth. Success. Stardom. Whatever they believed would give them the happiness they craved. Well, Jackson had all three of those things, and yet he hadn't known even a glimmer of real happiness until Danny had come into his life five years ago. Because Danny gave him that unconditional love Bree was talking about? Probably. But, damn it, a puppy…? Did he *really* have to let Danny keep the damned puppy?

'He really won't be any trouble,' Bree persevered eagerly, sensing a weakening in Jackson's resolve. The 'D' word had once again worked its magic charm on him. 'Your mother also brought a basket for the puppy to sleep in, and lots of food, and bowls, and brushes for grooming him—'

'Okay, okay, okay!' Jackson's voice rose in volume with each successive 'okay'. 'But the first time he gets into my camera equipment he's banished outside to the garden shed.'

'Woo-hoo! You're being allowed to stay, puppy!' Bree held the furry bundle up in the air.

Jackson watched in total surprise as his usually calm and unruffled assistant did a little victory dance around the sitting room. He felt completely taken aback by Bree's obvious happiness and the way it lit up her face, making her look almost beautiful: those smoky-grey eyes glowed, her cheeks were flushed, and her lips curved into a wide and happy smile. They were full and slightly pouty lips, he realised with a frown. The sort of lips that could drive a man crazy if applied to the right part of his anatomy...

'Isn't it time you got back to work?' Jackson rasped harshly as he straightened abruptly to glare down at her.

Bree came to an abrupt halt, the light fading from her eyes, the colour fading from her cheeks, and those sensual lips no longer smiling but once again set in their usual line of disapproval.

Jackson could deal with Bree's disapproval—hell, he was happy to deal with her disapproval! What he didn't need, didn't want to deal with, was that inexplicable, insidious physical awareness he had felt towards her just now...

'I'm going to get Danny from school,' he glowered.

'Fine.' She nodded dismissively, no longer looking at him but at the puppy held comfortably in her arms.

No, it wasn't 'fine' at all, Jackson thought to himself, frowning as he walked slowly outside to his car.

Bree had worked for him for almost a year. Lived in his house. Spent time with his son. She wasn't just good at her job, she blended perfectly into his life—organising his appointments, taking his clothes to be laundered, deciding on the menus for the week with the housekeeper, Mrs Holmes, looking after Danny when Jackson had to be elsewhere. It was like having a wife without any of the complications. Or the sex, of course—

Where the hell had *that* thought come from?

Wherever it had originated, it could go right back

there again. It would ruin everything if he even started to think of Bree in a sexual way!

In fact over the past year Jackson had made a point of never seeing or treating Bree as anything more than his assistant and occasionally Danny's babysitter.

To the extent, he now realised, that he had never even bothered to enquire about her private life before she came to work for him. He had likewise had no reason to enquire about it during the past year: to his certain knowledge Bree didn't *have* a private life now. She never went out in the evenings. If she had family and friends she never invited them to her apartment.

Moments ago, when she had danced so spontaneously around the sitting room with the puppy in her arms—when she had looked so nearly beautiful—for the first time Jackson had found himself wondering exactly why that was…

CHAPTER THREE

'Now, aren't you glad you changed your mind and decided to let Danny keep the puppy?' Bree murmured softly, smiling down indulgently at the little boy and the puppy an hour or so later.

She had come to tell Jackson that she was leaving for the day, and the first thing she'd seen was Danny and the puppy rolling about on the carpet together—luckily avoiding contact with the eight-foot-tall Christmas tree standing in the corner of the room surrounded by presents! Danny's happy chuckles filled the room as the puppy licked his nose.

'The jury's still out on that one,' Jackson muttered, looking up from where he slouched in one of the armchairs. 'Beau,' he growled across at Bree. 'He named the damned puppy *Beau*!'

Bree had to bite her lip to stop herself from laughing at his obvious disgust. 'Ah, how sweet—he named his puppy after you!'

'Very funny!' Jackson rose lithely to his feet before striding across to where she stood in the doorway.

'It suits him, don't you think?' Bree couldn't resist teasing.

'No, I don't think!' Jackson scowled down at her.

She looked up at him quizzically. 'My, you're in a cheery mood this evening!'

Jackson was well aware of his dour mood. Just as he was aware that the main reason behind that mood was standing in the doorway.

He felt surprisingly little lingering annoyance over Danny's puppy; anyone with eyes could see how happy Danny was with his grandmother's Christmas gift. No, he was willing to admit defeat where the puppy was concerned. Danny was so excited, what with Christmas being only six days away, that Jackson very much doubted whether he would be able to prise the puppy out of his son's arms now!

It was that sudden stirring of interest in Bree earlier—interest in her past as well as her present—that had continued to unsettle Jackson for the last couple of hours. It had unsettled him to the extent that he felt the need for company. Female company.

'Bree, could you sit with Danny later this evening while I go out?'

'Ah…' A perplexed frown creased her brow. 'Ordinarily you know I would have been happy to, but… Actually, I'm going out myself this evening,' she explained reluctantly.

'Your offer to take care of the puppy didn't last very long, did it?'

'I believe my exact words were "during the day",' she reminded him primly.

Was it Jackson's imagination or was that a blush spreading across Bree's slightly freckled cheeks? A guilty blush? As if she were hiding something…

He raised his eyebrows. 'Can it be that you're going out on a date this evening?'

'Well, there's no need to look so surprised, Jackson!' She was suddenly irritated. 'I'm twenty-six, not eighty-six!'

That might be the case, but as far as Jackson was aware not only did Bree *never* go out in the evenings, but she hadn't been out on a date since she'd come to work for him a year ago. Which, when he thought about it, was decidedly odd.

And Jackson *had* thought about it—for the past couple of hours. Several times. Several times too many as far as he was concerned!

For Bree to suddenly reveal that she was going out on a date this very evening—the first since he had known her—was a coincidence that only added to his already unsettled mood.

'Meeting up with an old friend?' he prompted curiously.

'A new one, actually,' she mumbled softly.

'Anyone I know…?'

She bristled. 'I don't think that's any of your business, Jackson.'

Jackson forced himself to relax at the deserved rebuke. 'I just thought perhaps I could vet him for you when he arrives.' He arched a mocking brow. 'You know—a man-to-man thing, to see if he measures up.'

Bree's lips thinned. 'He isn't coming here. I'm meeting him at a restaurant.'

'Oh, that's bad, Bree.' He shook his head, taunting her. 'You should never trust a man who isn't gentleman enough to call and collect you for a date!'

'Says the *gentleman* who rarely—if ever—collects his own dates!' she retorted tartly.

'I make a point of it.' Jackson gave an unrepentant

grin. 'That's how I know you shouldn't trust a man like that!'

Bree eyed him darkly. 'I'll bear your advice in mind.'

In actual fact it was precisely due to Bree's uncertainty about having dinner with Roger Tyler that she had decided to drive to the restaurant alone: at least that way Bree could drive herself home if Roger behaved in any way she found in the least objectionable.

Jackson's assumption when he went out earlier that the incoming telephone call would be Roger Tyler, confirming their two o'clock appointment, had been totally wrong; it had been someone else completely—another client confirming an appointment for next week. Roger Tyler hadn't telephoned back at all, and neither had he answered any of Bree's calls when she had attempted to inform him that Jackson was no longer available that afternoon. Instead Roger had appeared in person at Beaumont House promptly at two o'clock.

Tall and dark, probably in his late thirties or early forties, and with a craggily handsome face, Roger Tyler hadn't seemed too perturbed when Bree had smoothly delivered the excuse that Jackson wasn't there because he had been called away on business. In fact the other man hadn't seemed bothered at all—instead he had chatted away quite happily with Bree for over half an hour, culminating in an invitation to dinner that evening.

Bree could only suppose that the 'bimbo' Jackson had referred to earlier hadn't been willing to reschedule their date for the evening! Whatever the reason for Roger's invitation, Bree had surprised herself by saying yes.

She had no idea why.

No, that wasn't true; Bree knew exactly why she'd

acted so completely out of character by accepting Roger Tyler's dinner invitation. Because earlier she had realised that today was the one-year anniversary of her wedding that never was. In the circumstances Bree would probably have accepted a dinner invitation from the devil himself as a distraction from those crushing memories! Except the devil she knew hadn't asked...

Whenever Bree thought back to a year ago—which she tried to do as seldom as possible—it was never without feeling that same sting of humiliation she had suffered on the day in question. The day that had changed her life.

Meaning to put up some curtains, Bree had gone to the house she and David had purchased together and had planned to move into after their Paris honeymoon only to discover David was already there. Not just David, but also her married sister Cathy. And, as Bree had discovered painfully, the two of them had been in bed together—in what should have been Bree and David's marital bed.

Not only had Bree called off the wedding, but the scandal of David and Cathy's several-months-long affair had ripped a hole in Bree's family that still hadn't completely healed.

So, yes, Bree knew exactly why she had so impetuously agreed to go out with Roger Tyler this evening. Her acceptance was based not on any attraction Bree might or might not feel towards him, but because she desperately needed a diversion from her feelings of hurt and betrayal. Of inadequacy. Because David had so obviously preferred her older sister to her.

Feelings like that didn't seem half so important when a man like Roger Tyler had invited her out to dinner!

Doubts had begun creeping in after Roger had left Beaumont House—to the point where Bree had spent the afternoon toying with the idea of telephoning him to say that she couldn't make it this evening after all!

Jackson's obvious surprise that she was going out on a date, along with his cynical teasing, had brought about a complete change of heart on her part. Bree no longer cared whether or not Roger Tyler was a man she could trust—she had every intention of going out to dinner with him now. If only to prove to Jackson that she wasn't the unattractive piece of furniture he obviously believed her to be!

Her chin rose stubbornly. 'I'm sorry I can't help out with Danny this evening, Jackson. Now, if you'll excuse me, I have to go and get ready.'

Jackson reached out and placed a hand on Bree's arm as she turned away.

'What aren't you telling me...?' He looked down at her searchingly.

She laughed lightly, dismissively. 'I don't believe we've ever had the sort of relationship where we've confided about our private lives to each other, Jackson!'

No, they hadn't, Jackson acknowledged with a frown. And he had always been grateful for Bree's silence on the subject before today; he couldn't abide women who wanted to fill you in on every minute detail of their lives. Yes, in the past Jackson had always been *glad* that Bree kept her own counsel. Until now.

There was something different about Bree this afternoon. A brittleness. An air of recklessness he had never seen in her before. Almost as if she were standing on the edge of a cliff, about to jump over—

What the hell...?

As Bree had already pointed out, she was a grown woman and could do exactly as she wished in her free time. And if her dinner date this evening meant that Jackson couldn't go out after all, then that was just too bad. Hell, Bree was as entitled to a social life as he was.

Except she'd never had one until tonight...

He gave a tense, irritated shrug. 'I feel a sense of responsibility for you—'

'Oh, for goodness' sake, Jackson!' Bree snapped with irritation. 'I'm not your daughter!'

'You live in my house...'

'I live in the basement apartment as part of the wages you pay me—not in your house.' She shook her head impatiently. 'And if I were a man you wouldn't be asking me these ridiculous questions!'

If Bree were a man Jackson wouldn't have felt that stirring of physical interest in her earlier either!

'Come and play with me, Bree.'

Jackson had been so deep in thought that he hadn't noticed Danny joining them until he spoke at his side. Looking down, he saw that his son carried the now-panting puppy in his arms. It had been love at first sight for both of them when Danny had come home from school and rushed into Bree's office to see his Christmas present from Granny.

Jackson took great delight in seeing the way his mother cringed every time Danny called her that; only her deep love for the little boy kept her silent on the subject. Jackson found that he could forgive his mother for a lot of things when he saw the genuine love she had for her grandson.

'Bree can't play right now, Danny, because she has to

go and get ready to go out this evening.' Jackson sank down on his haunches beside his son.

Danny looked up at Bree with guileless blue eyes. 'You're going *out*?'

'Oh, for heaven's sake!' Jackson heard her mutter under her breath as she shot him an irritated glance before forcing a smile for Danny. 'I'll only be gone for a little while,' she reassured him lightly.

'Don't worry, Danny, I'll wait up and make sure that Bree arrives home safely,' Jackson drawled smoothly.

Bree narrowed her eyes at him. 'I'm sure that won't be necessary, thank you.'

'No problem,' he dismissed lightly, straightening up. 'Be sure and come into the main house to let me know you're back, won't you? Otherwise I'll only worry.'

Bree wasn't fooled for a moment by those innocent blue eyes Jackson levelled on her—he was enjoying himself now, damn him. At her expense. And all because she had impulsively accepted a dinner invitation from a man she didn't even have any real interest in!

It had all seemed so romantic eighteen months ago, when she and David had decided on a pre-Christmas wedding. An occasion and a time of year that would always have special significance for them both. As it turned out that Christmas had been nothing but a nightmare for Bree, lost in a haze of crying and heartbreak, of family rows and the slamming of doors, until she hadn't been able to stand it any more and had moved into the anonymity of a hotel in order to escape it all. Which was the very reason she had been so desperate and homeless when she'd come for her interview with Jackson almost a year ago.

Bree had so wanted it to be different this year, had

so wanted to be able to enjoy Christmas again—and had been sure that she could do so with Danny's help. There was something about children and Christmas that no adult could resist.

And Bree had almost managed to fool herself—until she had realised earlier that it should have been her first wedding anniversary today. Not that Bree had even a residual ounce of love for David left inside her, but that didn't mean she couldn't still grieve for her own lost hopes and dreams.

To now find herself the butt of Jackson's warped sense of humour was just too much!

She gave him a sweet, insincere smile. 'Of course, Daddykins!'

Danny gave a giggle. 'Did you hear that, Daddy? Bree called you Daddykins!'

As Bree had hoped, Jackson's mocking blue eyes were now totally devoid of humour. 'I heard what she called me,' Jackson bit out tersely, glaring at Bree over Danny's head. 'Just make sure you let me know you're back so that I can be sure everywhere is locked up after you.'

When he put it like that it was a reasonable request; there were security gates at the end of the driveway that Bree would have to come through, and an alarm system fitted in her apartment as well as in the main house. Human safety apart, Jackson had some very expensive photographic equipment in his studio, as well as several original paintings in the house.

'Will do,' she breezed flippantly. 'Have a pleasant evening, you two.'

Jackson knew he should have wished her the same,

and yet as he watched Bree leave something held him back.

It was that recklessness he sensed in her, perhaps, and the image he'd had of her earlier, standing on the edge of that cliff...

CHAPTER FOUR

IT WAS ALMOST midnight when Bree quietly let herself into the darkness of Beaumont House, moving softly through the silence to the kitchen and out into the entrance hall, before making her way to the sitting room, where she could hear the low murmur of the television. Jackson had evidently waited up for her to return from her dinner date as promised.

Or not, Bree realised with wry amusement as she entered the sitting room and observed Jackson, sleeping peacefully in one of the armchairs. The fire in the hearth had burnt down to just a few hot coals; only the flickering television and the coloured lights on the Christmas tree illuminated the comfortable room.

Bree crossed the room with the intention of switching off the television, only to hesitate beside Jackson's chair. She had never seen him asleep before—there was no reason why she should have—and she couldn't help noticing how much younger he looked without that mocking glint in his eyes and that cynical twist to those sensual lips. His golden honey-and-molasses hair had fallen untidily over his brow, which only added to that illusion of boyishness.

Because it *was* an illusion, Bree told herself sternly; Jackson was both mocking and cynical. And sarcastic. And rude. And completely impossible. And—

And quite possibly the most sensually handsome man Bree had ever set eyes on.

She had been both hurt and hurting when she'd first come to work for Jackson almost a year ago. Totally disillusioned with all men. And the often outrageous, too-handsome Jerome Jackson Beaumont was a man who enjoyed the constant stream of women coming and going in and out of his life—and his bed. Or rather the woman's bed; Danny's presence at Beaumont House meant that Jackson never brought women back here to spend the night with him.

All that had only served to confirm Bree's belief that men simply weren't capable of faithfulness and love for one single woman.

Which didn't mean that she couldn't appreciate what all those other women saw in Jackson!

He was certainly a handsome devil—if a devil could have long golden hair and mocking sky-blue eyes. And a wicked sense of humour. And a lean and muscled body that had to be every woman's deepest fantasy…

Exactly when had Bree stopped feeling so hurt by David's betrayal and become so aware of all those things about Jackson? Was it only today? Or had she noticed these things before but just never acknowledged them?

'What the—? Bree, is that you?'

Bree had been so lost in thought as she gazed down at Jackson appreciatively that she hadn't noticed when he awoke. Now he was gazing up at her—not with cynical or mocking blue eyes, but with the slow, lazy appreciation of a man who liked what he saw. Which happened to be Bree!

She took a couple of wary paces backwards. 'Well, of course it's me!'

Of course it was, Jackson acknowledged sardonically as he heard the familiar sharpness in Bree's tone. But this was a Bree he had certainly never seen before...

In the office Bree wore businesslike dark tailored trousers or skirts, usually teamed with jumpers in the winter and blouses in the summer; the soft, silky black dress she was wearing this evening could never be considered even remotely businesslike!

It was a sheath of a figure-hugging dress. Strapless and knee-length, it showcased a large expanse of her bare shoulders and the soft swell of the tops of her breasts, along with the shapely length of her legs, and her feet, tiny and slender, in black strappy three-inch heels.

Very, very nice. And yet, despite all the femininity on show, it was Bree's hair that held Jackson's fascinated gaze. Earlier today he had wondered briefly how long her hair would be when loose, and now he had his answer: it was so long and thick and curly that it almost reached down to her shapely bottom, and it was the rich colour of sable!

She looked, Jackson realised as he sat up slowly, like a woman out of a Renaissance painting, with the softness of her skin appearing a pearly and lustrous white against the darkness of that long, flowing hair and the fitted black dress. Hers was skin that tempted a man to touch and taste it. As for those incredible sexy smoky-grey eyes and the long dark lashes that framed them...

'Jackson?'

Bree had no idea what thoughts had been going through Jackson's head during the past few moments, but whatever they were she had become increasingly aware of the deepening tension that crackled in the air:

a physical awareness that she sensed was no longer just her own...

'What have you done with Beau this evening?' she prompted, as a distraction from that awareness. 'I didn't see him in the kitchen earlier when I came through, and he obviously isn't in here, either...'

A rueful smile curved Jackson's lips as he saw the concern in Bree's face. 'Well, I haven't sent him to the stray dogs' home, if that's what you're imagining!' He grinned.

She gave him a reproving glance. 'I'm pretty sure Danny wouldn't have allowed you to do that!'

Jackson arched a mocking brow. 'Well, for your information I tried putting Beau and his basket in the kitchen when Danny went to bed, but he cried and whined so much—Beau, that is,' he explained drily in response to Bree's questioning look, 'that I eventually brought him in here with me. Where he continued to cry and whine.' Jackson frowned at the memory of that piteous sound.

Bree nodded. 'Obviously he's grown as attached to Danny as Danny has to him.'

'Obviously,' Jackson snapped.

Bree eyed him quizzically. 'So where's Beau now?'

Jackson grimaced. 'I put his basket upstairs in Danny's bedroom. Normally I wouldn't approve of allowing dogs in the bedroom, but it was the only place where he would stop whining,' he explained defensively.

Bree was having trouble holding back a smile. 'Of course it was,' she said, humouring him lightly.

'If you dare to laugh—' Jackson broke off the warning as Bree did exactly that. 'It isn't funny, Bree,' he muttered gloomily, but she seemed unable to contain her amusement at his expense; those velvety soft grey eyes were glowing with humour.

'Of course it is,' Bree chuckled finally. 'Big, strong, I-don't-want-a-puppy Jerome Jackson Beaumont, worn down by the cries of that same little puppy!'

'You would have done the same in my position,' he muttered gruffly.

'Undoubtedly.' Bree felt herself softening at the realisation that beneath his gruff exterior Jackson was as tender-hearted as she was when it came to a defenceless, cute little puppy like Beau.

Jackson sighed. 'I told Danny to make sure Beau stays in his basket.'

An instruction that Danny—and Beau—had probably completely ignored, as they were both well aware. The puppy was no doubt curled up fast asleep on the little boy's bed at this very minute.

'You really are just a big softie!' Bree smiled at him teasingly.

Jackson's gaze, glittering brightly, continued to hold hers and a derisive smile curved those sensuous lips. Bree took another step backwards.

Her eyes widened in alarm as Jackson countered that movement by taking a stealthy step forward, standing so close now that Bree was able to feel the heat emanating off his body.

'What are you doing…?' she breathed softly.

'Nothing…' he murmured.

She swallowed hard. 'That's goo—'

'...yet,' he added huskily.

Bree had been aware of the stillness of the house when she'd first come in, but now that silence was charged with something else: a tense expectancy much like the loaded pause before a predator pounced on its prey!

She moistened lips that had gone suddenly dry. 'I only came in to let you know that I'm back.'

'And did you have a nice evening?' Jackson asked softly.

'Very nice, thank you,' Bree answered warily, not fooled for a moment by the casual pleasantry when she could still see that speculative gleam in Jackson's eyes as he continued to look down at her so unblinkingly.

It was a wariness that Jackson's next comment proved was completely warranted.

'Did you go out in that dress?' he enquired as his gaze swept over her from head to toes.

Bree swallowed. 'I… Yes, of course.'

It was one of the dresses Bree had bought a year ago to take on her honeymoon to Paris. Bought but for obvious reasons never worn—before this evening…

'It's…very nice.'

'Thank you.'

The speculation deepened in Jackson's eyes. 'Did you come home alone?'

'Well, of *course* I came home alone!' Bree snapped, glaring at the impertinence of the question.

Jackson shrugged the wide and muscled shoulders that were clearly defined in the fitted black T-shirt he was wearing. 'Just checking.'

Bree still frowned her irritation. 'Why?'

'Before I do this.'

Jackson took the single step that separated them, sliding his arms about her waist and pulling her into the heat of his body before his head lowered and his mouth claimed hers in a searingly hot kiss that totally took Bree's breath away.

She clung to those wide shoulders as her knees buckled slightly. Not that there was any possibility of her falling when Jackson's arms were clamped like steel bands about her waist. His hands stroked the length of her spine, his fingers a hot and arousing caress against the bare skin above her gown as his lips continued that plundering exploration, his tongue moist against her lips as he parted them before thrusting deep into the heat of her mouth.

His tongue stroked intimately against hers, evoking an explosion of pleasure, an aching response deep inside Bree. She felt heat burning between her thighs. Her breasts swelled and her nipples hardened as they pressed against the material of her dress, and she became fully aware of the hard throb of Jackson's answering arousal as his hands cupped her bottom to pull her up and into him.

A hard and throbbing arousal that was entirely in response to *her*, Sabrina Jones!

Bree felt empowered by that realisation, moving her hands up as she gave in to the temptation to entangle her fingers in that honey-and-molasses hair, finding it just as she had always imagined it would be: thick and long and silkily soft, and so—

As she had always imagined it would be...?

She had *imagined* something like this happening between herself and Jackson?

Since when?

What—?

All thoughts fled—Bree even forgot to breathe—as

Jackson's hand cupped her breast before his questing fingers sought the swollen tip.

Bree gasped as Jackson's lips left hers and his other hand moved to twist the long waves of her hair in his fingers. He arched her neck back, exposing it to his lips, teeth lightly nipping the lobe of her ear, before he softly kissed the swell of her breasts.

'Your skin is like velvet!' Jackson groaned.

His lips found her aching nipple through the silky material of her dress, his tongue stroking intense heat through the fabric to her breast for long, pleasurable seconds before he clamped his lips around her nipple and pulled it deep into the heat of his mouth.

An almost unbearable burning coursed through Bree's body as she gazed down at him, his lashes long and thick against his sculpted cheekbones. His hand moved to cup her other breast, the soft pad of his thumb rubbing against the nipple in the same rhythmic caress. Raging fire burned between Bree's thighs and she felt herself swelling and moistening there in a deep and aching throb that beat with the same rapidity as her heart.

She realised that it was *Jackson* kissing and caressing her so intimately!

Jackson of the wild and dangerous good looks. Jackson of the lean and muscled body. Jackson who had to be every woman's wildest fantasy in the flesh. Jackson who could—and did—have any woman he wanted.

But at the moment he seemed to want Bree.

At the moment.

Chilling reality hit Bree with the force of a physical blow, erasing all pleasure, all arousal, as she acknowledged that this couldn't—shouldn't!—be happening. Not between herself and Jackson, of all people!

She knew for a fact that Jackson never became involved with the women in his working life. Not the models he occasionally used for commercial photo shoots, and certainly not his assistants. He had several times stated—as a warning, perhaps?—that he wouldn't work alongside any woman with whom he had been intimately involved.

Tonight could definitely be described as intimate involvement.

How on earth was Bree going to extract herself from this explosive situation without also finding herself out of a job?

CHAPTER FIVE

'JACKSON, IS IT possible that you've been drinking?'

'What—?' Jackson staggered backwards, dazed, as Bree pushed him away with a suddenness he hadn't been expecting, before turning her back on him to re-arrange her dress.

Expecting?

Hell, Jackson hadn't been expecting a single thing about the way he had reacted to Bree this evening!

Not the way she looked with that beautiful waist-length hair loose about her shoulders. Not how sexy that thin scrap of a dress was, leaving so little to the imagination. Not the lure of those smoky-grey eyes. He certainly hadn't expected her to taste and feel so good. Or the way she'd responded so readily to the caress of his lips and hands on her soft, creamy flesh...

And Jackson hadn't expected to become aroused just by looking at her—nor the fact that he was still aroused, his shaft a hard and throbbing ache against his denims!

In spite of the accusatory way Bree was now glowering at him.

'Have I been drinking?' Jackson repeated harshly, stepping away and running a hand through the tousled length of his hair. 'You're the one who walked in here a few minutes ago looking like some slinky *femme fatale* from a forties movie!'

She raised her eyebrows. 'It's just a dress, Jackson. You've been photographed with dozens of women wearing far less than I am tonight!' she added defiantly.

And truthfully, Jackson admitted with a dark frown. In fact Bree's dress could be called modest in comparison with some of the evening dresses he had seen on other women. Except those other women weren't Bree!

What the hell was wrong with him this evening? He had worked alongside Bree for almost a year now without so much as a single sexual thought.

Well…maybe the odd thought. But he wouldn't be a healthy thirty-four-year-old man if he didn't have the occasional fantasy about an attractive twenty-six-year-old woman, whether she worked for him or not!

Yet he was now totally physically aware of Bree.

Because he didn't like the idea of her spending the evening with another man?

Or because of that small but tangible difference he had sensed in Bree today?

There was absolutely no reason why it should matter to Jackson if Bree went on a date, so it had to be the difference in her that had ignited this physical awareness.

But it was a physical awareness he must have been out of his mind to act upon.

'I still can't believe you went out in that dress!' Jackson was more comfortable on the attack than on the defensive.

'Don't be ridiculous, Jackson,' Bree snapped irritably.

'It's positively indecent!'

'Roger didn't seem to find anything wrong with it!'

'I don't—Roger Tyler?' Jackson gaped. 'Your dinner date this evening was with *Roger Tyler*?'

'That's right,' she replied coolly. 'And I must say that, unlike some people I could mention, he behaved like the perfect gentleman all evening.'

'Roger Tyler was the man you went out to dinner with this evening…' Jackson repeated, as if to himself.

It was a little difficult for him to comprehend the fact that his assistant—a woman who hadn't been out on a single date since she'd begun working for him—had just spent the evening with one of the most infamous womanisers in the public eye.

Damn it—of all men, Bree had been out with the reprehensible Roger Tyler!

Jackson's eyes narrowed ominously as he sat down on the arm of the chair. 'And exactly how did that come about?'

Bree shrugged her shoulders. 'He arrived for his two o'clock appointment, after all.'

The muscles in Jackson's jaw clenched. 'And the two of you enjoyed a pleasant hour or so chatting, no doubt?'

'More like half an hour, since we're splitting hairs,' she replied sharply.

'Long enough, in any case, for the man to invite you out on a date!' Jackson growled.

Bree stuck out her chin challengingly. 'Is there some unwritten rule I'm not aware of that prevents your assistant from dating any of your clients?'

Jackson hesitated, frowning. 'Not exactly, no…'

'Then what *exactly* is your problem, Jackson?' Bree demanded, hands on hips.

In spite of her earlier apprehension about the dinner date, Bree had actually enjoyed Roger Tyler's company this evening. Besides his obvious good looks and confidence, he was amusing and fun to be with, and not at all the egomaniac she had expected him to be. He had been charming and attentive all evening: the 'perfect gentleman' Bree had claimed him to be, in fact.

The restaurant where they had eaten dinner was obviously an exclusive one—the fact that there had been no prices on the menu confirmed that!—and Bree had tried hard not to stare at any of the other diners, many of whom she'd recognised from either the big or the small screen. The food and wine had been delicious, the service unobtrusive, and the company more pleasant and entertaining than Bree could ever have imagined. All in all it had been a surprisingly relaxing and enjoyable way to spend the evening.

Until her return to Beaumont House and this awful scene with Jackson. Well…the first part of it hadn't been awful at all, but the aftermath was certainly far from pleasant!

She would never admit as much to Jackson, but she was still reeling from her response to him just now. It had been an out-of-control response that was totally at odds with her usual reserve. An out-of-control response that Bree had never felt in the arms of the man she had planned to marry a year ago…

'Do you intend to see Tyler again?' Jackson enquired coldly.

'I don't believe—'

'And don't even *think* about telling me it's none of my business who you go out with!' he growled warningly. 'You're my assistant and Roger Tyler is my client—of course it's my business if the two of you are now dating!'

Was it? Bree wondered. Or was Jackson just being difficult?

Bree had only brought Roger Tyler into the conversation at all because she'd thought attack might be the best form of defence in what had become a very awkward situation. But perhaps in retrospect she would have been wiser not to mention that Roger Tyler had been her date this evening!

She grimaced, frustrated. 'We aren't dating. We've just been out to dinner together.'

'And I asked if you intend to see him again,' Jackson repeated evenly.

Bree sighed heavily before answering. 'He said he would call me tomorrow.'

'And?'

Bree was so annoyed by the interrogation she almost stamped her foot. 'And if he does call tomorrow and wants to see me again I'll decide then and there whether or not I want to see *him*!'

Jackson barely managed to bite back his frustration.

Just why the hell should it matter to *him* if Bree had finally decided to come out of her shell and start dating?

It shouldn't. As he had told himself earlier today, Bree was as entitled to a private life as he was.

Except Jackson had just kissed her.

He had acted against every self-imposed rule he'd ever had concerning his assistants. Against every instinct telling him not to ruin a good thing when he found it: namely, the best damn assistant he had ever had!

Damn, damn, *damn*!

He rubbed his temples, trying to rein in his anger. 'Do you actually like Tyler?'

Bree raised cool brows. 'Well, obviously—seeing as I've just spent the evening with him.'

Jackson paused to let his irritation subside. The woman could be so infuriating!

'No. I meant do you *really* like him?'

She shook her head impatiently. 'I know what you meant, Jackson—and, again, I don't consider that to be any of your business. I certainly don't need some big brother figure breathing down my neck, checking up on every man I choose to go out with!'

Big brother? Jackson had just almost made love to her, damn it! He could still see the damp patch on Bree's dress where his mouth had been exploring only moments earlier!

The memory instantly reawakened the aching throb in Jackson's jeans—and the fact that he was sitting down made it all the more painful!

He stood up abruptly, in the hope of easing that burning ache, and realised immediately how obvious his arousal was against his denims.

'Perhaps it's time you returned to your apartment?' he suggested abruptly, his tone clipped. 'We can talk about this again in the morning.'

'I don't think so, Jackson,' Bree replied firmly.

He rolled his eyes. 'What do you mean?'

'I mean that I am your employee, Jackson—that's where my responsibilities begin and end. As such, I don't believe I have to answer to you for anything I might choose to do in my private life!'

Jackson tightened his jaw in an effort to stop himself from giving Bree the reply she deserved: what the hell had just happened between the two of them if Bree was just an employee?

Damned if he knew.

And it was probably best if it remained that way.

Kissing Bree in the first place had been a mistake on Jackson's part. Almost making love to her had been an even bigger one. It would be better all round if they both tried to forget it had ever happened.

If either of them *could* forget.

'You're right: it *is* time I went to my apartment,' Bree agreed suddenly, still totally unsettled by their argument over Roger Tyler—not to mention the fact that she and Jackson had almost made love just now!

A fact that would definitely make it difficult for the two of them to work together in future.

Was that the only thing worrying her about this evening? Whether or not she and Jackson would be able to continue working together?

Bree didn't dare to think about the reasons *why* she and Jackson had almost made love.

'Fine. I'll see you in the morning.' Jackson nodded curtly and looked away, a frown darkening his brow.

A similar frown remained on Bree's brow long after she had returned to her apartment.

CHAPTER SIX

'GOOD MORNING, BREE! And how are you on this—?'

Jackson's deliberately cheery greeting was cut off abruptly as he entered Bree's office the following morning, after dropping Danny off at school. A small bundle of dark grey and white fur rushed across the room, becoming entangled in his legs and almost tripping him up in the process.

'Damn it, Beau!' Jackson regained his balance, bending down to pick up the squirming puppy before he could cause any more mayhem.

So much for Jackson's bright and breezy entrance!

He had debated long and hard with himself as he'd stood in front of the mirror shaving this morning, considering the best way to behave towards Bree today. They had stepped over an imaginary but definitive line between work colleagues and lovers—a line Jackson had only yesterday told himself must never be crossed if he and Bree were to continue working together...

Never be crossed? Last night Jackson had trampled it completely underfoot in his haste to kiss Bree!

The memory of which had not been in the least conducive to his having a dreamless and trouble-free sleep...

In fact Jackson hadn't slept well at all, as his reflection in the mirror had confirmed: he had dark circles under his eyes and a grim expression on his face. The dark circles wouldn't fade until he'd had a decent night's sleep, but the grim expression definitely had to go! Hence his attempt at a hearty good morning—an attempt that had been totally ruined by Beau's exuberant greeting.

'He likes you!' Bree put down the Christmas card she'd been reading, chuckling softly as the puppy licked Jackson's chin enthusiastically. 'Or not,' she added when Beau sneezed loudly, his expression one of doggy surprise.

'I think it's my aftershave he doesn't like,' Jackson remarked distastefully, before putting the puppy back down onto the carpeted floor.

'Probably,' Bree agreed, suddenly feeling shy and more than a little embarrassed by memories of the previous evening's intimacy. Now that Jackson had had the whole night to think about it, Bree was half worried that he might have decided to tell her they could no longer work together.

Which would be awful.

Worse than awful!

She liked working and living here. More than that, Bree had realised whilst lying sleepless in bed the previous night, Jackson and Danny had become like family to her. This was no doubt partly due to the still-strained relationship between Bree and her own family. But, whatever the reason, Bree couldn't bear the idea of being asked to leave, of never seeing Jackson or Danny again...

The events of last night meant she might not be given any choice in the matter!

Bree still had no explanation for what had happened.

One minute they had been talking and the next... The next was the part Bree had no explanation for. Jackson kissing her. And her own response to those kisses.

Bree had never thought of herself as a sensual being. She'd had no reason to think of herself that way—having feelings like the ones Jackson had incited the previous night had never happened to her before!

She and David had started going out together during their last year of university. Casual dates, mainly, to the cinema or out for a pizza. After graduating they had lost touch for a year or so, then met up again at a party given by a mutual friend. David, by then a stockbroker, had invited Bree out to dinner. After that they had dated regularly, and got engaged on Bree's twenty-fifth birthday. They had arranged their wedding for the following Christmas.

Never in all the years that Bree had known David had she been as excited by his kisses, as aroused by his caresses, as she had been in Jackson's arms the night before!

Which meant precisely what?

That she had somehow become a sensual being in the last year?

Or that she hadn't loved David as much as she thought she had?

Certainly Bree had never felt the thrum of excitement in David's company that she felt again now, just from looking at Jackson and remembering their intimacies of the night before!

Her mouth firmed resolutely and she looked down at the open appointment book on her desk.

'You have a meeting with Lord Caxley at ten o'clock this morning, a lunch date with Jennifer Greaves, and as it's Danny's last day of school before the Christmas holidays there's a present for his teacher on the—'

'What happened to "Good morning, Jackson"?' he cut in derisively, leaning against the side of her desk and looking down at her with teasing blue eyes.

Too close! Jackson was standing far too close to her. So close, in fact, that Bree could feel the heat his body exuded through the white T-shirt and faded blue denims; she could smell the aftershave that had so disagreed with Beau a few minutes ago, and the more earthy, male smell of clean skin and the lemon shampoo Jackson must have used on his hair.

The same golden honey-and-molasses hair that Bree had threaded her fingers through the night before as Jackson's mouth latched onto her breast—

Oh, dear Lord! What was happening to her?

She wasn't this person. Had never been this person. And Bree didn't *want* to be the sort of person whose breasts swelled, nipples hardening, as a hot rush of moisture burned between her legs, prompted simply by the close proximity of a man! And not just any man, either. Jerome Jackson Beaumont, to be precise.

But Bree couldn't deny that she was feeling all of those things now. Her fingers gripped the edge of her desk and she shifted uncomfortably in her chair, an urgent throbbing between her thighs, her breasts tingling, the nipples hard and ultra-sensitive against the soft material of her bra.

'Bree…?'

She drew in a ragged breath, forcing her fingers to relax their grip on the desk, before looking up at Jackson from beneath long dark lashes, trying in vain to remember what they had been talking about.

'I thought you would want to know what appointments you have lined up for today,' she explained quietly.

Jackson looked down searchingly into Bree's smoky-grey eyes, not in the least reassured by the way her gaze avoided his. As he had feared, something had changed, shifted, in their relationship. But was it to the point where they really couldn't continue working together?

Jackson felt a sinking feeling in his stomach at the thought of that happening. Was that because he didn't want to have to go to the trouble of training another personal assistant? Or was there something else?

He decided the first reason was the least complicated option to go with.

'Bree, do you want to talk about what happened between us last night?' he prompted softly.

'No,' she replied curtly, continuing to avoid his gaze as colour warmed her cheeks.

'Do you want me to apologise?'

She glanced at him sharply. 'Do you want to apologise?'

He grimaced. 'Hell, no.'

She swallowed. 'Then I suggest the best thing would be for us both to try and forget the whole incident.'

Jackson wasn't sure he would be able to do that. How *could* he forget it? It had been Bree he had almost made love to last night. *Bree!* And she might be wearing tailored black trousers and a charcoal-grey sweater this morning, her hair scraped back from the pale delicacy of her face and secured on the crown of her head, but now Jackson knew exactly how long and beautiful her hair was, how velvety soft her skin was to the touch, how perfect the weight of her breasts felt in the palms of his hands, how sensitive her nipples were…

'Do you want to read through the correspondence we've had with Lord Caxley before you meet with him at ten o'clock?' Bree asked, standing up abruptly.

Maybe she would be able to breathe if she wasn't quite so close to Jackson and the warm caress of those sky-blue eyes! She avoided even looking at Jackson as she picked up the pile of discarded envelopes from the morning's post, dropping them in the bin on her way over to the filing cabinets on the other side of the room.

Jackson shrugged. 'I'm just supposed to photograph him for posterity, aren't I?'

'For the reception room at his parliamentary offices in Westminster, I believe,' Bree corrected drily.

He nodded. 'Just in case any of his constituents decide to pay him a visit and have no idea what their MP actually looks like, I presume?'

Bree smiled. 'Probably.'

'No, I don't need to see his file.' Jackson dismissed the idea with a wave. 'Oh,' he added casually, 'I forgot to ask. Has Roger Tyler called you yet this morning?'

Bree eyed him warily. 'It's only nine o'clock…'

'And?'

She shrugged. 'And I very much doubt that Roger has even *seen* nine o'clock in the morning for some years, let alone been *compos mentis* enough to make a telephone call!'

'You have a point there,' Jackson muttered, straightening up—and in doing so accidentally knocking over the pile of Christmas cards that had arrived in the post that morning.

'Damn!' He sank down on his haunches to gather them up from the floor.

'It's okay. I'll do it!' Bree rushed across the room, eager to help him pick up the cards. Well, one card in particular: the same card she had been looking at when he'd first come into the room.

'No problem.' Jackson continued to gather up the dozen or so cards. 'I don't suppose any of these are remotely interesting. I don't know why— Hello, what's this?' He frowned as he read the inscription inside the card he had just picked up. '"To Bree, with love from David…"' He turned to look at her enquiringly.

Bree's face had paled when she'd seen Jackson picking up the one Christmas card she hadn't wanted him to see—and her silent prayer that he wouldn't look inside had obviously gone unanswered!

'No one important.' She made a grab for the card and missed as Jackson lifted it tantalisingly just out of her reach. 'Give it to me, Jackson.'

'Not until you tell me who David is.' He stood up slowly, keeping the card out of Bree's grasp. 'I don't know what's happened to you, Bree.' He shook his head mockingly. 'Dinner with Roger Tyler last night. A Christmas card from another man called David today. I had no idea you had such a hectic social life!'

Bree winced inwardly, noting that Jackson had missed out the part in between dinner with Roger and the card from David—namely, the part where he had kissed her!

She hadn't been able to believe it herself either, when she'd opened the envelope addressed to her and found a Christmas card from David inside!

The day that Bree had found him and Cathy in bed

together David had come to her parents' house and tried to speak to her. He'd done the same thing again and again for days, and each time Bree had refused to see him. There had been absolutely nothing she wished to say to him after seeing him with Cathy, both naked in her bed—the same bed she and David had planned to share after their wedding!

The Christmas card that Jackson now held out of reach so tormentingly was the first communication Bree had received from David since she had written to him a year ago, informing him that she had cancelled their wedding and never wished to see him again.

Bree knew from visiting her parents that the affair between David and Cathy—now divorced from her husband—was over. Her parents had told her about David's frequent visits to their house to ask how Bree was. No doubt, she thought bitterly, her parents had seen nothing wrong in supplying him with her new address so that he could send her a Christmas card. And if Jackson hadn't read the card Bree might have just accepted it as the olive branch it was obviously meant to be before dismissing it completely from her mind.

'Bree?' Jackson prompted sharply, deeply concerned at how pale her face had become. 'Who is David?'

He wasn't in the least reassured by the haunted expression in those smoky-grey eyes as Bree looked up at him.

CHAPTER SEVEN

A SHUTTER CAME down quickly over those expressive grey eyes as Bree moved sharply back towards her seat, putting the width of her desk between them.

'And would your lunch today with Miss Greaves be business or pleasure?' she enquired icily, looking up at Jackson in a direct challenge.

His eyes narrowed to sky-blue slits. 'I don't see what that has to do with anything.'

'No?' Bree raised cynical brows.

'No,' Jackson bit out sharply. 'It isn't the same thing at all.'

'It is in as much as your lunch today is no more my business than David's role in my life is any of yours,' she spat, her slender hands flat on the desktop.

David's role in Bree's life?

The two of them had worked together in harmony for almost a year now, though in the past two days Jackson knew that harmonious relationship had been blown completely and utterly to pieces. Some of it was his own fault; Jackson freely admitted that. He had been totally out of line last night in kissing Bree—let alone what followed.

But where the hell had all these other men in her life come from so suddenly? Roger Tyler was obviously a relatively new acquaintance, but had this David been around all the time and Jackson just hadn't known about it?

And what if the other man *had* been in Bree's life for some time? Why should that matter to Jackson?

It didn't! Or at least it only mattered in as much as it showed him that he didn't know Bree as well as he'd thought…

'I really don't want to talk about this, Jackson,' Bree said with finality.

He continued to look at her searchingly for several long seconds before slowly lowering his arm to place the Christmas card down on the desk in front of Bree.

'You're right. It's none of my business.' He took a step backwards, exhaling deeply.

'Thank you,' she murmured huskily.

Jackson nodded tersely. 'I won't be back here today until after I've picked Danny up from school.'

In other words, Bree guessed dully, Jackson's lunch with Jennifer Greaves was going to last way beyond the time they spent in the restaurant together…

And just what had Bree expected? Had she imagined that Jackson might cancel his lunch date with the beautiful supermodel after what had happened last night? Had Bree really thought there was even a possibility of that happening?

If so, why had she been so determined—even more determined than Jackson—to put the whole of last night behind them?

The disappointment Bree felt at the very thought of Jackson spending the early afternoon in bed with Jennifer Greaves was totally illogical!

Inexplicable…

And it was certainly something she didn't want Jackson to notice!

She straightened determinedly. 'In that case I won't be here when you get back,' she announced, adding in response to Jackson's frown, 'I'm taking the afternoon off to go Christmas shopping, remember?'

Jackson had forgotten that earlier in the week Bree had asked whether she could take this afternoon off. As he had no appointments on this particular Friday afternoon, Jackson had been only too happy to agree to the half-day holiday. Following Bree's reaction to his having seen her Christmas card from David, Jackson couldn't help wondering if Bree intended to spend *all* of the afternoon Christmas shopping...

'I seem to remember your saying yesterday that you would look after Beau during the day,' he reminded her tersely.

'This afternoon off was arranged before I made that agreement,' she came back impatiently. 'I'm sure Mrs Holmes won't mind having Beau in the kitchen with her while I'm out.'

'It would seem to be irrelevant whether she does or not,' Jackson muttered bad-temperedly.

Bree gave a sigh. 'I'll try to get back as quickly as I can, okay?'

'I suppose it will have to be.'

She grimaced at his unreasonableness. 'You'll be late for your appointment with Lord Caxley if you don't leave now,' she said softly when Jackson made no move to go. 'And don't forget to take the Christmas present for Danny's teacher with you.'

Jackson frowned down at her in frustration for several long seconds, aware that he had to leave now or, as

Bree said, he'd be late for his appointment with Caxley. He knew he was only delaying because he still felt unsettled by the strained atmosphere that now existed between himself and Bree. He felt as if there ought to be something he could do or say to take away that tension. But he had no idea what that something might be!

Oh, to hell with it! He would talk to Bree again later this evening and try to sort the whole mess out then.

The telephone on Bree's desk began to ring.

'Bye, then, Jackson,' she said tightly, reaching for the mobile.

Jackson had absolutely no intention of going anywhere until he found out who the call was from, knowing it could be Roger Tyler or the mysterious David. Or it could be neither of them, Jackson acknowledged, reproaching himself.

'Oh, hello, Roger,' Bree greeted brightly, even as she shot Jackson an irritated glance. 'Just a minute, Roger.' She put her hand over the mouthpiece and looked at Jackson enquiringly. 'Is there something else I can help you with before you go…?'

Jackson's nostrils flared. 'I guess Tyler does know what nine o'clock in the morning looks like after all!' he growled.

The other man had certainly been quick enough off the mark in calling Bree today! Not that Jackson was in the least surprised. Bree had looked beautiful last night. She was also warm, with a dry sense of humour that made her fun to be with, and—damn it! Damn, damn, *damn* it!

'I'll see you later,' he rasped harshly when Bree gave no reply to his taunt, striding out into the hallway and picking up the gaily wrapped Christmas present for Danny's teacher from the hall table before leaving.

Well, he hadn't so much left the house as slammed out of it, Jackson recognised with a self-disgusted wince as he slid behind the wheel of his sleek black sports car.

What the hell was the matter with him today?

Bree was the matter, came the instant reply. Bree and the two men who had suddenly appeared in her life and now vied for her attention.

Attention Jackson realised he wasn't at all happy to share...

BREE WAS TIRED and bad-tempered by the time she struggled back from the hot, crowded shops later that evening, loaded down with bags.

She'd only had a few Christmas presents to buy—things for her parents, Danny and Jackson, and a little something for Mrs Holmes—and after only an hour in the shops she had managed to find suitable presents for everyone except Jackson.

Jackson.

Bree had absolutely no idea what to buy for the man who had everything—and what he didn't have he could easily go out and buy!

No—it wasn't just that, Bree acknowledged wearily as she removed her shoes before putting the kettle on for a much-needed cup of tea. It was the change in her relationship with Jackson that was causing the problem—not Bree having no idea what to buy him. The previous month she had chosen a nice sweater to give him for his birthday without any trouble whatsoever. The previous month. Now it wasn't so easy to choose something suitable.

She couldn't buy Jackson another jumper, and he didn't wear formal shirts unless he absolutely had to—and even then he had pure silk ones specially made. A book seemed too impersonal. As did aftershave.

After three more hours of wandering fruitlessly around the shops Bree had had to admit defeat: she simply had no idea what to get Jackson for Christmas!

Now, in the emptiness of her apartment, she briefly wished that she had accepted Roger Tyler's second invitation to dinner. But only briefly. She had enjoyed his company the evening before, but not enough to encourage him by going out with him again tonight. Her life already seemed complicated enough without—

'What on earth...?'

Bree hurried out into the hallway. After the briefest of knocks, the internal door to her apartment had been slammed open with such force that it crashed into the wall before springing back again.

Jackson easily caught the edge of the door as it rebounded, his expression grim as he glared down the hallway at her.

'It's about time you got back!' he snarled accusingly.

Bree recoiled slightly from the vehemence of his tone.

'I was only gone a couple of hours—'

'And while you've been out enjoying yourself the whole household has been in uproar!' Jackson roared, stepping into the apartment and closing the door firmly behind him before striding purposefully down the hallway, muscles flexing beneath his fitted black T-shirt and faded denims.

Bree would hardly call shopping for Christmas presents in shops that were hot, stuffy and crowded 'enjoying herself'. But Jackson didn't look as if he was in the mood to argue the point.

She hurried after him. 'I'm sorry to hear that, but— Wait—what sort of uproar?'

Jackson continued to scowl as he turned. 'Beau escaped out of the kitchen, and Mrs Holmes didn't notice he was gone for several minutes. By which time he had chewed his way through the wrapping paper on half a dozen Christmas presents under the tree, before proceeding to knock the whole damned tree over on top of himself.'

'Is he all right?' Bree gasped anxiously, imagining that tiny puppy buried under the eight-foot Christmas tree.

Jackson's eyes narrowed in warning. 'I should have known you would be more concerned about the puppy than the chaos he's caused!'

'Yes... Well...' She had the grace to look briefly apologetic. 'Christmas presents can easily be rewrapped, and the tree righted, but if Beau has been hurt—'

'The puppy's fine,' Jackson snapped. 'And the tree is now standing—even if some of the lights are broken and the decorations slightly askew. And even as we speak Danny, with the dubious help of Beau, is rewrapping the Christmas presents.'

Bree visibly brightened. 'Then it would appear that the crisis is over.'

The renewed anger glittering in Jackson's eyes as he glared down at her didn't give the impression that he agreed!

CHAPTER EIGHT

BREE SHIFTED UNCOMFORTABLY as she followed Jackson into her small sitting room.

'Shouldn't you be going back upstairs now...?'

'Mrs Holmes is supervising the rewrapping of the Christmas presents—she felt it was the least she could do after allowing Beau to escape,' Jackson explained distractedly.

'Oh.' A frown creased Bree's brow. 'I... You aren't going to send Beau back as you threatened to do yesterday, are you?'

He raised derisive brows. 'What do you think?'

She gave a wry smile. 'I think you might have a fight on your hands from Danny if you tried to do that now!'

Jackson tilted his head to one side and looked at her speculatively. 'You like doing that, don't you?'

She looked puzzled. 'Doing what?'

Jackson smiled knowingly. 'Invoking Danny's name as a stick to beat me with!'

'Oh!' Bree gasped as guilty colour warmed her cheeks. 'I— Well, I—'

'Didn't think I'd noticed?' Jackson taunted. 'Oh, I've noticed, Bree; I've just never had reason to argue the point.'

'Until now...?'

'No, not even now.' He sighed. 'When you're right,

you're right. Danny would never forgive me if I even attempted to part him from Beau!'

'No,' Bree agreed softly.

He gave a rueful smile. 'I'm really not a complete monster, Bree.'

'I don't think you're a monster at all,' she murmured.

'No?'

'No.' She suddenly looked very serious. 'I think you're a wonderful father to Danny.'

'You do?' Jackson looked surprised.

'Most certainly I do,' Bree confirmed without hesitation.

'Several times I've had the impression that you think I should have married and given him a mother and some brothers and sisters.'

Bree felt her heart sink at the very thought of Jackson with a wife and several more children—but only because a married Jackson would probably be even more impossible to work for, she told herself firmly. What other reason could there possibly be?

She shook her head slowly. 'Marrying for those reasons would be completely wrong—for both of you.'

'I couldn't agree more.' Jackson nodded. 'Which is why I would never consider marrying any woman who couldn't accept and love Danny as I do.'

Bree grimaced. 'It's really none of my business, is it?'

No, it wasn't, and if Jackson hadn't had such a lousy day so far maybe he wouldn't be talking about it now either.

Jennifer had been her usual charming and beautiful self, and she'd made it obvious throughout lunch that she was expecting them to spend a couple of hours in bed together afterwards. Ordinarily Jackson would have been only too happy to oblige—as he had several times in the past.

But not today.

Today Jackson hadn't been able to work up even a spark of enthusiasm for making love with Jennifer. In fact he'd felt quite the opposite; just the thought of her tall and willowy body had been a complete turn-off when compared to the softness of Bree's body. A body that Jackson had found himself thinking about far too often during a lunch date with one of the most beautiful women in the world.

He looked at Bree now, attentively and appraisingly. She looked adorable, despite the weariness from her shopping trip evident in her expression. Several dark wavy strands of hair had escaped their confines to curl wispily about her cheeks and throat. The blue jeans she wore moulded perfectly to the slenderness of her hips and bottom; a blue sweater clearly outlined the curve of her breasts.

In spite of that weariness and untidiness Jackson knew he found Bree's natural beauty infinitely more appealing than he had found Jennifer Greaves's ultra-perfect looks!

Bree looked pained. 'You seemed to imply earlier that there had been more than one crisis since you got back,' she reminded him carefully.

'I did, didn't I?' He paced the room restlessly, his considerable height and the width of his shoulders dwarfing her cosy sitting room. And causing Bree's heart to start pounding and her palms to dampen...

These conversations with Jackson were...unsettling. Particularly so when she found his rakish good looks and the barely leashed power of his lean and muscled body just so—so overwhelmingly male!

'Well...?' she prompted warily as he continued to pace.

His eyes glittered with displeasure as he turned to look at her. 'You had a visitor earlier.'

'I did?' Bree's wariness increased as she wondered who that visitor could possibly have been. Certainly not Roger; they had parted amicably enough on the telephone earlier. And on the rare occasions when she met with family or friends it was always in town or at one of their homes; Bree had certainly never invited anyone to visit her here at Beaumont House. She'd always preferred to keep her work and her private life completely separate. Although she and Jackson hadn't been too successful at doing that lately!

'Yes,' Jackson bit out tersely.

Bree bristled at the censure she heard in his tone. 'I trust I am *allowed* to have visitors here?'

'Of course,' he snapped.

'Well? Aren't you going to tell me who it was?' she demanded impatiently—really, Jackson could be one of the most infuriating of men!

As well as one of the most dangerously attractive...

His was a dangerous and disturbing attractiveness that Bree had found herself thinking about far too much today. She'd thought about him as she'd worked that morning. She'd thought about him as she'd eaten a light lunch before going out. And as she'd wandered around the shops, searching in vain for his Christmas present, she'd thought—of course—of nothing but him.

The cocoon of emotional and physical numbness that Bree had wrapped herself in over the past year had, she realised, been forced wide open by the intensity of the previous night's lovemaking with Jackson!

So much so that her senses were running riot with physical awareness just from being in his presence again. Jackson made her pulse race, and the smell of him—clean and earthy, with the underlying musk of a male in his prime—sent shivers of sensation down her spine. Her hands—hands Bree now clasped firmly together behind her back—ached to reach out and touch him. All of him. From the impressive width of his shoulders to the hardness of his muscled chest and stomach, and lower still to his—

Oh, dear Lord!

Bree swayed slightly on her feet as the heat of desire rushed through her. Her whole body was feeling hot, her nipples tingling as they became engorged, that warmth seeming to burn as it ached between her thighs.

She sat down abruptly on the sofa—it was that or risk falling down!

Bree had always believed that going weak at the knees was just a romantic expression; now she knew it to be absolutely true. If she hadn't sat down when she had, she would probably have collapsed in a heap at Jackson's feet!

What was happening to her?

Whatever it was, it was distinctly uncomfortable! And totally, utterly stupid if she wanted to continue working for Jackson.

Which she did.

Just the thought of leaving—of never seeing Jackson again, of being separated from Danny—was enough to make Bree's chest ache. And not in a pleasant way either!

'What are you thinking about?'

Bree looked up at Jackson warily, her breath catching in her throat as he focused all the intensity of his glittering blue eyes on her. She moistened her lips nervously, averting her own gaze and looking into the flames of the gas fire.

'I'm still waiting for you to answer my question,' she said softly.

'But that wasn't what you were thinking about, was it?' There was a quiet, knowing triumph in his voice as he spoke.

Colour warmed Bree's cheeks even as she raised heavy dark lashes to look up at him. 'You can't possibly know that.'

'Can't I?'

'No!'

He raised his eyebrows, taunting her. 'I know that whatever you were thinking about it hardened your nipples!'

The colour deepened in Bree's cheeks as she looked down self-consciously and saw the clear outline of her aroused nipples against the soft wool of her sweater. She closed her eyes, groaning inwardly with mortification.

'Maybe you were imagining your visitor was Roger Tyler?'

'Of *course* I wasn't imagining that!' Bree protested, looked up with a frown.

'No?' Jackson took a moment to savour her protest before his expression hardened again.

Was Bree even wearing a bra? If she was, then it was worse than useless at concealing the smooth curve of those full and tempting breasts, let alone the firm outline of her aroused nipples.

Nipples that Jackson ached to expose to the ministrations of his lips, tongue and teeth!

'Who do you think it was if it wasn't Tyler?'

'I have absolutely no idea. Nor am I particularly interested—least of all in playing your childish little guessing games,' she spat impatiently. 'I think it's time you left.'

'I'm not going anywhere until you tell me who David is.'

'David?' She was completely taken aback. 'Are you saying that my visitor was *David*?'

'Would it matter to you if it was?'

Would it? Bree asked herself dazedly.

Last week—yesterday, even—the answer to that question might have been yes. But did it matter to her today, here and now, after what had happened with Jackson last night…?

CHAPTER NINE

BREE'S CHEEKS PALED as she avoided answering that question—even to herself.

'I've never asked you about any of the women you've been involved with, have I?'

His jaw tightened, his mouth thinning into a hard line. 'And is David someone you're involved with?'

'I believe I used the past tense, Jackson,' she snapped, fuming with annoyance.

His expression was grim. 'Past tense as in years ago or recently?'

Bree moved impatiently. 'What difference does it make as long as it's in the past?'

'You tell me…' He raised his eyebrows, looking deep into her eyes.

She shook her head. 'I have no idea what you want from me, Jackson.'

'I believe, for the moment, a simple answer to my question will do,' he said softly.

Bree frowned at him and took a deep breath. 'Look, I'm sorry if David came here earlier and…and was a nuisance. He's obviously annoyed you somehow.'

'I don't know enough about the man to be annoyed with him, Bree,' he assured her briskly.

'Does that mean you're annoyed with *me*?' she asked incredulously.

'I don't remember saying I was annoyed with anyone!'

'Well, you're definitely in a snit about something!'

Jackson hesitated. 'A...*snit*?'

'A snit, yes. That's the only explanation I can think of for this ridiculous conversation,' Bree snapped.

'Is it ridiculous to show an interest in your friends?' Jackson took a slow, predatory step towards her as he continued to hold her gaze with his own.

Wariness darkened those smoky-grey eyes. 'It's definitely something,' she insisted firmly.

Jackson shrugged his shoulders dismissively as he moved to stand behind her.

'Nevertheless...'

Standing this close to Bree, he could detect the enticing, delicate fragrance of her perfume, and somewhere deeper, beneath the artificial scent, he sensed her arousal: a hot spiciness that caused his shaft to thicken against the rough denim of his jeans as he gave in to temptation and threaded his fingers into the silky hair at Bree's temples.

'What are you doing?' Bree breathed, her back stiff with shock, her neck tense.

'What does it feel like I'm doing?' Jackson whispered huskily.

Whatever it was, it felt marvellous. Bree was almost purring as Jackson's fingers moved lightly through her hair. Her eyes closed and her back arched with pleasure when she felt the full weight of her hair falling about her shoulders as Jackson removed the clip, shaking the lustrous length of curls loose before continuing that soothing caress.

She knew she should stop him—knew that they were once again stepping over that line between employer and employee. Knew it and yet couldn't prevent it. Didn't *want* to prevent it, she amended, as Jackson's hands moved to rest lightly on top of her shoulders. She felt the warmth of his breath against her earlobe, gasping as his lips began a slow and leisurely exploration down the length of her throat.

The muscles in Bree's neck loosened and she leaned her head back, dark lashes brushing her cheeks as her eyes closed, breasts thrusting forward, hands clenched at her sides. She could no longer contain a groan of ecstasy as an electric current of pleasure travelled down her spine, culminating almost unbearably between her thighs.

Jackson's hands slid down over the tops of her breasts, lightly skimming the sensitised tips before cupping the firm rounds beneath, gently squeezing and massaging their soft weight.

Bree's breath caught in her throat as the soft pads of his thumbs moved back and forth across the hardened peaks of her breasts. Her hands moved up to clasp his forearms—not to push him away, but to press him closer still.

'Oh, God...' she groaned weakly as Jackson gently squeezed those throbbing nipples between finger and thumb.

Her breasts quickly rose and fell as Jackson increased the pressure on her nipples. Her eyelashes fluttered weakly as she tried to raise the lids and couldn't. The pleasure of Jackson's caresses was all she could feel or think about.

Bree moaned protestingly when those hands left her breasts, then gasped when cool air hit her feverish skin as Jackson lifted her sweater up over her breasts, bar-ing them to the heat of his palms as he plucked at her throbbing nipples.

She writhed restlessly on the sofa, desperately aware of that uncomfortable throb between her legs as she felt excitement building. She needed—oh, God—she needed—

'Tell me what you need, Bree,' Jackson encouraged, moving from behind the sofa to nudge Bree's legs apart. He knelt between them, lowering his mouth to her breast hungrily before raising his head to look down at those full rose-tipped orbs. 'Tell me, Bree!'

One of his hands cupped her breast, caressing, squeezing her swollen nipple, as he slowly kissed his way down her abdomen to her navel. His other hand moved purposefully to the fastening of her jeans, sliding the zip slowly downwards until he could see the white lace of her panties.

'Bree…?' His voice was a muffled rasp: the sight and scent of her arousal had only deepened the aching throb of his shaft.

'Touch me, Jackson!' she gasped achingly. 'For pity's sake, touch me!'

'I *am* touching you, Bree.' He added pressure as he squeezed her breast.

'Lower, Jackson…!' Her thighs moved restlessly, invitingly. 'I need…!'

She tasted so damned good, and her skin was like silk to the touch as Jackson's mouth moved lower still, almost tasting Bree's arousal as he kissed her through those white lace panties. He heard her gasp as his tongue found and gently stroked the crux of the heat raging through her. His hands once again moved up to cup and caress her breasts, tugging at the swollen nipples as Bree stretched against him in a silent plea, and he took the throb of her against his tongue as evidence that Bree was fast approaching her climax.

'Harder, Jackson!' Bree sobbed in desperation, her fingers entangled in the thickness of Jackson's hair as she held him against her and arched into the rhythmic caress of his tongue. 'Please!'

She cried out in protest as his mouth left her to latch on to her breast, sucking hard as he shifted to the side, pushing her jeans and panties down and throwing them aside before pulling her further down the sofa and parting her legs. Bree was completely open to him as his lips claimed hers and his tongue plunged into the heat of her mouth, as he thrust first one finger inside her and then another, thrusting again and again, whilst caressing her swollen nipple with his other hand, taking her higher and higher towards release.

Bree wrenched her mouth from Jackson's, whipping her head from side to side as her first ever orgasm hit her with a force that completely took her breath away. Pleasure unlike anything Bree had ever experienced claimed her in wave after earth-shattering wave.

'You haven't—didn't—'

'Does that bother you?' Jackson lay on the sofa beside Bree and held her in his arms, the hardness of his arousal warm against her thigh as she continued to tremble and quake from the aftershocks of her release.

'Of course it bothers me,' she breathed.

Jackson smiled. 'It doesn't bother me.'

'Really?' She stared up at him, eyes wide with disbelief.

'Really.'

Giving Bree such pleasure, and then watching her plunge over the edge of that pleasure into orgasm and beyond, had been the most satisfying physical experience of Jackson's life. He could only imagine, only anticipate, how much more satisfying actually being inside Bree would be…

'Oh.'

Jackson chuckled. 'You sound surprised.'

'A little, yes.'

Bree could say nothing more at that moment, when she was so full of embarrassment over what had just happened. Inwardly she groaned with mortification every time she remembered the way she had completely unravelled as Jackson pleasured her with his mouth and hands!

Jackson.

The man Bree had worked with so harmoniously over the past year.

The same man who had an unwritten rule about never becoming personally involved with the women he employed.

Bree had a feeling, lying there half-naked in Jackson's arms, wearing only her sweater now pulled down over her sensitive breasts and the lace panties she had put back on moments ago, that this went way beyond personal involvement!

'Who's David, Bree?' Jackson murmured softly. 'And why did he come here to see you?'

'Oh, for goodness' sake—!'

'For mine, actually,' Jackson amended drily.

Bree drew in a deep breath. 'I have absolutely no idea why David should have come here to see me.'

Jackson raised his brows. 'You could always try asking him…?'

She smiled contentedly. 'I'm quite happy where I am for the moment, thank you.'

'That's good to know.' Jackson's arms tightened around her. 'Although I doubt that David is going to leave until you tell him to do so.'

Bree frowned. 'What?'

He nodded. 'He's upstairs in the sitting room, with Danny and Mrs Holmes.'

'What?' Bree raised herself up on her elbows and stared down at him incredulously.

'He didn't seem to mind waiting until you came home,' Jackson explained evenly.

Bree paled visibly, all the colour draining from her face. At the same time, Jackson observed, she looked not just anxious but actually *hunted*. She wrenched herself out of his arms and rose agitatedly to her feet before pulling on her jeans.

'You mean that while we—while I—all this time David has been sitting upstairs waiting to see me?' She could manage little more than a whisper.

Jackson inclined his head. 'He was still there when I came downstairs earlier, yes.'

'You—' Bree's hands clenched into fists at her sides, her grey eyes glittering darkly as she stared down at him in complete disbelief, two angry spots of colour blooming in her cheeks.

'You—I—you complete *bastard*,' she finally spat out forcefully. 'You absolute one-hundred-percent *bastard*!'

With one last disgusted look in Jackson's direction Bree turned on her heel and strode forcefully from the room and down the hallway, slamming the door of the apartment behind her.

CHAPTER TEN

'IT'S CHRISTMAS EVE, Bree; surely you aren't going to keep up this stilted politeness all over Christmas?'

Bree shot Jackson a brief glance from where she sat behind her desk, opening the post on Wednesday morning, with snow falling steadily outside the window behind her.

'I can't see that being a problem when I have no intention of being at Beaumont House over Christmas.'

'What?' Jackson exclaimed in surprise, crossing the room to her desk in three long strides.

Bree remained unruffled as he towered over her ominously. 'I'm not going to be here for Christmas,' she repeated evenly.

Jackson was dumbfounded. 'Since when?'

Bree gazed at him steadily. 'Since I decided not to be,' she explained with cool nonchalance.

Jackson shook his head in frustration. 'If this is because of the other evening—'

'I have no wish to discuss Friday evening with you, Jackson. Now or at any other time,' she interrupted in a brisk, businesslike tone, her back stiff and unyielding.

Jackson had put up with four days of this treatment from Bree. Admittedly it hadn't been too much of a problem over the weekend—Jackson had decided that it was probably best to leave Bree to her own devices once she had refused his invitations to accompany him and Danny to a pantomime on Saturday and ice-skating on Sunday. But the past two days in the office had been damned uncomfortable as Bree continued to give Jackson the cold shoulder, not speaking to him unless she absolutely had to, and even then only in the briefest of terms.

He gave an impatient sigh. 'Damn it, I've apologised to you; what more do you want from me?'

Bree stood up, turning her back on Jackson as she put a letter away in the filing cabinet. Yes, Jackson *had* apologised to her for his behaviour on Friday evening—and it had been one of the most embarrassing conversations of her life! Especially when Bree had had no idea whether Jackson was apologising for not telling her earlier about David's presence upstairs, or whether he was apologising for making love to her!

Bree cringed with embarrassment every time she so much as thought of that time with Jackson. Of the intimacies they had shared. Of her complete loss of control...

She had never—*ever*—behaved like that before. And she very much doubted that she would do so again.

Because she had realised that she was in love with Jackson.

Totally and irrevocably.

Ironically, the truth of her feelings had hit Bree as she and David had sat talking in the bar they had gone to on Friday evening, once Bree had told him she would prefer to go out. Jackson had still been downstairs in her apartment, and there was nowhere private enough for them to talk in the main house.

She had looked across at David as they'd sat together, two untouched glasses of white wine on the table in front of them, and acknowledged that he was still as dark and handsome and charming as he had ever been—and she had known without a doubt that she felt absolutely nothing for him.

She had always thought if she ever saw David again that the pain of his betrayal would return. Instead, as Bree had listened to him telling her that he still loved her, begging her to give him another chance, she had realised that she felt nothing. No residual anger. No hurt. No disappointment. No love. Not even mild affection. Just a vast wasteland of emotion that she had been as eager to escape as she had been keen to get away from the man himself.

It was a realisation that had saddened Bree more than anything else. A year ago she had wanted to marry David. A year ago she had believed she loved him, and that her heart had been broken when she'd discovered he was having an affair with her own sister.

But a year ago Bree hadn't known Jerome Jackson Beaumont. Or fallen in love with him…

She knew herself to be in love with him now. And it was a love so futile that it made the pained disillusionment of a year ago pale into total insignificance.

'Are you going away with David?' Jackson rasped harshly into the silence that had fallen over the room.

It was an uncomfortable, dead silence that made Jackson want to say something, do something—anything to shock Bree out of the coldness she had shown towards him over the past four days!

She turned around to face him, her expression coolly remote. 'Not that it's any of your business but, no, David and I have no intention of meeting again.'

Jackson breathed an inward sigh of relief for that small mercy at least. 'Then perhaps Roger Tyler...?'

Bree raised derisive brows. 'Don't be absurd. Again, it's none of your business, but the answer to that is also no.'

Jackson's mouth thinned with frustration. 'Then where the hell *are* you going?'

She shrugged, crossing the room to return to her desk. 'I haven't made any definite plans yet.'

'Then why go anywhere?' Jackson scowled. 'Danny is expecting you to spend the holidays with us,' he added petulantly.

Bree gave a rueful smile. '*Now* who's using the D-word as emotional leverage?'

Jackson wasn't averse to using whatever leverage was necessary, emotional or otherwise, if it meant that Bree would spend Christmas with them.

'Well?' he prompted tersely.

She gave a sigh. 'I do have a family of my own, you know.'

'No, I *don't* know!' Jackson snapped with impatience. 'How could I, when you've never talked about any of them?'

'There hasn't been any reason for me to do so before now.' Bree shrugged.

Jackson narrowed his blue eyes in speculation. 'And what's happened to change that?'

The change, as Jackson called it, was all within Bree. The revelation of her complete lack of emotion towards David—a lack of emotion which had allowed Bree gently but firmly to turn down his pleas for reconciliation—had helped her to realise that she no longer harboured any anger towards her sister either; hurt and disappointment, yes, but not anger. In fact Bree's newfound feelings for Jackson meant that she might even owe Cathy a debt of gratitude for saving her from a marriage that would ultimately have been pleasant at best and a disaster at worst!

As it was, Bree had decided that it was time to put the past behind her; her heart had moved on without her mind even realising it, and it was time for her to do the same. As such, she was toying with the idea of going to visit her parents for Christmas, and at the same time making her peace with Cathy.

'Nothing has changed, Jackson,' she said.

'Hmm…' Jackson didn't believe her. He knew that even though he had apologised Bree was still angry with him. And with good reason. Jackson had behaved badly on Friday evening. His only excuse was that he had felt threatened by the advent of first Roger Tyler in Bree's life and then the arrival of David from her past. A past she resolutely refused to share with him.

A past Bree could have no reason to *want* to share with him when he had been just as reticent about his own history…

'Believe it or not, Jackson, it's normal to want to spend Christmas with your family,' Bree remarked sardonically.

'I've had the increasing impression throughout the year that you think of Danny as part of your family.'

'I do,' she confirmed sadly.

'But not me?'

She felt colour warm her cheeks. 'Jackson, you have your own family—'

'Try telling my mother that!' He grimaced in distaste.

Bree felt relieved at the change of subject. 'Have you and Clarissa ever been close?'

'Once upon a time, yes,' Jackson acknowledged gruffly. 'Before my sister…before Jocelyn died.'

'I'm sorry, I didn't mean to pry.' Bree frowned.

'*Why* didn't you?' Jackson eyed her in frustration, not sure why he was so angry with Bree, only knowing that he was. 'Doesn't my behaviour on Friday evening give you the right to ask me whatever questions you damn well please?'

Bree looked pained. 'I thought we had agreed, during your apology, that it would be better if we didn't refer to that incident again?'

Jackson shook his head violently as he began to pace the room. He felt restless and frustrated.

'I think we can safely say that we've tried doing that and it obviously isn't working!'

Bree avoided that piercing blue gaze. 'Jackson, I really would prefer not to—'

'We're way past what you would *prefer*, Bree,' he snapped harshly. 'Way past.'

He stopped pacing and looked at her with a directness that made her blush.

'In fact, I think it's time we shared a few truths about our respective pasts.'

Bree eyed him uncertainly, not sure if she wanted to have this conversation; not sure if the fragile shield behind which she had managed to hide her feelings for Jackson could cope with the two of them revealing 'a few truths' to each other!

She licked her lips nervously. 'I don't think, if we're to continue working together, that sort of honesty between the two of us is completely necessary, Jackson—'

'It's *very* necessary!' He leaned forward across the desk until his face was only inches away from Bree's, the warmth of his breath a soft caress against her cheeks. 'In fact I believe that if we don't have this conversation and at least try to clear the air between us we won't be able to continue working together at all!'

Quite what Bree would have said in answer to that disturbing statement she wasn't altogether sure; in any case she was spared the trouble as a knock sounded on the office door.

Jackson's nostrils flared with frustration and impatience as he straightened up.

'Yes?' he roared in the direction of the door.

Mrs Holmes opened the door and smiled across the room at him. 'You asked me to let you know when Danny and I had finished baking cookies, Mr Beaumont, so that you could take him and Beau out into the garden,' she reminded him brightly.

Jackson let out a deep, controlled breath. 'So I did,' he acknowledged lightly. 'I'll come through in a couple of minutes,' he added, waiting until the housekeeper had left before turning back to Bree, his expression hard and unyielding.

'It's Christmas Eve and I promised Danny I would build a snowman with him. Do you want to come outside in the snow with us?'

Bree wasn't sure *what* she wanted to do after hearing Jackson's shocking statement about them not being able to continue working together if they didn't clear the air between them.

Except she knew that she didn't want to go outside with Jackson—let alone Danny and Beau. Jackson was right: she *did* think of Danny and Beau as part of her

family. And Jackson too. So how could she go outside
with any of them when she could barely breathe, when
her heart felt as if it were being squeezed in her chest at
the mere thought of Jackson asking her to leave? She did
need to get out of here, though. To distance herself—
and most of all to be alone.

'Probably not,' Jackson answered himself drily. 'Just
don't try leaving for the holidays before I come back
in, Bree,' he warned softly, as if guessing that might
be her intention. 'This conversation is very far from
over,' he added grimly, before following Mrs Holmes
down the hallway.

Bree felt totally numb as she stood up and stared
bleakly outside into the garden, not seeing the snow that
still fell lightly, or the beautiful white landscape it had
produced. Her thoughts were totally turned inwards as
she became lost in the miserable possibility of having
to leave Beaumont House. Having to leave Jackson.

She was vaguely aware of Danny's excited chatter
and Beau's equally excited barking outside in the hall as
father and son put on warm outdoor clothing together.
The back door of the house slammed shut behind them
moments later, before they reappeared in the garden
outside the office window and began to pelt each other
with snowballs. She watched as Danny fell into a fit of
giggles when Beau, rushing to defend his young master,
attacked Jackson's ankles and unbalanced him, causing
him to fall over into the soft snow. His response to the
hoots of laughter was to pull Danny down with him,
and the two of them rolled about in the snow together
as he began to tickle the little boy.

Alone inside the office, Bree could only look on si-
lently at the magical family scene outside as the snow

fell gently on father, son and the fluffy little puppy playing so happily together.

Her family.

She stepped back from the window abruptly, her face paling as she realised that without her even becoming aware of it Jackson and Danny truly had become her family this year.

But it was a family she could never rightfully claim as her own.

CHAPTER ELEVEN

'I THOUGHT I told you not to even *try* leaving here until the two of us had finished our conversation!' Jackson roared furiously as he slammed the door to Bree's apartment behind him. Bree herself was tossed over his shoulder as he strode purposefully down the hallway.

'Put me down this instant, Jackson!' Her protest was as violent as the fists she pounded against his back. 'How dare you—?'

'How dare *you*?'

Jackson didn't even break stride as he kicked open the door to her bedroom, a nerve pulsing in his clenched jaw, his expression grim and his eyes bleak as he recalled the lurching feeling in his chest when he had heard the sound of Bree's car starting up in the garage. He and Danny had been sitting together in the kitchen, drinking hot chocolate to warm up after being out in the snow for over an hour.

'You simply can't manhandle me in this ridiculous way—'

'Too late—I just did!' Jackson threw her unceremoniously down onto her bed and stood glowering down at her. 'Where did you think you were going?' he demanded through gritted teeth.

Bree glared back at him just as angrily as she struggled to sit up. 'Just for a drive, if you must know—'

'Oh, I believe I must, Bree.' His voice was danger-ously soft.

This was a danger that Bree recognised—even if she had no intention of responding to it after the sheer indignity of having the ignition of her car switched off and the keys deposited in the pocket of Jackson's jeans, of being hauled out and thrown over Jackson's shoulder like a sack of potatoes and carried down to her apart-ment before being dumped unceremoniously onto her bed! She was far too angry to heed the warning signs.

'Don't move,' Jackson bit out harshly as Bree tried to get up.

Her eyes flashed darkly. 'Maybe someone should have told you that the time of the caveman is long past—'

'Maybe someone should have told *you* not to push your luck,' he warned, putting one knee on the side of the bed.

'I—what are you doing?' Bree attempted to scoot across to the other side of the bed as Jackson loomed over her ominously.

'Guess!' He smiled humourlessly and his hand grasped her leg, preventing her from moving any fur-ther away.

'Jackson...?' Bree eyed him warily as he knelt fully on the bed before nudging her legs apart. She was barely breathing, and certainly unable to move as he lowered himself in between her denim-clad thighs, taking his weight on his elbows as he looked down at her. 'Danny is—'

'Danny is perfectly happy upstairs in the kitchen with Mrs Holmes.'

Jackson's face was so close to hers that his breath stirred the hair at her temples.

She swallowed hard, very aware—how could she not be?—of the heat of Jackson's arousal nestled between her thighs. 'I—I don't think this is sensible, Jackson—'

'I've tried being sensible for the past four days!' he exploded. 'For all the good it did me!' He shook his head in disgust. 'You've barely been able to look at me, let alone speak to me! So to hell with being sensible, Bree,' he finished grimly. 'I want answers and I want them now. And once I have them I'm going to make love to you until you don't have the strength to move, let alone think about leaving!'

Bree breathed shallowly, knowing by the glittering intensity in Jackson's eyes that he meant exactly what he said.

'I don't understand…'

'You will,' Jackson promised grimly. 'Now, I want to know *exactly* why David came here to see you on Friday.' He gasped with arousal as she ran the tip of her tongue across her lips. 'And it might be better for all concerned if you didn't do *that*, Bree…'

Bree's cheeks warmed as she felt once again the throb of Jackson's arousal between her thighs.

'David is—I was engaged to him. A year ago we should have been married.'

'Why weren't you?' Jackson's voice was hushed.

Bree grimaced. 'Because I found out a week before the wedding that he was having an affair with someone else. My own sister, as it happens.'

'Holy—' Jackson stopped himself, scowling darkly, his gaze once again sharpening in intensity. 'This all happened a year ago, you said…?'

She nodded. 'It was the anniversary of our supposed wedding day last Thursday.'

The same day Jackson had noticed a difference in Bree—that new recklessness, as if she were standing on the edge of a cliff and about to jump...

Jackson's eyes narrowed. 'Why did he come to see you?'

Bree smiled ruefully. 'He thought that a year was probably enough time for me to have forgiven him—'

Jackson drew in a sharp breath. 'And was it?'

'Oh, yes,' Bree confirmed, knowing she had only been able to feel that forgiveness because of the way she now felt about Jackson. She was in love with him. And it was a love totally unlike anything she might once have felt for David.

Just being with David again on Friday evening had been enough for Bree to realise that it had been her pride more than her heart that was hurt a year ago.

She had realised just as surely that her heart would never recover from loving Jackson.

'I see,' Jackson snapped. 'So the two of you are now back together?'

'Hardly!' Bree dismissed the idea with a dry smile. 'Forgiving him and Cathy doesn't mean that I want to pick up where the two of us left off!'

'It doesn't?'

'No,' she said firmly. 'I don't love him. I'm not sure that I ever did.' She gave a rueful shake of her head. 'We met at university, parted for a while, and then met up again. I realise now that going out together became something of a habit; when he asked me to marry him it just seemed like the next step in the relationship. I know now it would have been the wrong step,' she concluded quietly.

Jackson nodded. 'So are the two of you going to see each other again?'

'I told you earlier that we aren't.' Bree shook her head firmly. 'We've made our peace and said goodbye.'

'And going out to dinner with Roger Tyler on Thursday…?'

Bree sighed heavily. 'That was just a knee-jerk reaction to the anniversary of my wedding-that-never-was.'

Jackson looked down at her searchingly, deducing from the unblinking steadiness of her eyes as she returned his gaze that she was telling the truth.

'Okay.' He breathed deeply. 'So now we come to the biggie: did our own lovemaking last week happen for the same reason?'

Bree's gaze no longer met his and she began to push against his chest. 'You're too heavy, Jackson—'

'I'm not going anywhere until you answer me, Bree,' Jackson assured her grimly.

Her hands grew still against his chest and she frowned up at him. 'I don't know what else you want me to say. Obviously these…lapses between the two of us have made things very difficult. To the point where, as you suggested earlier, we may not be able to continue working together.'

'And would that bother you?' he demanded sharply.

Would leaving Beaumont House, leaving Jackson and Danny, *bother* Bree? Just the thought of it was enough to create a huge hollow inside her. And it was a hollowness that Bree knew would never be filled once she was forced to leave Jackson.

'Yes, it would bother me very much to leave Danny and—and you,' she admitted huskily.

'Why?'

'It's like you said earlier: I've come to love Danny… to think of him as part of my family.'

Jackson eyes gleamed. 'And…me?'

She swallowed hard, a haunted look entering her eyes.

'Sorry, it's unfair of me to expect you answer that now.' He frowned in self-disgust, rolling to the side and taking Bree with him, his arms like steel bands about her waist, holding her beside him as he stared up at the ceiling. 'You've been honest with me about your past, and now I'm going to reciprocate by telling you something that only one other person besides myself is aware of.'

'Jackson…' Bree raised her head to look at him uncertainly.

He smiled ruefully. 'It's nothing bad, Bree, just… very personal.'

'About you and Jennifer Greaves?'

'Me and…?' Jackson shook his head in bewilderment. 'There *is* no me and Jennifer Greaves!'

'You went out to lunch with her on Friday.'

'And that's all I did.' He looked hard at Bree for a moment. 'It would appear that, for me, La Greaves and women like her have completely lost their appeal.'

Bree's heart gave a leap in her chest. 'They have?'

'Yes,' Jackson assured her decisively. 'Now, will you allow me to finish what I started telling you?'

'If it really is that personal, are you sure you want to tell me about it?'

'*Very* sure,' he stated firmly. 'It's about Danny's mother.'

Bree drew in a sharp breath as curiosity and confusion battled inside her. Loving Jackson as she did, how could she help but feel curious about Danny's mother? At the same time she felt deeply confused as to Jackson's reasons for wanting to confide in her.

Unless…

No, she mustn't let her imagination run away with her. Jackson was only reciprocating after she had just told him about herself. Not that Jackson had given her much of a choice in the matter, but even so…

Bree shook her head. 'You don't need to tell me anything—'

'Yes, I do—damn it!' Jackson swore vehemently, rolling over to look down at her whilst holding her firmly against him as he smoothed the hair back from her soft pale cheeks. 'Maybe after what happened to you a year ago you aren't ready to hear this yet—maybe you never will be,' he added grimly. 'But I'm damned if I'm going to let you walk away from me without first telling you how I feel.'

'About what?'

'*You*, damn it!'

She stared up at him. 'Me?'

Jackson sighed with frustration. 'Bree, if these last few days of floundering around like a—like a jealous moron have shown me nothing else, they've shown me that I've fallen in love with you. Completely, crazily, head-over-heels in love with you.'

Bree's breath caught in her throat. Had Jackson just said…? Had he just said that he…?

'There's no need to look quite so horrified, Bree,'

Jackson muttered sardonically. 'I told you—I'm not expecting anything back from you. God knows, I'm well aware of how impossible I can be! But—'

'You're in love with me?' Bree finally managed to gasp incredulously.

'Well past the point of no return, I'm afraid.' He nodded gently. 'Admittedly it took the threat of two other men in your life for me to realise the truth, but now that I have I must be honest with you about it. I owe you that much. I love you, Bree. So very much.'

Bree was speechless. Absolutely, completely speechless.

Jackson cocked his head to one side thoughtfully. 'It took the appearance of Roger Tyler and David in your life for me to finally admit it to myself—and even then I still initially thought I was just annoyed at the possibility of one of them stealing the best personal assistant I've ever had.' He shook his head. 'I hated it when you went out with Roger Tyler. Then I went through absolute hell when you disappeared with David on Friday evening after the two of us had made love. I didn't know who I wanted to strangle more—him or you!'

The wall Bree had built to shield her emotions over the past few days had begun to crumble the moment Jackson told her he was in love with her, and it fell away completely now, as he continued to explain his feelings for her—in typical Jackson fashion, of course!

Jackson loved her.

Jackson was in love with her!

Bree's heart felt full to bursting as she looked up at him. 'And now...?'

He grinned. 'Now I just want to keep you all to myself, so that no other man can steal you away from me—ever!'

She swallowed hard. 'Ever...?'

Jackson nodded. 'I would very much like to marry you, Bree.'

Bree's eyes widened. 'You want to *marry* me?'

She was aware that she had sounded somewhat moronic during these last few minutes, but the things Jackson was saying...the prospect of a future together implied by his words...it was almost beyond belief.

Jackson's arms tightened around her again. 'I've realised these past few days that I want it all with you, Bree.' His voice deepened solemnly. 'Marriage. Babies. Years and years of loving, arguing, growing old together.'

Bree gazed at him—at the sincerity in his expression and the love shining in his eyes. It was all more than enough to convince her that Jackson meant every single word.

'And what if I were to say that the reason I've been behaving the way I have over the past few days is because I've realised I want all that too?'

Jackson became very still. 'And have you? *Do* you?'

Bree smiled shyly. 'Oh, yes.'

He swallowed. 'You...*love* me?'

She chuckled at his expression. 'There's no need to look quite so horrified, Jackson,' she teased, repeating his words from earlier. 'Impossible as you undoubtedly are, you're also incredibly loveable.'

'You really are in love with me?' Jackson could still only stare at her dazedly.

'More than I've ever loved anyone or anything.'

'Enough to marry me?'

She nodded. 'And have your babies. Lots of them. At least four would be—Jackson!' Bree only had time to gasp before he swept her up into his arms and proceeded to show her just how much he loved her.

CHAPTER TWELVE

'THERE'S SOMETHING I have to tell you before you agree to marry me, Bree…'

'I thought I already had.' Bree stirred sleepily in Jackson's arms as they lay naked in bed together.

'You might want to reconsider that decision once I've finished speaking…'

Bree's attention sharpened as she noted the seriousness of his tone. 'Whatever is it, Jackson, I'll still want to marry you,' she promised.

'I hope so.' He sighed shakily. 'Bree—Danny isn't my biological son. In every way that counts he's mine, and he always will be,' he continued firmly. 'But I'm not his biological father.'

Bree felt completely awake now and she looked up at Jackson searchingly, seeing the truth of his words in the steadiness of his deep blue gaze.

'But he looks so much like you…'

Jackson's jaw tightened. 'Yes.'

'But how can that be if—?' Bree frowned as her thoughts tumbled over each other in an effort to make sense of Jackson's statement. 'Your sister Jocelyn?'

'I always knew you were too intelligent for my own good.' Jackson smiled at her ruefully. 'Yes, Danny is Jocelyn's son.'

Bree shook her head in disbelief. 'But how…? I know

your sister…I know Jocelyn died…but where's his real father?'

'Still married to his wife, I imagine.' Jackson frowned.

'Ah…' Bree grimaced. 'Tell me what happened, Jackson,' she invited soothingly.

It was a familiar tale: a university student falling in love with one of her married lecturers, the two of them embarking on an affair that culminated when Jocelyn found out she was pregnant.

'My mother was horrified,' Jackson continued grimly. 'Refused to have anything to do with Jocelyn unless she agreed to have an abortion.'

'Which she obviously didn't.'

'No, thank God!' He gave a shudder. 'There was never any question of it in Jocelyn's mind. The baby was hers and she was going to keep it.'

Thinking of Danny, of how adorable he was, Bree felt eternally grateful for Jocelyn's determination.

'But Clarissa absolutely adores Danny.'

'Yes,' Jackson agreed drily.

'And she knows he's Jocelyn's son?'

'Oh, yes.' Jackson nodded. 'She adored him from the first moment she saw him—shortly before Jocelyn died.'

Bree swallowed. 'Did the two of them manage to make their peace before…?'

'Yes,' he said gratefully. 'And it's because of my mother's genuine love for Danny that I've been able to forgive her for so many other things,' he added.

Bree could understand that. 'You continued to love Jocelyn, though, didn't you…?'

Jackson nodded. 'She was and always will be my

baby sister. I wanted her to come and live here with me once I knew she was pregnant, but she was adamant she was going to manage on her own. And she did. I helped her financially once the baby was born, of course, and visited her often during her pregnancy and afterwards, but otherwise Jocelyn was very independent. She did agree to let me be with her at the birth, though,' he recalled, close to tears. 'It was…truly amazing. The most profound experience of my life.'

'What went wrong, Jackson?' Bree asked softly.

He gave a shaky sigh. 'The doctors discovered that Jocelyn had breast cancer when Danny was only six months old. It— She— By the time they realised it was too far advanced for them to do anything about it. I moved in with her—cared for Danny when she was too sick to do it herself. One night she asked me if I would take Danny, bring him up as my own son once she was gone. Hell, there was no question of my not agreeing to do that; by that time Danny was my son in every way that mattered! We had the adoption papers drawn up and signed only weeks before Jocelyn died. She held him at the end, and—' He broke off, overcome with emotion.

'It's all right, Jackson.' Bree held him tightly in her arms.

'Is it?' He looked at her intensely. 'Is it really all right, Bree?'

She looked down at him in gentle reproach. 'You didn't really think my knowing the truth about Danny was going to make any difference to how much I love you both, did you?'

He frowned. 'I've always held off becoming too involved with any woman because I didn't think she would be able to accept that Danny being adopted makes him as much my child as any other children I might have...'

He stopped speaking as Bree placed her fingertips across his lips.

'He won't ever be anything less, Jackson,' she assured him emotionally. 'I love him as much as you do. I—I would be honoured to be allowed to become his mother.'

'Oh, you'll be "allowed", Bree.' He smiled. 'Danny already thinks the sun rises and sets with you, anyway,' he added. 'All he could talk about earlier was how much more fun it would have been if you had come outside and helped to build the snowman.'

'That must have rankled.' She laughed merrily.

Jackson grinned. 'Only because inwardly I agreed with him. Everything...*life* is so much more fun with you, Bree!'

'We'll all go out tomorrow and build another snowman,' she promised.

'And then we'll come back inside and make love again,' Jackson added, winking impishly.

He paused to demonstrate that love with a slow kiss.

'There's just one other thing,' he added, breaking off the kiss reluctantly. 'I would like to tell Danny about Jocelyn when he's old enough to understand.'

'We'll tell him together,' Bree promised. 'Talking of Danny...' She looked at him in playful reproach. 'It's Christmas Eve and our son will be wanting his dinner. Then he has to have his bath before we take him up to bed and read him a bedtime story because Father Christmas comes in the—' Bree broke off in horror. 'Oh, my Lord, I haven't got you a Christmas present!'

She gasped. 'I couldn't find anything suitable when I went shopping on Friday and— What are you laughing at?'

'You, my darling Bree.' Jackson chuckled, throwing back the bedclothes as he got out of bed, then picked her up in his arms, twirling around the room with her. '*You're* my Christmas present, Bree!' He kissed her. '*You!*'

He kissed her again, deeply, hungrily, with every ounce of love he had for this incredible, beautiful woman—this wonderful woman who was going to be his wife and Danny's mother.

For ever.

* * * * *

THE SOLDIER,
THE PUPPY AND ME

Myrna Mackenzie

Dear Reader,

When I discovered that I would be writing a book about a puppy at Christmas, I was thrilled. I love puppies. Who doesn't love puppies?

Then Trey McFadden, the hero of the story, dropped in. He was damaged, he kept his heart to himself, he didn't want a wife (especially not his former next-door neighbor, Ella Delancey) and he didn't want a puppy. Puppies were for people who could offer commitment. Trey wasn't ever going to be that guy.

Hmm, that could be a problem, I thought. Because Trey was going to be home for a short visit and not only was Ella still living next door, she was Christmas-sitting a puppy from the local shelter. But surely I could depend on good-natured Ella to help me save the story. After all, she had once loved Trey from a distance.

But no. Ella had grown up and now she knew that Trey wasn't the man for her. She didn't intend to risk her heart again.

Sigh. It was beginning to look as if there was no way to get these two together.

Then Fizz, the puppy, took over. He was a natural matchmaker. Too bad that Trey, Ella and Fizz had only until Christmas to find a happy ending. Fizz and I had our work cut out for us. I hope you enjoy the results.

Best wishes for happiness during this special season,

Myrna Mackenzie

CHAPTER ONE

TREY MCFADDEN HADN'T seen or wanted to see his family home in Eagleton, Illinois, for ten years. But despite the fact that it was nearly three in the morning, the full moon enabled him to tell that the house was pretty much as it had been on the day he'd walked away when he was eighteen years old. Except for all the Christmas lights.

Christmas lights? Who in heck had hung Christmas lights? The house had been empty for…he wasn't sure how long, but he knew it had been a very long time. His parents wintered in warmer climes, and there were no servants. No anyone.

But there were lights. In fact, almost every single house on the block was lit up with bright blue, red, green and yellow LEDs. Frowning at the mystery of the lights on his own house, he parked the rental car in the driveway and went to the door. A note was sticking to the door knocker.

I just heard today that you were arriving and that you have agreed to be the Grand Marshall of our inaugural Christmas Festival. Hope you don't mind the lights. If you do, just follow the cord and unplug them. E. Delancey

Agreed? Not exactly. More like he'd been pressed into service at the last minute and had only *agreed* because he had a debt to pay off. As for the lights and the note…

E. Delancey? Trey glanced next door. Wasn't that the name of the teenage girl who had lived there when he'd left ten years ago? Maybe. Or had her mother's name begun with an E, too? He couldn't remember what the elder Ms. Delancey's first name had been. What he remembered…

"Nope. Not going there," Trey muttered.

The last time he and Eleanor Delancey had spoken at length—pretty much the *only* time they had spoken— things hadn't ended well at all. There had been anger. Insults, embarrassment and despair. Bad memories all round. And he for one preferred not to think of that time, or of Eleanor, either. She was a milk and cookies daydreamer who believed in unicorns, princesses and happy endings, while he was something else entirely. But with a little luck their paths wouldn't cross and they wouldn't have to do the "polite neighbor" act during the brief week he would be here.

Trey followed the cord of the lights. It connected to an extension cord that clearly trailed next door to the Delancey house. With one quick pull he shut off the lights. And ended any connection to E. Delancey.

"Sorry, Eleanor," he said with a twist of his lips as he entered the house he'd hoped never to enter again.

AT THREE IN the morning Ella woke with a start. She looked down at the squirming bundle of golden fur in the basket on the floor. She had made no sound, but as if he had heard her thinking, the puppy immediately sprang up and started dancing around.

"It must have just been you that woke me, Fizz," Ella whispered, even though the puppy hadn't been doing anything when she awoke.

Sometimes it was just better to believe the easiest answer was the right one. Much better than imagining pretend ghosts and ghouls. Or robbers. Because those were probably just as unlikely as her guess about the puppy. Eagleton, Illinois, was a sleepy community where everyone knew everyone and a few people still left their doors unlocked. The most likely reason she had awakened in the middle of the night with a start was the one Ella didn't want to think about.

Trey McFadden was coming home. And she had once been hopelessly, futilcly in love with him, while he had been painfully uninterested in having anything to do with her.

No. I wasn't in love. It was just a crush, of course. That's all. But—

"Darn it, Fizz," she said to the puppy. "Let's get up and take you for a visit to the great outdoors. Would you like that?"

Fizz gave a little yip and danced around as if he understood exactly what she was saying. She'd only been fostering him for two days, but already it was clear that Fizz was a lively one. He'd say yes to anything; he'd try anything; he was probably going to run her ragged before the holidays were over.

But she smiled and shuffled downstairs with him. "Just let me get your leash," she said, glancing out the window. With one deft move she fastened the leash on

Fizz's collar and opened the door. She glanced next door again. The lights were off. They'd been unplugged.

"He's here," she said.

Her heart raced faster; she missed a step. Unfortunately, it was the step leading down into the yard and, trying to keep her balance, she lost the leash. Instantly Fizz was off and running. He had discovered puppy freedom and he was going to make the most of it.

"Fizz!" she called in a loud whisper, not wanting to wake the entire neighborhood. "Where are you?"

A rustling in the bushes next door at the McFadden house was her answer. Thank goodness for the full moon. And for the flashlight she had grabbed on her way down the stairs.

"Fizz, you get back here right this instant!" she whispered as loud and as commandingly as she could, given the fact that she was trying to be quiet…and also trying to maintain her dignity. Not an easy task in December, when she was outside in her pajamas and slippers rustling around in Trey McFadden's shrubs.

Not that any of that mattered. Fizz was still an untrained puppy. He didn't yet respond to commands. To him, "Get back here" was no different than "Let's have a party" or "Let's dig a hole in our neighbor's lawn." Thank goodness there was snow on the ground. He couldn't do much damage to the grass, and his digging enabled Ella to get close enough to catch him.

Almost.

As she reached down for him Fizz wagged his tail wildly, his little body squirming, seemingly overjoyed at the prospect of being held. But a slight noise sent him darting away, up the steps of the big red-brick mansion that made every other house on the block look like baby houses in comparison.

Oh, no, he was scrabbling at the door, jumping around and yapping.

"Fizz, stop! Come here this minute!" Her whisper was still a whisper—barely—as she ran up the stairs and grabbed the little dog. Whirling around on the concrete porch, she took the first step, making her escape.

The metallic sound of the door opening behind her made her heartbeat click up a notch.

"Stop right there. Don't take another step."

She didn't.

"Not exactly prime visiting hours," he said, his voice deathly calm. "So I suggest you tell me who you are and what you're doing here in the middle of the night."

That deep voice slipped through her, and Ella shivered slightly. Her heart was pounding hard, but at least he didn't know who she was. She still had her back to him. Now, if she could just scurry away... But...

What was the point? He'd see her go next door, and anyway she was still holding Fizz, who was wriggling and snuffling and trying to see who was behind them. No doubt he would see the dog again during the next week. She couldn't conceal her identity without looking like a total idiot and a cowardly sneak afterward. Which was too bad, considering...everything.

Slowly, she turned. "It's just me. Just Ella Delancey, your neighbor."

"The light lady." He said it as if he'd never met her before. As if he'd never *known* her before. Which was pretty much the truth.

She couldn't help blushing. Thank goodness even the

full moon couldn't reveal her heightened color. "Sorry about the lights. Stuart asked me to do things up right."

"Stuart?" Trey said when she mentioned his cousin, the mayor.

But at that moment the squirming puppy wriggled his way right out of Ella's arms. She managed to break the brunt of his descent as he leaped but, seeing the open door, he made a beeline for Trey's house, dashing past the man and disappearing inside.

"Fizz, stop!" Ella called, her voice rising in despair as she moved to the door, then looked up into Trey's eyes. "May I?"

He stepped to the side slightly and she squeezed past him, her body brushing his. She was suddenly very aware that she was in worn pink flannel pajamas with white hearts parading in a line across her chest. Her long light brown hair was a tangled riot of waves. With those silver blue eyes studying her as if she were a lab experiment, she needed to regain her composure quickly. But first she had to capture Fizz. And she'd never been inside this house.

"Did you see which way he went?" she asked, her voice coming out a bit too breathless as she took her soggy slippers off, leaving her in her bare feet.

"In the back. The rooms back there connect in a circular pattern. I'll take the right. You take the left."

And they would trap Fizz in the middle.

Ella wasted no time following Trey's directions. She could hear the scrabble of little doggie toenails on what had to be expensive wood flooring. She followed the sound, saw him, bent and scooped just as Trey slid in to do the same from the other direction. He was in his stockinged feet and went to his knees in an intentional slide. Ella had made her move a half-second before Trey, and his hands ended up cupping hers as he looked up at her and rose to his feet.

"Do you have him?" he asked, his voice low and dark.

"I—yes." Her voice came out shaky. The warmth of Trey's palms against the backs of her hand sent a sizzle of awareness through her. Immediately he moved away.

"Thank you," she said.

He shook his head. "Does he get out like this often? In the middle of the night?" There was a judgmental tone to his words.

She frowned. "I don't know. I'm just fostering him over the holidays. The shelter he was at doesn't like people to give their puppies as gifts. Too much risk of buyer's regret after the holidays or animals ending up with inept owners, you know?"

He shook his head. "No. I've never been a pet person."

"Why?"

The word slipped out without her thinking. She blinked.

"I'm sorry. That's none of my business."

It was a reminder that she had one long-ago day interfered in his business in a way he might have forgotten but she never would.

CHAPTER TWO

"No SECRET. I'M not the ideal candidate for the responsibility of long-term relationships, and a pet is definitely both a responsibility and a long-term commitment. As you said, no one wants to deal with buyer's remorse. I don't take on what I won't keep."

She nodded tightly, wondering how many women he had walked away from, how much buyer's remorse he'd avoided. With his dark good looks and those broad shoulders, women would want him even if he didn't want them back.

And the mere fact that she was wondering that meant she had stayed too long. It was far too late and it was time to get out. Fast.

"Well...thank you," she said. "I'll just get back to my house. And I'll be more careful with Fizz in the future."

She moved back toward the front of the house.

"Eleanor."

Her name on his lips stopped her. She turned around again.

"Why the lights? Why did Stuart ask you to do things up right? I know it's Christmas, but...an entire block blazing like a multi-colored flock of fireflies?"

She shook her head, her long hair sliding over her shoulders. "It's the festival. This is Stuart's first year in office. He only won the election by a few votes, so he feels he has something to prove. He hopes having the festival and doing it up right will bring people together in a way they haven't been for a long while. The festival has to be perfect. The town has to look like the type of old-fashioned Christmas scene we all have in our minds."

He blinked. She knew what he was thinking. He *wasn't* one of those people who coveted old-fashioned Christmases.

"All right," he said. "I get that. But…why were you the one decorating my house?"

This time she didn't even have to try to read his mind. She had once interfered in his life. Or tried to. He was afraid she was doing that again.

She opened her eyes wide. "Don't think what you're thinking. I'm not seventeen and a ridiculous idealist anymore. I don't intend to do anything that would concern you. But I have a duty. It's part of my job as Stuart's assistant. I'm in charge of the festival."

"So…I'll be taking my marching orders from you?"

"I wouldn't put it that way. You're the Grand Marshall—the guest of honor."

"Who was called in last minute when someone else canceled."

Ella hoped she wasn't blushing again. She shrugged. "You were Stuart's first choice, but I—I knew the other person and you—"

"I wasn't likely to be willing?"

"Yes." She didn't add that she hadn't wanted to ask him any more than he had wanted to come. She had managed not to think of him for a long time. Now here she was in her pajamas, in his house, feeling…awkward, girlish, uncomfortable…as if she was lacking in some way. He had always made her feel that way. She hated that. She really wished that Stuart had chosen someone else and that Trey had stayed away forever.

But that couldn't matter. Things were what they were, and she had spent a lifetime learning to deal with less than ideal circumstances.

"But when my ballet dancer broke her leg Stuart promised that he could talk you into coming. And you're here. I…appreciate you coming on such short notice."

He shrugged. "It's Stuart, and I owe him. Although I think this will settle my debt. Five days of activities before we even get to the Christmas Eve parade?"

She couldn't help blushing. "It has to be big, but more than that it has to be meaningful."

Trey crossed his arms over his chest. "And you'll be…directing me?" His voice was deceptively calm, but she could tell that he wasn't happy. Darn the man for looking sexy even when he was angry.

And darn *her* for feeling even more awkward than she had before. She wished she was wearing more clothes. As it was, she pulled herself up to her full height and stared up at him. The man was far too tall.

"As Grand Marshall you'll be expected to show up to a few events."

"A few. I see. And those events are…?"

She wanted to look away, and because she wanted that so badly she forced herself to keep staring. "A party at a local preschool where most of the children are underprivileged, a walk-around to visit with the local business people, and a presentation on the history of the town."

"Damn Stuart. I'm not the guy for this kind of thing."

"You're balking? No, you can't do that. Trey, I know

this isn't the way you'd like to spend Christmas, but Stuart needs this and so does this town. Eagleton has been hit hard by the loss of the auto-parts factory. The people need a good Christmas, and you're a war hero, a homegrown son who made a success after he left the military. It would mean so much to them just to be able to shake your hand. If you're uncomfortable with any of this I'll be a resource. I'm good at hand-holding."

As if to demonstrate, she reached out, just stopping before reaching his arm.

Her breath stopped. She had Fizz in a football hold beneath the other arm, but for once even he was still. Trey looked down at her hand.

"No hand-holding needed," he said quietly. "I'll do my part."

And clearly he wished he could do it without her.

"Don't worry, Mr. McFadden, I'm not as impulsive as I once was. Despite my slipup earlier tonight, I don't butt in where I'm not wanted anymore. I'm a complete professional these days."

He raised one dark eyebrow and raked his glance over the hearts on her pink pajamas. Beneath those hearts was nothing but her bare breasts. Somehow she managed to keep staring at him as if she hadn't noticed his insolent look at all.

"I meant that. Do not underestimate me, Trey. I'm not the girl I used to be." She tromped off, slipped her bare feet into her wet slippers at the door and, pulling back the massive door, stepped into the still dark night. She glanced back over her shoulder. "Tomorrow I'll be back to fill you in on the details of the week. At ten o'clock sharp. Be ready."

For some reason he seemed to find that amusing. His lips lifted in a slight smile.

"What?" she asked. "I didn't say anything funny."

He shook his head. "You're right. You didn't. But I've never been lectured by a woman wearing fuzzy bunny slippers before."

"You've probably never been lectured by *any* woman before."

"Not true. It's happened before." From the tone of his voice she was pretty sure that it had happened in the most intimate of situations.

That wasn't going to be what this was like. She was over Trey McFadden.

"Tomorrow," she said, "I'll go over the details of the schedule. Then, if you're fine with that, you can be on your own for the rest of your time here. Good night."

Trey gave her a curt nod.

Fizz, who had been quiet through most of this, gave a little puppy woof. Just as if he knew what was going on and was saying goodbye.

"Forget it," she told him as they made their way back to their own tiny house. "He doesn't like dogs."

Fizz wagged his tail.

"And don't go trying to win him over, either," Ella warned. "Don't go all puppy on me. I had planned on being completely businesslike with Trey, from my grey suit down to my sensible ballet flats and stoic exterior. Because of you I ended up wearing nothing but pajamas with my hair wild and crazy. That's not happening again. So no funny stuff, Mister Fizz. I have my job, he has his, and your job is to be a quiet, happy puppy— who stays in his own yard. Because the less we think about Trey McFadden the better."

Fizz wagged his tail, then wriggled over and tried to curl his little body around her leg.

She laughed and picked him up, holding him to her heart and cuddling him close. "I didn't mean any of those criticisms. You're perfect as you are…or you will be once you're old enough to learn to follow basic commands. You're my Christmas companion and I'm not letting anyone or anything spoil our Christmas together. It's just the two of us, Fizz. Just you and me."

Trey, with his hot blue eyes and broad shoulders, was just a fantasy from her youth. And she was a grown woman who knew better than to give in to impossible fantasies.

CHAPTER THREE

THE CLOCK WENT off at nine-forty-five and Trey slammed his hand down on it. After Ella and her bouncy little puppy had left the night before he'd been unable to get to sleep. He'd kept seeing her sticking out her chin and trying to boss him around. It was cute as heck. And he knew darn well that he shouldn't be noticing that. She was still the unicorn fairy princess, the happily-ever-after lady. That made her untouchable.

Still, she was going to be here in less than fifteen minutes. He sprinted for the shower, threw himself under a stream of hot water and tried to prep himself for the day. No, make that the next *several* days. She had said she was going to stay out of his hair. Immediately the memory of a day when she had crossed an invisible line zinged into his memory. He shoved it aside. Ella had been told not to interfere, and she had done it anyway. She'd seen a side of him no one had ever been allowed to see. The vulnerable side.

She was darn well never going to see it again. That side of him no longer existed.

As he turned the shower off and wrapped a towel around himself he heard a tentative tapping on the door.

Darn it, she was three minutes early.

He stalked down to the door and threw it open. She gazed up at him with those big gray, thick-lashed eyes.

Innocent eyes that still believed that puppy dogs could cure any heartache. In fact she was holding the puppy now.

"What's his name again?" he asked, trying not to notice that the puppy was looking up at him with eyes every bit as innocent as Ella's.

"It's Fizz, but it might change when someone…you know…adopts him."

Her eyes were everywhere but on his chest, which was cute and somehow…erotic.

He frowned at his thoughts, opened the door wider and motioned her inside. "Why not you?"

"Me?"

"Why aren't you adopting him? You seem to like him."

"Who wouldn't?" Then she looked at him. This time her glance did take in his chest before she hastily looked away. "Oh, yes, I remember. You're not a pet guy. Anyway, no, it wouldn't be fair for me to keep him. Right now Stuart is letting me bring him to the office, but that can't last forever, and he's too friendly a dog to leave alone all day. He'd be lonely."

The way she said the word *lonely* made him think she knew something about the emotion. He shook his head. He was just being fanciful.

"Let me put some clothes on," he said, which made her turn a pretty shade of pink. Ella wasn't really a pretty woman—her nose was just a touch too thin and her mouth a bit too tiny for classical beauty—but she had those big eyes and an interesting face. The blush did amazingly intriguing things to her features. It made it difficult to see her as just a neighbor and not a woman who possessed all the delectable parts that kept a man tossing and turning at night.

But thinking those kinds of off-limits thoughts was his signal to duck out. As he set up coffee and got dressed, he could hear her talking to the dog downstairs.

"You'll have to be good for a few minutes, sweetie. Mr. McFadden and I have to discuss a few things. I won't be long," she said, just like a mother talking to a child. Or at least the way he imagined most mothers would talk. His never had. Neither of them.

When he rejoined her, he saw that she had created a play area for the puppy. She'd set up the large basket she'd carried Fizz in and had brought out a collection of toys.

"All right, I suppose you'll want to get right to what will be expected of you this week." She pulled out a sheet of paper. "It's not really too bad. I'm sure you can duck out of one of these. Stuart is pretty easygoing."

"I know."

She blushed again and he tried to hide a smile. If not for the fact that Eagleton brought back so many bad memories, and if not for the fact that it was clear that Ella wasn't the type of woman a man toyed with, he would enjoy making her blush this week—and then…

No. None of that. He reached out for the paper. There was a map of the town with several locations starred and numbered. On the bottom of the map the date, time and details of each event were matched with the numbered stars.

"Why do you have things like 'pride,' 'community,' 'strength' and 'warmth' listed?"

She looked slightly embarrassed. "I meant to take those out…but those are the types of feelings we're trying to instill. You have no idea how much of a beating the people of the town have endured since the plant shut down and so many of them lost their jobs. Their pride and self-esteem have been wounded. Stuart and I want to restore some of that, even if it's only for an hour or two."

The scent of coffee drifted out and Trey motioned Ella into the kitchen. "I'm…sorry to hear that things have been so bad."

"Stuart didn't tell you?"

"Stu and I tend to gloss over bad things unless we think there's something the other person can do to alleviate the problem. Always been that way."

She nodded and sipped her coffee. "Do you mind…? It's none of my business, but I know you don't really want to be here. You said that you owed Stuart a favor. What did he do for you?"

"No secret. He bought me a ticket out of here." His voice was flippant, but there had been nothing light or minor about what his cousin had done for him. "And he didn't ask me to spill my guts."

"I never asked that of you!" she said.

"Sweetheart, your eyes asked it every time you saw me."

"I didn't even know you! I still don't know you!"

"Exactly."

She glared down at the piece of paper. Her cheeks were twin roses, bright pink. Lovely. Not that he was going to say so.

Finally she took a deep breath. "I've put the internet link to the town on the sheet," she said, clearly putting the past behind her. "You won't be expected to do much of anything at the events except be there and smile…and not contradict anything that Stuart or I say about you."

Her head had drifted lower as she spoke and her last words caught him by surprise. Without thought he reached out, slid his fingertips beneath her chin, coaxing her to look at him. "What exactly does that mean?" he asked.

She wet her lips. He wanted to groan. Her mouth might be small, but there was something enticing about it. Something elusive, sensual.

"You were a soldier. Everyone here is proud of you."

"For living? Others died while I didn't."

She blinked and those pretty wide eyes teared up a bit. "Yes. For living. People lost jobs and it's killing them. Losing a son would be so much worse. They know you were out there battling for them."

"I was doing what I was ordered to do. And then when it was over I built a business and made a veritable ton of money halfway across the country in San Diego. You don't think people will resent that?"

"Yes. Some. But most will see you as proof that it's still possible to succeed."

And that kind of wide-eyed innocence, naiveté and trust was just why he needed to get out of here quickly.

A tiny yip and some snuffling, then the sound of tearing paper and scratching came from the next room. Ella jumped to her feet and ran into the other room, Trey following behind her.

"Oh, no! Fizz, no!" she said, clapping her hands.

The little dog was up on the coffee table, his mouth full of newspaper. There was a scratch on the table. Instead of looking guilty, the little guy wagged his tail and tried to lick Ella's face when she got close.

"No!" she said, picking him up and putting him in his basket. She offered the puppy a chew toy. "No," she told him.

"No big deal. I never liked that table," Trey said.

"It doesn't matter. He has to learn not to chew. It can be dangerous for him. He might chew an electrical wire or chew on something that might poison him. And, from another perspective, it can also be expensive. I—that table—it was probably worth more than my whole living room."

"Like I said, forget it."

"No. I'm not like that. It's damaged, and I can't fix it completely, but I can repair it so that it looks better than it does now."

"Ella…"

"Trey…" She put her hands on her hips.

"It's not worth the trouble." He knew how to command. He stared into her eyes, modulated his voice.

For a minute they stood there, staring into each other's eyes. She started to drop her head. Then she closed her eyes and raised her chin instead. "It's worth the trouble to me. My pride is at stake here."

The puppy was looking back and forth between them as if they were batting a tennis ball around.

"You can help me carry it home and I'll repair it there," she said. "There's no need for us to invade your house any longer. All right?"

She stared at Trey. He didn't want to admit it, but she had him. He knew about the need to salvage one's pride. It would be childish to tell her that he wouldn't mind taking a sledgehammer to every piece of furniture, every brick in this house where his pride had been slammed against the wall every day.

"Trey?" she asked again.

He glared back at her and blew out a breath. "You never did listen very well," he grumbled. But he picked up the table and carted it to her little house.

"I DID LISTEN," Ella told Fizz after Trey had gone. "I heard what he said about not wanting commitment or pets or obviously people. I heard it when I was young and I heard it now, too. And only one time did I ignore what he told me. I'll never make that mistake again."

She was pretty sure he still hadn't forgiven her for that time. It was part of the reason she was worried about the presentations in town. People were going to want to fawn over him. She was totally sure he wasn't going to like it. At all.

But it was Christmas. The fawning was a gift that worked both ways. She hoped. She also hoped she could forget that moment when he had touched her.

She reached up to feel the place where his fingertips had held her chin. Her heart had been pounding. It was still pounding. Which was just unacceptable. She wasn't seventeen anymore, unable to stop herself from dreaming about a boy who suspected that she had a crush on him and wasn't thrilled about it. She was old enough to know that caring wasn't enough to change hopeless situations. And she was well beyond old enough to know that when Trey left this time he would never return. Any more touching, even of the most innocent variety, would be a mistake.

"And as for you, young man," she told Fizz. "I can't believe you scratched his table. I was going to stay in the background from here on out. Now I'll at least have to see him again to return his table."

It was probably just hearing his name, but Fizz wagged his tail, licked her fingers. She could have sworn that he smiled.

"I mean it. It's over. I might even sneak this table onto his back porch under cover of darkness."

But, no, she wouldn't do that. Then he would be sleeping upstairs, and she had a hunch that Trey slept naked.

Bringing the table over in the daytime was a much better idea.

CHAPTER FOUR

ELLA WAS AS good as her word. The next day, when he attended the "Eagleton Through the Years" presentation and shook one hundred hands, received one hundred pats on the back and one hundred thank-yous, which he did his best to accept graciously, she kept her distance. When Stuart asked him to say a few words and his chest went tight because it was clear that they saw him as a hero, and this was a delicate situation where he needed to be positive, she stayed away.

He couldn't say *It's good to be home.* This had never been home. So... "It's good to see everyone," he said instead, and that felt...okay. That was right. There were people he had all but forgotten, and if shaking his hand or thinking he was more than he really was made someone feel better, then he was glad he could help. "Hello, Mrs. Blevins," he said, accepting a hug and cookie from the older woman. "Hi, Bob."

The man gave him a hearty slap on the back.

Trey almost said, *How's the farm?* but just then he looked at Ella. She was looking worried. Had Bob lost the farm? He quickly changed his comment. "I remember when you beat the stuffing out of me. I deserved it, too, for saying something I shouldn't have."

Bob looked sheepish. He smiled. "You were just messing, Trey. It was fun beating on you, though. Anytime, buddy. Anytime. I wouldn't mind saying that I bested a soldier."

Trey laughed. "I guess I'd better watch my mouth."

Bob walked away with a grin on his face.

Ella looked as if she'd received a gift. But she stayed on her side of the room. She didn't even appear to look his way again. But for the rest of the next hour Trey was always aware of exactly where she was in the room, just as he'd been aware all those years ago that she had watched him. That she had known at least something of the angry fights that went on at his house.

Despite the bad memory, he almost wanted to smile. Maybe even then he'd been as aware of Ella as she had been of him. Good thing he'd played the tough guy and told her not to hang around his house. Good thing he'd been humiliated and embarrassed and never tuned in to that quiet, thrumming attraction. Just look at her now. She had come to this town skinny and quiet and scared, and here she was smiling at every person, reaching out her hands, hugging people and helping the elderly. And smiling at all the young men who seemed to hang on her every word.

There did seem to be a lot of men hanging around Ella. Trey frowned, then kicked himself for frowning. None of his business. In a few days he'd be gone again, and this time he would never come back. As for Ella, she would probably eventually marry one of those guys.

"So what do you think?" Stuart asked, coming up beside him.

"About what?" Had Stuart seen him looking at Ella?

"The town. Has it changed much? I see it every day, but you're looking at it after having been away a long time."

Trey glanced out the big plateglass windows. Clean white snow dusted the tops of the parking meters, evergreen garlands hung in big loops between the light poles, with a wreath and a big red bow on each pole. The trees were decorated with white lights. Lots of white lights. Christmas carols played softly in the background. "It's definitely more Christmassy than I remember."

Stuart laughed. "Ella took it to heart when I told her to do it up right. Every space is decorated. But that's not exactly what I meant."

"I know. You meant the people. They're afraid," Trey said, nodding toward the people at the refreshment table.

"A lot of them left. No work."

"But you stayed. So did Ella. Why?"

Stuart shrugged. "You know me. I'm an optimist. As for Ella—you'll have to ask her that. When her father died, and her mother passed away soon after that, I thought she might move away. She has no family here. But I don't think she'll ever leave. There's a determination in her to make things right for people."

There always had been, Trey remembered. *She'd been into causes even when the cause had been hopeless. Even when she'd known nothing about the situation and after she'd been told to stay away.* "They like her," he said. "The townspeople."

"They *love* her. And why not? She props them up and makes them feel good about themselves. She's that way about everybody. Except you. For some reason she wasn't big on inviting you here. Any idea what that's about?"

Trey raised an eyebrow. "Not like you to pry, Stu."

To his credit, Stuart looked sheepish. "You're right.

Not my business. But I worry about her, and Linda does, too. I love my wife to death, but she wants to make a match for Ella and so far it hasn't happened. She dates now and then, but nothing ever comes of it. The way she reacted to me inviting you…I just wanted to make sure you hadn't done anything in your youth to sour Ella on men. But—" he held up a hand "—I'm not asking."

"Good," Trey said, as he noticed yet another man approaching Ella with hope in his eyes. "I was a jerk when I was younger, but Ella and I never had a relationship. You know that."

"I know." But the sound in Stuart's voice told Trey the rest of the story. Stuart knew that Trey had lived next door to Ella, and that his bad-boy reputation meant that a full-fledged relationship wasn't necessary for a girl to get hurt.

"It wasn't that way with us. Ever," Trey said.

Ella might have had a schoolgirl crush on him, but he had cured her of that on the night he'd told her to get out of his house, his yard and his sight forever. A sensitive girl like Ella would have been hurt, but a smart girl—also like Ella—would have quickly realized that he wasn't worth her hurt. She would have cut him loose… and must have hated the thought that she had to work with him on the Christmas Festival.

She'd done her best to keep him from being invited; she was holding her nose and working with him despite her distaste; she was even repairing his damn table. He owed her for that.

And she didn't look as if she wanted to talk to that guy, who didn't appear to know how to take no for an answer. Trey frowned. Not his problem, not his concern, not his business. She was an adult, and she clearly knew how to handle herself if Stuart had put her in charge of the entire festival. So why had he even noticed that guy or her response?

He glanced her way again. She was giving the guy a sad smile and walking away. Probably letting him down easy. He wondered how many times she'd done that over the years.

He wondered what she'd do if *he* ever tried to kiss her.

And now we're done thinking about Ella, he told himself. Because that was *so* not appropriate. He was never going to kiss Ella. Surely the only reason he was even thinking about touching her at all was to stop thinking about the fact that everyone here seemed to think he was a real hero, when he had done nothing more than any other soldier during his years in the service.

Ella must have seen him looking at her, because she faded even more into the background. No, she disappeared completely. When next he saw her she was holding Fizz.

He couldn't help himself. He gave her a look, raised an eyebrow.

She shook her head. What did that mean?

He took a step toward her.

To his surprise she moved away. Subtly but most definitely she retreated.

He tried again.

Again she moved. He looked down at Fizz, who she was absentmindedly petting. The puppy looked at him and wagged his tail. Then he looked at Ella, before glancing back at Trey and giving a little woof.

What did that mean? It almost felt as if Fizz was telling him something.

More likely it meant that he was losing his mind. Fizz was a dog, and while Trey conceded that there might be people who had special connections with animals, he wasn't one of them. Still…Fizz *was* kind of cute, and he had clearly won Ella's heart. In fact he was the only male she seemed to want to spend time with here. Had to give the puppy credit for that.

But when Bernadette Dixon got up and began delivering her slideshow on the history of the town, and twenty minutes later had barely reached the mid-eighteen-hundreds, Fizz was clearly beginning to squirm in Ella's arms. People were beginning to snooze in their seats and Ella was looking distressed.

Trey raised a quizzical brow. Reluctantly she came toward him. "It was supposed to be a very brief feel-good presentation about a few of the most memorable Decembers in Eagleton," she whispered. "Followed by a period dance by our Grand Marshall."

He tried not to smile. "I assume you mean the ballet dancer and not me?" he said.

"Of course. Unless you'd like to step in and save us by performing," Ella said.

Their whispering must have been too loud, because Bernadette was giving them evil looks.

Ella sighed. "Bernadette is a sweetheart, but once she gets started she won't stop, and this isn't going to endear Stu's festival to the cause. Time for a quick change of plan. I hate to ask you to do this, but can you hold Fizz for just a minute? He was in Stu's office and on the verge of snacking on Stu's leather briefcase. It wasn't fair to leave him alone any longer. I need to get up on stage and make an announcement. We need to wrap this up with something more fun."

She appeared to be thinking as Bernadette went on and the sound of shifting chairs and feet got louder.

"More fun? And what will that be?" he asked.

She hesitated, then looked him in the eye. "I'd tell you, but then you might refuse."

With that announcement she moved toward the stage, leaving Trey wondering if this was going to be one more of those Ella moments he'd experienced when he was young—the ones that had turned out so badly and ended with that horrific day.

In the next few minutes Ella had expertly applauded Bernadette for her "intro" to the town's history, promised everyone that what Bernadette had offered was the merest taste of what they would find if they stopped in at the local historical society, and suggested that they wrap up the meeting with a rousing chorus of Christmas carols.

"I'm sure that our hero and guest of honor, who used to be the lead singer in a…a fine garage band, would love to start us off."

And that was how Trey found himself up on stage, trying to keep up with a crowd who called out the names of their favorite Christmas songs. He gamely tried to remember the words, and was doing all right and even getting into the spirit of things until someone called out, "I'll Be Home for Christmas."

"I love that song," someone else yelled. "I always cry. Put your heart in it, Trey."

Trey knew the song. He liked the song. But for him it was too much of a lie. He looked at Ella. She and Stu were probably the only ones here who knew that this wasn't his home, had never been and never would be.

For half a second her gaze locked with his. He knew

the minute she'd made a decision to do something very Ella-like.

"Oh, Fizz," she said suddenly, her eyes growing round, as if she'd actually forgotten the puppy.

She reached out to take the puppy from Trey. The little dog had fallen asleep while Trey held him, but at the overly loud sound of his name he roused up and began licking Trey's hand.

"Thank you so much for holding him," Ella said. "And thank you all for coming today. Don't forget that we're having a Christmas Walk with the merchants the day after tomorrow. Shall we end this meeting with a rousing chorus of 'We Wish You a Merry Christmas?' That's such a perfect song to sing us out of here. Let's bring the roof down, everyone!"

Without waiting for an answer Ella began singing, and Mr. Murchant quickly caught up with her on the piano. The rest of the crowd quickly got into the spirit and joined in.

Trey glanced to the side. Ella had left the stage. By the time the song was over she had disappeared.

Now who's the hero? Trey wondered. No one had even noticed that Ella had changed the song on them and prevented him from having to pretend that he was a man who dreamed of home and all the things that home implied.

Ella had saved him…just as she'd tried to once before.

But this time it was different. This time he appreciated the gift. And conceded that he owed her.

And he was a man who paid his debts.

CHAPTER FIVE

ELLA CURSED HERSELF for having enjoyed the afternoon. Standing there next to Trey, his deep voice joining hers, little Fizz in his arms, she had felt a twinge inside her—a sense of belonging, of being in the right place. Which was so...*stupid*.

Trey hated Eagleton. This town had never brought him happiness, and he was a success in a distant city now. No doubt he had plenty of exciting women who wouldn't do something foolish like handing him a dog when he'd told her he wasn't a dog person, or asking him to get up in front of a group of people and sing.

"But what does any of that matter?" she asked Fizz as she took the puppy to the enclosed backyard to let him romp in the snow.

She'd known when Stu asked him here that he wouldn't want to come, and she'd promised him that she'd keep her distance from him. Spurred by concern that Stu's festival was listing to one side, and by her knowledge that everyone loved a soldier, she'd manipulated Trey onstage and broken her promise today, but tomorrow things would be different. She would stay out of his hair.

"You and I will make better arrangements tomorrow," she told Fizz. "Maybe I'll hire a...a puppy-sitter. Just for the day, you know."

Fizz almost seemed to be looking at her accusingly. Sadly.

"That is *so* my imagination," she muttered.

But it wasn't her imagination that she was still affected by Trey. She'd seen how gentle he was with Fizz, how he'd done his best to make everyone else feel at ease—even though he wasn't comfortable with being the hometown hero, and even though it must make him uneasy when he was doing so well and so many people here weren't. No one had said a word to him about his father moving the car-parts business out of state. Probably because they knew that no one had ever had any sway with Darren McFadden—least of all his son.

"Stop it," she muttered. Fizz cocked his head.

"I'm sorry. Not you. It's me, Fizz. I'm the one who's messed up here."

Because she just couldn't seem to keep her mind off Trey.

Trey had wandered upstairs to change. He was just peeling off his shirt and had not yet put on his T-shirt when he glanced out the window and saw Ella next door, tossing a red rubber ball to Fizz. The little dog tore across the yard in a kind of hop-run, then wrestled with the ball, slinging his head one way and then another.

"Bring it here, Fizz!"

Ella's voice was muffled through the glass. He remembered how sweet she'd sounded during the Christmas carols today. He'd hazarded a glance at her for a second when they'd been singing, and her eyes had been like stars. It was clear that she loved what she did, that she loved this town and the people who lived here, that she fit. Just like she fit that little puppy she was clearly already falling for. She belonged here. And despite the fact that he didn't belong, didn't *want* to belong to a home and family place like this, he had been entranced watching her. Her lips had been soft, pink. Fresh. As if they'd never been touched. Though of course she'd been kissed. With that many guys hanging around and the fact that she was so eminently kissable... His body ached at the thought.

He frowned at that. And saw that Ella had looked up at the window and seen him watching her.

For a second he thought she was blushing, although at this distance he couldn't really tell that. In the next instant he was sure she was distressed.

Caught staring at her, he felt a bit like a stalker. He remembered a day when he had used that harsh word with her. It hadn't been his finest moment. And now when she'd thought she was alone...

Trey opened the window. "Sorry. I wonder...is there anything I need to know about the day after tomorrow?" Not the greatest attempt at conversation, but the best he could do on short notice.

Immediately she looked guilty. "No, I—I won't be ambushing you again like that. I'm sorry about the singing. And about Fizz. I don't know what I was thinking."

"Probably that Bernadette, well meaning though she might be, was going to cast a pall over Stuart's festival, and that no one wants to be remembered as the man who killed Christmas."

She stared at him for a couple of seconds, then...yes, she really was blushing.

"It's my job to make sure things go right, and there are always going to be minor glitches. I'll keep you out of them from now on. You're the guest of honor, not one of the planners, and as far as your part is concerned everything from here on out will be perfectly perfunctory. You won't need to worry. About anything. You've got all the info you need. We're done. You can spend tomorrow free of any distractions. No one is going to bother you. I mean that."

With that, she picked up Fizz, said a curt goodbye and rushed inside.

ELLA CLOSED THE door, then stood there with her back against the wall. She felt hot, then cold, then hot again. Trey had been shirtless. Had she been staring? Had he noticed her staring?

She pressed her palms to her hot cheeks.

"Fizz, we have *got* to stay away from that man. It's not good for us—not good for him."

Why *had* she asked him to sing today, when there'd been half a dozen other people she could have asked?

But she knew. She knew. Trey had always felt at loose ends here. He'd been wanting to escape Eagleton forever. Despite the fact that they'd only known each other for one year, he'd said as much that awful day when he had confronted her with the truth: that she'd been watching him, spying on him, interfering in his life.

He hated Eagleton and yet she'd known that all it would take was a hometown soldier to set foot on stage and the crowd would love him. The fact that he had a fine voice would make them love him more, and maybe for once in his life he'd feel…right.

"That was presumptuous of me, Fizz. He already feels right, but it's his new life in San Diego that suits him so well. He said as much. And I'm doing it again.

Trying to fix things, to make them right." And maybe this time she realized that her motives were selfish. Because she wanted Trey to see *her* in a different light.

That was wrong, because what Trey wanted—what he'd always wanted—was to be left alone.

And I need some self-respect, to know that this time I did the right thing with him. I stayed away and left him alone.

The feelings that evoked might be a lot more hollow than her made-up fantasy feelings, but at least they were real. They were adult. They were…right.

"So we keep ourselves busy, we don't look next door, we line up all our tasks and we get things done. All without thinking of Trey McFadden. What do you think, Fizz?"

The little dog cocked his head. Did he look sad? Ridiculous.

THE NEXT DAY Ella busied herself. She lined up all her lists. The merchants had collection boxes full of toys for the disadvantaged children at the preschool, but she would pick those up tomorrow, before the merchants' Christmas Walk. In the meantime she went to the store and hurriedly bought ingredients for the cookies she needed to make.

Fizz was home alone, so Ella rushed through the store.

"How's Trey liking his vacation home?" someone asked.

"Not sure. We're both so busy," she lied. She had no idea what Trey was up to.

"Ella, about Trey—" someone else began.

"Sorry, sweetie, I have a puppy home alone and dozens of Christmas cookies to make. I'd stop if I could."

In truth, she hated brushing people off this way, but she could not talk about Trey. If just thinking about Trey made her blush and imagine him with his shirt off, what would happen if she talked about him?

What would people think?

They'd think she had a crush on him. And she didn't. No, she didn't. He was just a very good-looking man, a very virile man, and one she had once long ago had a crush on. It wasn't the same thing at all.

When she got home Fizz was chewing on Trey's table again. She squealed and pushed it into an empty bedroom and shut the door. If she didn't have to give Fizz up she would start to train him. As it was…

"We're on borrowed time, you and I, Fizz," she said softly. *Just like Trey.*

She closed her eyes at that thought, then started slamming cookbooks around and getting pans, bowls, measuring cups and spoons and all her ingredients out. A half hour later she put her first batch of cookies in the oven.

It had started snowing an hour earlier, and now the kitchen was getting dark. Ella flipped on the light. She went to the window to close the shades and saw that Trey was shoveling snow, his tall form easily pitching the white fluffy stuff. He looked like…

A vision of him in the window yesterday popped into her head.

"*Grr*, stop it, Delancey," she told herself.

Suddenly everything seemed very quiet. Where was Fizz?

"Fizz?" she called.

A small woof came from the next room. A little tail was sticking partially out from beneath the sofa, and as she watched, he slithered farther under it. His next woof sounded distressed.

Getting down on her hands and knees, she saw the problem. His ball had rolled beneath the sofa, but it was behind one of the far legs. Stuck. And it was clear that Fizz was not going anywhere without his favorite toy.

She had barely gotten the ball out from behind the couch and Fizz from beneath it when the smoke alarm went off.

Ella went running into the kitchen, grabbed a mitt, opened the oven and retrieved the cookies. They were charred bits of dough now.

And the kitchen, indeed half the house, was full of smoke. She opened several windows, made sure the screens were in place, and faced her disastrous batch of cookies. She sat down at the table and thought about how she hadn't anticipated Bernadette's protracted speech, how she had taken Fizz to the meeting and ended up passing him off to Trey, how she had actually conned Trey into singing. None of this was like her. She was competent; she loved her job; Stuart had chosen her for a reason, hadn't he? So…why was she acting as if she'd lost half her brain? What was wrong with her?

But she didn't really have to think very hard. The truth was obvious. Trey McFadden had come back home and now she was aware of him…just as she'd always been. He made her nervous, hot, itchy—as if she didn't fit into her own body.

And this afternoon when she'd been baking the cookies she'd been thinking about Trey and had lost track of Fizz. She'd burned the cookies and might have done worse if not for the smoke alarm. Once again she was far too focused on Trey McFadden. That was just asking for trouble. This had to end. Now.

CHAPTER SIX

TREY TOSSED ANOTHER shovelful of light, fluffy snow. There wasn't much left to do, but he preferred the biting briskness of the cold and concentrating on the task to allowing himself to think about the fact that he had clearly made Ella feel as if she had to hide in her house to keep from antagonizing him.

Not that he should mind that she had gone inside. The less they saw of each other the better. Right?

The sudden sound of Fizz's mini-bark brought Trey's head up. It wasn't a muffled sound, either. And the dog sounded distressed. There it was again. And again.

Trey rushed around the corner to where the sound seemed to be coming from.

Fizz had his face pressed against the windowscreen. He was still barking, but when he saw Trey he stopped and cocked his head. He gave a little woof, then moved away.

In two seconds he was back, barking again. And then he was gone again. The barking grew more pronounced.

Trey moved closer. He could see now that when Fizz moved away he ran toward the door leading into the next room, then returned. It was almost like one of those old films where the dog was trying to communicate with the person.

And… Trey sniffed. That definitely smelled like smoke.

Smoke?

Where was Ella?

"Ella!"

No answer.

"Ella!"

"Trey?"

Suddenly she stumbled into the room. Her hair was falling loosely around her face, she was barefoot, and she looked like she'd just lost her last friend.

"Open the door, Ella. Let me in," he coaxed.

"Why?"

"Just do it. All right?"

He could see that she didn't want to. For some reason that made him angry. But she went to the back door and let him inside. "Are you all right? Fizz was going nuts."

She looked at the little dog. "Tattletale."

But she sounded…he supposed *loving* was the right word. It wasn't a word he wanted to think about.

"Your house is full of smoke," he said.

"Oh…not so much. It was worse before." She looked up at him. "I burned the cookies."

She sounded so guilty and her voice was so sad that he wanted to laugh, but he could see that it wasn't a laughing matter to her. "Were they…special cookies?"

"They were for tomorrow. I wanted to make four batches, and I've already burned the first batch." She was looking at him as if he had personally turned the oven up too high.

He held up his hands in front of him. "I swear I didn't have anything to do with it."

"No. I—that is, I know you didn't. I'm just…I don't

operate well around you. I never have. I'm normally good at my job, and I know how to bake a simple batch of chocolate chip cookies. But apparently not today."

"Chocolate chip? Homemade?"

She gave him a look. "It's not that big a deal."

"It is to me. My mother never made cookies."

"Have *you* ever made cookies?"

He blinked. "Good point. I can't blame someone else for something I've never done myself. Maybe I should give it a try. You said these are for tomorrow? I'll help. Come on."

She looked at him as if he'd just spoken in a language she didn't understand. "Excuse me?"

"I said come on. What do you need to bring?"

"I'm not going to your house. You're not making cookies. You're the guest of honor and I've told you twice that I'm not going to…to stalk you again."

Ah. There it was. "Ella, I'd hoped to avoid it, but we're going to have to talk about that day sooner or later."

"No. I don't want to. Ever. And I'm not going to your house."

"You can't stay here. Breathing in all this smoke can't be good for you."

"I'll be fine. The smoke will dissipate."

"It's going to linger for a while."

"I'm okay with that."

"What about Fizz? He's just a puppy. He's got those little, pristine, not yet totally formed lungs. Don't you, boy?"

Fizz did his part, managing to do that cute little cocked head, sad-eyed look. Ella was no match for a pro like Fizz.

But, to her credit, she tried. "I'll stay here and make the cookies. You take Fizz home with you, where the air is clearer."

"Nope. Not a puppy guy." Which was still true. He appreciated the dog's intelligence and inventiveness, and conceded that he was a cute one, but Fizz still represented a whole laundry list of things that Trey did not want to deal with in his future. "Plus, what would the shelter think of you, palming your foster-puppy off on someone who is an avowed puppy-hater?"

She gave him a look. Okay, that might be stretching things a bit.

"Ella…" he drawled. "It's cold in here. It's smoky. And, like it or not, you and I have to deal with each other for another few days. I came here for Stu. You're making cookies to help Stu. Let's call a truce. Come to my house. I have a big kitchen and probably all the requisite kitchen appliances. Despite my puppy aversion, I'll find an empty room and set it up so that he can run around safely while we get busy in the kitchen."

A luscious pink rose up her cheeks. He could see where it disappeared beneath the collar of her white blouse. Something hot and dark made Trey think of what it would be like to back Ella up against a cabinet and let his lips dip beneath her collar to explore all that pale skin. *Dammit!* That was not going to happen. He cleared his throat.

As if she was afraid he was going to say something even more suggestive or embarrassing, Ella straightened up. "Okay, you win. Your house. We'll bake cookies. You probably have a gigantic oven. I'll be done and back here in no time."

She certainly sounded eager to get away from him.

Trey felt like frowning. Instead he just nodded. Could he really blame her for wanting to sever their relationship? It was amazing that she'd even agreed to talk to him. Her memories of him couldn't be pleasant ones. He'd been a total jerk. So what was he going to do about that?

ELLA HOPED THAT Trey couldn't see how nervous she was. And *why* was she nervous? She was just here to bake the cookies. He was just going to help. The fact that he had volunteered both to help and to offer his home still amazed her. But then it sounded as if he and Stu had a special relationship.

She tried not to feel glad, not to be happy that Trey, who was such a loner, had someone he could talk to. That was the old Ella thinking, the nosy Ella, the stupidly sentimental Ella, and Trey detested her brand of nosiness and sentimentality.

"What's first?" Trey asked, coming up behind her.

She somehow managed not to jump, but she could not remain unaware of him, of his nearness.

"First we assemble the ingredients," she said, showing him her recipe and naming the ingredients as Trey gamely tried to locate measuring cups, spoons and bowls.

"Then we mix."

Trey mixed.

"And then?"

His voice was low and deep. He was so close… She glanced up at him from beneath her lashes. He was gazing at her. Waiting.

She swallowed. "Then we…these are chocolate chip…so we just drop them."

He raised a dark, quizzical brow. "We drop them?"

Ella couldn't hold back her smile. "Not on the floor. Like this."

She showed him how. Trey followed her lead. Soon the first batch of cookies was in the oven.

"And now?" he asked, coming up behind her. She could barely breathe.

"Now we make sugar cookies. And we decorate them. And we don't let the other cookies burn. Cookies don't take long to bake. So we can't get distracted."

No question that reminder was for herself more than for Trey. *She* was the one who was far too aware of him. *She* was the one who was susceptible.

"Right. No distractions," he said, and frowned. He took a step away.

Within minutes the chocolate chip cookies were out and Ella was batting Trey's hand away. "You'll burn yourself. They're hot."

He grinned and stopped reaching for a cookie. "You can't blame a guy for trying." He stared straight into her eyes.

"You have to wait," she told him, her voice breaking.

Trey nodded. "I'm doing my best not to step out of line," he said. "I'm trying to wait, to stop myself."

Ella looked up at him again. His silvery blue eyes were so beautiful. They always had been. And his lips...

She reached for one of the still too warm cookies and handed it to him. "Just one. They're for tomorrow."

He looked at her palm with the warm, chocolaty cookie resting on it. Then he lifted her hand, took the cookie. A smear of chocolate remained on her skin. He closed his eyes, then touched his lips to her palm.

His kiss—and it *was* a kiss of sorts—sent her heartbeat into overdrive. Her nerve endings tingled, reacted.

She sucked in a deep breath. Did she make a sound? She must have made a sound, because his eyes turned fierce. He leaned toward her. Then he looked down. It almost sounded as if he was counting.

"Trey?" Her voice was shaky.

"I didn't mean to do that," he said, and she could tell that he meant it.

"It's all right." But it wasn't. She was already too susceptible to him. Touching would only make it worse. "Maybe we should get back to making cookies."

He nodded, and soon she was coaching him in the intricacies of frosting sugar cookies.

"What is that, exactly?" she asked, gesturing to something green.

"It's a Christmas tree."

"Really? Does it look like any that you've ever seen?"

He laughed. Soon she was laughing, too. And Fizz was jumping around and woofing, clearly entranced with his two adults even if he didn't have a clue why they were acting so silly.

"Fizz, would you like a Christmas tree, buddy? Can he have it?" he asked Ella.

"It's not the best thing for him, but there's no chocolate in it, so yes. Just one."

He held out the cookie. "Fizz, what is this?"

Fizz gave his little baby bark.

"See? He said, 'Christmas tree.'"

Ella chuckled. "It sounded more like 'green blob' to me."

"Are you making fun of my artistic abilities?"

"You can't be good at everything, can you?"

He shrugged. "I don't know why you keep implying that I'm good at so many things and that I'm some sort of hero. You know it's not true. I'm just a man, Ella, and a very fallible one at that. That's always been true. No one knows that better than you." And now he was no longer laughing. He was staring directly into her eyes.

Ella knew she couldn't handle that kind of close scrutiny. He had always made her too aware of herself. Aware of him. She turned back to the cookies, quickly finished decorating the last one and started to wrap them. "It's not that I don't know that you're…human," she said, still with her back to him. "It's just that when I moved here you…your family was so much larger than life than mine was. You almost didn't seem real."

"But that was an act. You know it was an act."

She knew. At least she knew part of it. She'd heard the yelling. "Yes. I knew that things weren't…right, and that there was no harmony in your house."

"Did you know why?"

He came up next to her and took the container of cookies out of her hands. The pads of his fingertips brushed her skin and she trembled. Quickly she shoved her hands behind her back.

"Your father…" She struggled for words. "He didn't approve of your activities."

"He didn't approve of *me*," he clarified. "And neither did my mother. You knew that."

She looked up at him and nodded slowly. "Yes. I knew."

She'd heard them one day when the windows were open. It was what she'd tried to stop in her naively childish way. Seventeen years old and filled with puppy love, she'd rung the doorbell and confronted Trey's parents—total strangers whom she'd known even less than she'd known Trey. But she'd thought she'd known him. Because she'd made up dream scenarios in her mind; she'd raised him up on a pedestal, given him godlike characteristics that no human could ever live up to. And, filled with all of that young-girl naiveté, she'd told his parents they were wrong. She'd painted a picture of a young god, tried to tell them that they should be proud to have such a son. Not old or wise enough to know how to be tactful, and filled with self-righteous indignation, she had rebuked them.

And promptly and icily been turned out of the house.

"What happened that day? After I left? You never said."

"No, I didn't, did I? I merely took a page out of my father's book and ripped you to shreds."

She looked down at her hands, reached down and picked up Fizz and began to pet him as he nestled against her. Maybe it was wrong to use the puppy to hide her nervousness, but Fizz, despite his own frenetic behavior, was somehow calming—or at least as calming as anyone or thing could be under such circumstances.

"I suppose my interfering made things even worse."

"It wasn't that so much."

But she could imagine what a bully like his father would have said about a small skinny girl defending his football-player-sized son's honor.

"It was more that I'd spent my whole life hiding what was happening at home from the world. I was adopted, and when my birth parents gave me up it was because they already had three kids and I was an accident they didn't want. They didn't have good, honorable reasons for giving up a child, so I'd always felt like the runt of the litter. But my adoptive parents chose me because my birth parents had very high IQs and were physically attractive. They figured that with those genes and their own expectations and rules I would have to be a genius, an overachiever, someone who would be absolutely perfect and would live up to their expectations and needs in every way.

"I proved them wrong from the start. I didn't like being treated like a show dog, and I didn't turn out to be what they wanted. At school I swaggered, tried to act cool and uninterested. I took out my frustrations in sports. At home I rebelled. And I thought I had everyone fooled into thinking that I led a normal existence until you came along. Having you know...see...hear... I didn't deal with it well. I behaved badly."

"No. You were right. It was presumptuous of me to try to interfere with your personal life."

"You thought you were helping me."

"But it didn't help. It made things worse, didn't it?" Only the puppy in her arms kept her from losing control of her voice.

"It doesn't matter. It was your intention that counted."

"It *does* matter. I can only imagine what he said to you and—"

"Ella—"

"I always do this. I try to make everything perfect, and if they're not perfect I try to fix things when not everything can be fixed. That's what you said to me that day. And your voice—"

"I was embarrassed. You'd caught me outside feeling sorry for myself, angry at everyone, choked up and near tears. When you showed up and saw me on the verge of crying or kicking something I let loose on you. That was wrong."

"No, I—"

"Ella, shh." He stepped closer.

"But I want to explain."

"No. *I* want to apologize. For not thanking you for thinking better of me than I deserved."

"But—"

Fizz gave a little woof and clambered higher against her. Suddenly Trey smiled, a sly little smile. He stepped forward, right into her space, and took her into his arms. With Fizz still balanced against her shoulder Trey kissed her. Softly. Gently. Exquisitely. With such skill and tenderness that she thought she might cry.

It was over in a moment…and yet he was looking at her as if he wanted to kiss her again. Differently this time.

"Why?" she asked.

He smiled. "You wouldn't stop apologizing…and it seemed like the right thing to do. Fizz seemed to think so."

"Fizz is a puppy."

"A puppy with good instincts. See? He even made a space for me," Trey said, indicating the way Fizz had moved to her shoulder, enabling Trey to make his move without crushing the puppy.

She was blushing. She knew that she was blushing. Because she was totally discombobulated. Trey was an experienced kisser. He was probably bored being stuck here in Eagleton. Okay, he had been trying to apologize, and she had been dithering, not letting him.

"Thank you," she said.

"For the kiss?"

More blushing.

"No! I mean…for the apology. I know I must have

made things worse for you. I think I've always known and regretted that. And…I was embarrassed."

"I hurt your feelings that day."

"No," she said slowly.

"Yes," he insisted.

"Maybe. It was mostly that I was young and stupid and I had a crush on you. I'd built you up into some make-believe boy and it was a shock to have you speak to me that way."

"I really am sorry. I'll bet that no one else ever spoke to you like that in your life."

She pulled back and looked at him as she cuddled Fizz in both arms. But Trey was still close, and he reached out and scratched Fizz beneath the chin. The little puppy licked his fingers. Trey gave Fizz an appraising look, but quickly turned back to Ella.

In that moment, she made a decision. "Don't be sorry. When you yelled at me it helped me to move on. It woke me up out of my dream world of white knights and enabled me to live a happy life."

"You say that as if your life is over."

"Not over."

"Good, because some white knight is going to come along one day."

"I doubt that very much."

He frowned.

She shook her head. "That's not a negative thing. I'm not complaining. But it's like this. Your parents weren't happily married, I take it?"

"They weren't happy people."

"Mine were. They were exquisitely happy. My father's job took him here and there, but my mother would have lived with him on the bottom of the ocean if that

was where he needed to be. He would have moved us to
the top of a cloud if she said that was where she wanted
to go. We only moved here because my father got a
chance at stability, and they wanted that for me, but lots
of times they were so tuned in to each other that they
didn't even know I was there. I've never, *ever* seen any
two people as in love as they were. And that's why there
won't be any white knights for me. I want what they
had, but I don't think that kind of love comes around
more than…I don't know…once a century? Once an
eternity? And I won't settle for less. I want that, but I
doubt I'll ever find it."

"Ella…"

"Don't say it like that. I'm happy. I really am happy.
I fit here in Eagleton. I belong." And if he kept looking
at her the way he was looking at her now…if he kissed
her again…he might know that she had lied. A little.
She still had feelings for him. She wasn't at all happy
about that. And, oh, she wanted him to kiss her.

That thought stopped her cold. "I'd better take the
cookies home. Fizz needs his beauty sleep."

"Is that right, buddy?" Trey asked.

The little dog woofed and licked Trey's finger again.

"Are you sure you're not a dog person?"

"Never going to happen. You come from the perfect
couple. I failed the family test twice. Not going there
again. No wife, no kids, no pets. But, Ella?"

She had collected her box of cookies, had Fizz in
tow and was turning to go. "What?"

"If I'd known what you tasted like I would have
kissed you years ago."

There was a dangerous look in his eyes, an *I dare you
to put down those cookies and kiss me again* look. Ella

fought to keep from moaning, from going over there, taking his face between her palms and kissing him the way she'd always wanted to.

"You're just trying to sweet-talk me into giving you another chocolate chip cookie. Or excusing you from tomorrow's event. That's just not happening. I'll see you there, Trey. And there will be no more kissing."

He smiled.

She smiled back.

And then she walked out the door. She and Fizz stepped into her house and she shut the door behind them.

"That 'no more kissing' thing I said? That was a warning for *me*, sweetie. And if I ever decide to do something stupid like kiss Trey again, I want you to start barking, or nip me good. Anything to keep me from doing something totally stupid. You got that, Fizz?"

But Fizz was already playing with his red ball. His back was to her as if he didn't want to discuss the matter.

CHAPTER SEVEN

THE NEXT DAY looked like Christmas personified. There was snow on the ground, the sun was shining, and there was just enough of a breeze to set the Christmas bells in the trees outside City Hall to jingling.

After last night's confessions and kiss Trey was determined to be on his best behavior. He had embarrassed Ella, forced a confession from her, and this time when he left town he intended to leave on good terms with her. He was closing the door on his past, and that meant making peace with sweet, undeniably domestic Ella Delancey. And then putting her out of his mind forever.

But that was proving hard to do. She looked delectable in her red coat and white mittens, her long hair streaming down her back as she stood with him in the doorway outside City Hall. The big red-brick building was located right in the center of town, with shops flanking it and marching away down one block on each side. Today's Christmas Walk had been a rousing success, with the shops staying open later than usual and each shop serving treats to the steady stream of townspeople who oohed and aahed over the decorations and performers, the string quartets, guitarists, soloists and carolers dressed up as if they had just stepped out of *A Christmas Carol*.

"Ella, you've turned Eagleton's Christmas into a joyful one again. The town is smiling and shining, and we all know it's due to your hard work," said Bert Kilstrom, the pharmacist.

"And I know you were the wonderful secret Santa who contributed the lights," she said, kissing the man on his wrinkled cheek.

"And look at this young man." Bert slapped Trey on the back. "He's brought excitement to the town and has proven that he didn't forget us the way so many of the young ones do when they move away. We're proud of you, son," Bert declared. "Nice Christmas tree cookies, too. I hear you had a hand in making them."

"Thank you, sir," Trey said with a smile. "I'm happy you've forgiven me for the candy bar I filched."

"Well, you worked it off, didn't you, Trey? You're a fine one. You made us proud when you enlisted, and you made good in business, too."

He shook Trey's hand, then moved on as more people took his place. Trey smiled until his teeth hurt and struggled to remember names.

When the crowd finally dissipated, he turned to Ella. "Why are they all so proud of me?" he asked. "At least half a dozen people have told me that. I don't get it," he told her. "It has to be more than having been a soldier. There are other men in town who have served, and I mostly joined up just to tick off my father, because I knew he had no respect for anyone who ranked less than a general. That's nothing to be proud of."

Ella gave him a patient look. She sighed.

"What?"

"You're not going to like it."

"All the more reason to tell me."

"They're proud of you because they knew your father. You may have thought they didn't know what went on at your house, but anyone who met Darren McFadden knew what you went home to every night, and they knew that it took guts to defy him, to become a foot soldier and then to make a success of yourself with no help from him. How can anyone not admire that?"

"I was a screwup when I was here, a cocky jerk. Angry."

"So what? Who wouldn't be under those circumstances?"

He smiled down at her.

"What?" she asked. "Why are you looking at me that way?"

"If I told you my name was Lucifer and I was here to steal souls, I believe you'd find some way to make a positive out of that."

"I'm not a Pollyanna. I understand reality."

"Do you, now? What's reality, pretty Ella?"

She stared up into his eyes. "Reality is that I'm not all that pretty and that this is just a brief moment in time. You and I have made peace with a bad moment in our past, which is good, and soon you'll go on your way. I'll take Fizz back to the shelter, and some lovely family will give him a home. You'll go on to continued success and I'll have a lovely life here working for Stu."

"That's how you see the future, is it?"

"It's how the future will be. See? I'm a total realist."

"Hmm, I used to think you were a dreamer."

"I used to be a dreamer. But then, every young girl is. This one simply grew up."

A flash of anger slipped through Trey, followed by an intense sadness. Ella deserved so much more than she was going to allow herself. It was all wrong. But he had no right to say that. A man who had once accused her of sticking her nose in where it didn't belong had no right to interfere in her life or to lecture her on what he thought *she* should do. Especially because right now he was thinking that she should...

Kiss me, he thought.

He scowled at that, then caught himself. "Are we almost done here?"

"Yes. We're done."

The finality of those words reminded him how quickly time was passing.

"Last cookie?" she asked, indicating one lone tree on the plate.

"We'll save it for the puppy. He's going to be miffed that you left him with Bernadette today. She doesn't seem like the puppy type."

"She was the only person I could find who wasn't coming into town. Maybe...maybe he won her over."

"It could happen. He can be a wily one."

She shook her head. "He's just a puppy. An adorable little puppy. Not sneaky, not wily."

He winked at her. "You keep believing that," he teased. "That pup has wicked intentions where you and I are concerned. He warned me about the smoke. He moved aside so I could kiss you."

"Well, will you look at that?" said Alex Staunton, the owner of the grocery store, walking toward them. "Someone hung some mistletoe right over the doorway of City Hall. And the two of you have been standing there for hours. What *have* you been doing?"

"Alex!" Ella said. "You know what we've been doing, and it wasn't kissing."

But a crowd was forming now. Stuart was with Alex, and he always attracted a crowd of people with questions for the mayor. He gave Trey a questioning, not very happy look. Trey shook his head.

"But now you *have* to kiss her, Trey," Alex said. "It's the right thing to do beneath the mistletoe. It's Christmas, man."

Trey looked at the mistletoe. He looked at Ella. And he knew that if he kissed her again it wouldn't be like last time. It wouldn't be gentle or sweet. He'd been staring at her all day and he was wild to taste her lips.

But they had an audience. It just wasn't going to happen.

"Sorry, Alex, everyone," he said, smiling at them. "But Ella and I can't be your Christmas entertainment now. We have to get home to a baby."

"A *baby*?" someone called.

"It's a dog," someone else explained.

"Oh, do *not* tell Fizz he's a dog," Trey told them. "I'm pretty sure he thinks he's a person. Or a Christmas elf. There's just something about that puppy. Something special."

He held out his arm. "Ella?"

She rolled her eyes. When they were out of sight of everyone, she elbowed him. "Are you trying to make them think that you're insane?"

Trey shook his head. "I'm not quite sure what I was trying to do. I think I was trying to distract them from the fact that I had the chance to kiss a lovely woman and I turned down the opportunity."

"That just shows that you're smart. You're practical."

Trey was pretty sure that it didn't mean either of

those things. It most assuredly meant that he was a coward who didn't trust himself around Ella.

BERNADETTE ONLY LIVED two blocks away from Ella and Trey, so after they'd collected Fizz from the woman, who declared that Fizz was "too active," they turned toward home with Fizz leading the way.

"I wonder what he did to her," Trey said.

"He probably didn't do anything out of the ordinary. He's a puppy. Bernadette likes things tidy and neat. She doesn't like noises or messes."

As if he knew they were discussing him, Fizz backtracked and ran up to them.

"Poor boy. Women just don't understand the mess thing, do they?" Trey asked. "Always with the neatness and the quiet. 'Pick up your shoes…' 'If you didn't listen to such loud music you might concentrate more and earn an A instead of an A minus on your paper.' 'Try to be a normal person and not a disgusting pig.' 'Don't leave your chew toys around,'" he said, mixing together things his mother had undoubtedly told him with what he was guessing Bernadette would have told Fizz.

"Was your mother…?"

"She wasn't so bad. Mostly I think she took her cues from my dad. I was kidding about the neatness thing, you know. I didn't get that any more than any other kid, I don't think. She only got really verbally abusive when my dad was angry. Then I think she needed to appease him by coming down doubly hard on me. But, Ella, I only told you that stuff so I could apologize. It's long gone—done—and I've got a great life now. No complaints."

"I know."

He smiled to reassure her.

"Do you think Bernadette was mean to Fizz? Maybe I shouldn't have left him with her."

"Only one way to find out if he's irreparably scarred. Hey, Fizz?"

The puppy looked up.

"Want a cookie, Fizz?"

As if he already knew the word *cookie*, Fizz started jumping around. He ran back and forth. He ran in happy circles. Soon his leash was tangled around Trey and Ella's legs.

"Fizz, no!" Ella said.

She was up against Trey and in danger of falling. He wrapped an arm around her to steady her and himself. And now his body was planted against hers.

"Do you still think Fizz doesn't have ulterior motives where we're concerned?"

She gave him a *you have to be kidding* look. "You teased him with a cookie."

"I did not." He pulled the last cookie out of his pocket and gave it to the puppy. Fizz settled down to eat. He went at it voraciously, slobbering, throwing crumbs everywhere. "I guess that answers our question about his mental state. He looks ecstatic."

"And we're tangled up until he's done with his cookie."

Trey looked into her eyes. "You know how we didn't kiss under the mistletoe…?"

She took a deep breath. Her eyelids fluttered just a bit, but then she looked directly into his eyes. "Because you were being smart."

"Because I didn't want an audience."

She nodded as if she was agreeing.

"Well, we're alone now. There's no one on the street, and Fizz is otherwise occupied. He's holding us hostage. I'm going to kiss you now, Ella, as long as you don't mind."

Her answer was to rise up on her toes, cup his face in her palms and kiss him—long and hard.

Heat rushed through Trey. His mind and sanity disappeared. Reality ceased to exist. When they came up for air, he was breathing hard. "Ella, if I'd known you kissed like that... We should have done this years ago."

"No," she said, shaking her head. "No, we shouldn't—and we shouldn't be doing it now, either. But this is a moment out of time. Christmas is two days away and then you'll return to San Diego. Once you're gone, I'd like to be able to say that I'm no longer the only woman in Eagleton you haven't kissed properly."

He'd like to think that some other man wasn't going to be experiencing *her* kisses, but he had no right to say that.

Looking down, he saw that Fizz was finished with the cookie and staring at them as if he knew just what had been going on. And maybe he did. He'd taken just long enough to eat his treat to make sure that Trey had his chance to kiss Ella. And now, like a good chaperone, he was putting an end to things.

"Plans for tonight?" Trey asked.

"I'm wrapping the presents you and Santa will be giving to the underprivileged children at the preschool tomorrow."

"Okay. My place."

"Trey..."

"You want me to hand out presents without even

knowing what's inside? How can I play my part convincingly?"

"It's not a part. You just stand there and smile and that's it."

"Nope. I agreed to come here and help, and I'm not going to make little kids think I'm some large and forbidding authority figure standing silent like a statue. If I'm going to do it, I'm doing it right. There will be conversations."

She opened her mouth.

"Don't object or lecture," he said.

Her laugh was soft and silvery. "I was merely going to say thank you. Is that allowed?"

"Yes. And now I feel like a judgmental ass."

"You'll never be that in your whole life."

He stopped cold. "How can you be so sure of that?"

"Simple. That was your father's role, and you've rejected everything he was and all he stood for. In a way, he gave you a present. He taught you how to be the opposite of him."

And with that she trudged off with Fizz, leaving Trey to stare after her. Until Fizz gave a *Come on* woof.

Trey did as he was told.

CHAPTER EIGHT

TREY HAD NEVER wrapped a present in his life. That was apparent to Ella after less than five minutes. He was eyeing the wrapping paper from all angles as if it were a major engineering project.

"What exactly does your company do again?" she asked.

"We produce green building materials and search for new ways to use recycled materials."

"Sounds like a good idea. Is that what you're doing with that wrapping paper? Studying it to find a new way to use it?"

He gave her a sheepish smile. "I'm waiting for you to show me how, so I don't have to admit that this is outside my realm of experience."

"Like cookies?"

"Exactly. Now, if you'd like me to demonstrate how a turbine works, or how to make the most of a limited water supply, I'm your man. Wrapping a child's present with—" he eyed the paper "—penguins wearing Santa hats… Outside my comfort zone."

"Well, then, you're in for a treat. There's a process here."

"I'm assuming you're going to explain that process?"

"Absolutely. First we put on some Christmas music. Do you have some?"

He looked at her as if she were crazy.

"No? I thought not. That's why I came prepared." She pulled a CD out of the kangaroo-style center pocket of the royal blue hoodie she was wearing.

"You brought your own music? Was that necessary?" he teased.

She shrugged. "Only if we want to do this right. And I do."

"What else do you have in there?" He looked at the deep pocket. "A Christmas tree? More music?"

"I might have one more CD. But first this one. It's one of my favorites." She put it in the player and soon "Silver Bells" was wafting through the house.

"That's nice. Now what?"

His deep voice sent a shiver of awareness through her. She looked around. "We...I think we light a fire."

"You think?"

"My family always wrapped Christmas presents at the same time in different rooms of the house. We had traditions. Music. Cocoa. Christmas lights. Candles. But we didn't have a fireplace. If we had, I'm sure we would have lit a fire."

Trey had moved to the fireplace as she spoke. He was already stacking the wood he'd brought in a couple of days ago. "There are emergency candles and matches in the drawer next to the stove in the kitchen," he said. "Probably no cocoa, though."

"That's okay. I brought my own."

He glanced up at her and grinned as she pulled two packets out of her hoodie. "You didn't bring your own candles?"

She blushed.

"You did, didn't you?" he asked.

"I didn't think you'd have any."

"Traditions are important to you, aren't they?"

"They remind me of what it was like when my parents were alive. Of course I'm not doing a Christmas tree this year because of Fizz, and because there's just me, but for the rest I'll try to make things festive. My mom and dad loved Christmas. And maybe because we moved around so much they loved traditions. The kind that are portable. Like what you do on gift wrapping night."

"I never told you I was sorry that they passed away. I didn't know them well, but I know that they were good people."

"How could you know?"

"Your father always said hello to me, your mother once brought me a glass of lemonade when I was working outside, and I never heard anyone say anything bad about them." He looked away slightly.

"Except *your* parents."

"Well, then, that proves it. Your parents were the best." He smiled. The fact that he could smile about it told her that he really was okay.

"Do you call them? Ever?" she asked.

"Once a year. On Christmas, as a matter of fact. It makes me feel…"

"Superior?" she guessed.

"A little," he conceded. "Mostly it makes me realize that I moved on and they didn't."

"You're the adult."

"I don't know about that," he said. "Shouldn't an adult know more about wrapping Christmas presents?"

"Well, by the time tonight is over you'll know so much you never dreamed of," she promised.

The look he gave her was...*hot*. The hoodie suddenly seemed stifling, as if it was choking her. "I'd better get those outside lights on," she said, turning away.

"I'll do that. The switch is outside, and you have to be a much better cocoa chef than I am."

"Okay."

"Good. Then, let's get this gift wrapping party started."

He put his hand out. She tipped her head. He motioned for her to put her hand on his and she did, her heart thudding faster. He grinned at her.

"Okay, gift wrapping coach. One, two, three, break," he said, as they parted to go their separate ways.

"You do that often?" she asked when he returned.

He chuckled. "Actually, yes. We do a lot of team building at the office and at the plant. I want people to feel that we're involved in a common cause and that each person is important."

"That's nice—that you feel each person who works for you matters and belongs," Ella said. Trey, who had not felt a sense of belonging in his home growing up, still wanted that for other people.

He studied her for a moment. "I hope my employees think so."

"Maybe you should ask them?" she said.

"Excuse me?"

"My parents always asked each other what they wanted. I think that was part of what made them fit so well. They knew they were on the same page. I try to do that in my work with the town, too. You'll never know for sure what the other person wants if you don't ask."

Trey was studying her so intently that Ella felt as if

he could see right through her hoodie to the lacy underwear she was wearing. She had a bad feeling that he was going to ask her what *she* wanted.

"I already know what you want. And what I want," she said, determined to head him off. "You want to get back to your business and travels. I want the agency to find a good home for Fizz, and I want to enjoy my life here and to make a difference in the town."

"And to find that white knight."

"I should never have told you about my parents' fairy tale marriage. That's not likely to happen for me."

"I think you're wrong, but…"

"We'd better get started on these gifts," she said, ending the discussion of her marital prospects. "It's getting late, and I don't want to disappoint the kids."

Soon they were knee-deep in wrapping paper scraps, ribbons and bows.

Trey chuckled and gestured.

Ella looked down to see that Fizz had been frolicking in the wrapping paper scraps. An errant bow was stuck to his fur, and his nose had disappeared into one end of an empty wrapping paper roll. He was trying to sling it free.

"Here, boy. Let me help you," Trey said. "For a free spirit like you, that must seem like jail."

And for a free spirit like Trey had always been, her parents' kind of love would probably feel like a prison cell, Ella reminded herself. She was beginning to like him too much, to know him in a way she hadn't before. That made him even more dangerous to her deeply romantic soul. She could no more have Trey McFadden now than when they were teenagers.

But she could kiss him. She knew that he would

let her kiss him. Only the fear that kissing him would lead to something she couldn't handle held her back as she looked across the room and saw him gently freeing the little dog.

Once freed, Fizz looked at her as if to say, *Isn't he a wonderful person?*

He is, she thought. *He's wonderful. I'd better enjoy what little time I have with him.*

TREY KEPT HIS distance for the rest of the evening. Sitting in front of the fire with Ella opposite him and Fizz on her lap, he realized that everything felt different here this time. This house didn't feel like the terrible place he'd grown up in. The fire, the woman, the dog, the music…there was a sense of contentment in the air, of anticipation.

And yet anticipation of what? Nothing had changed. He was still here just as a favor for Stuart; he was still leaving as soon as Christmas was over. Fizz would be going back to the agency, and Ella would continue in her quest to make her world and Eagleton a better place.

Maybe all he was anticipating was Christmas. Maybe that was it. The holiday had not been a happy one in his youth, but this woman and this little dog were conspiring to make this one…pleasant, comfortable, homey.

And maybe that was all he could ask for.

Well, no, he could ask for one more thing. Before he left here he was going to do some serious kissing with Ella. That woman could certainly kiss. Where on earth had she learned that here in Eagleton?

What man had claimed those lips before him? And
how had the man managed to walk away?

Trey really needed to know the answer to that question.

CHAPTER NINE

TREY MIGHT NEVER have been near a lot of children before but he hid it well, Ella thought, watching him pass out the gifts to the children the next day. She had opted to bring Fizz along rather than hunt for a sitter, and when Trey or Santa got into sticky situations, such as a child asking for the impossible, Fizz was brought in as a distraction. It only took a few seconds and the child forget that he or she had even asked for some impossibly expensive gift that the down-on-their-luck parents of these children would never be able to afford.

"You're killing 'em, Fizz," Trey said when the party was almost over and Santa was taking a break.

Fizz gave his hand a lick, gave a little woof.

"Yeah, you know you're a charmer, don't you?"

He was grinning broadly. Ella was going to miss that smile. She was going to ache for it once Trey was gone. There were times when she almost wished he'd never come home. Then she wouldn't have known what she was missing out on.

Looking at Fizz now, a thought came to her. She frowned.

"Uh-oh, that doesn't look good. What's wrong, love?"

She glanced up at that, but then those teasing, flirting ways had always been part of the old Trey she remembered—the too awesome for words Trey, who'd won all the girls and hadn't seemed to think there was anything unusual about calling every girl in sight "love." Not that he'd ever called *her* that before.

But this wasn't about her. "I was wondering…worrying, actually, if we're doing Fizz a favor by introducing him to a lifestyle he'll have to give up soon. All these children…look how much he loves it. But he might not be adopted by a family with children. And if not…"

"Ella," he said, his voice gentle as he reached out and cupped her jaw, "you can't fix everything or everyone. You can't make life perfect for the world and for all the people you care about."

Or for myself, she thought.

"I know. But I want to. Look how little he is, how cute."

Trey looked. He sighed, then turned toward her, a fierce look in those gorgeous eyes. He moved closer, lowered his voice, still cupping her jaw. "I know I've said this before," he whispered, so that only she could hear, "but…he could be yours."

She shook her head, her skin sliding against his fingertips. "No. I told you. He'd be alone every day. It would be cruel. It wouldn't be fair."

"Or perfect," he said.

She nodded as he slid his hand away. It was all she could do not to lean into him and ask him to keep touching her, keep talking. She loved the sound of his voice. She loved being with him, and she loved that he saw her as she was. Mostly. There had been that silly moment when he had been the old Trey, telling her that she was pretty.

"Mister?"

The childish voice caught Ella—and obviously Trey—by surprise. Both of them looked down to see a pint-size little girl with curly brown hair and big blue eyes tugging on Trey's pants leg.

He dropped to one knee so she wouldn't have to crane her neck. "Yes?"

"I've been waiting and waiting for Santa to come back but he hasn't. They said you was his helper, so I want to know…what I want is…can I have a puppy for Christmas? I sure do want a puppy. Yours is nice. He licked my hand and he did not bite me one little bit."

Trey looked up at Ella. "I—"

She knew what he wanted from her. He wanted to see if it would kill her to lose Fizz. The lump in her throat grew to a gargantuan size, but she couldn't speak. She couldn't even nod or shake her head.

He turned to the little girl. "To be honest, I don't know if you can have a puppy. Puppies aren't like toys. They need to be cared for. Sometimes they get sick and have to go to the doctor. You have to walk them every day even when it snows or rains. And your m—that is, whoever takes care of you would have to be cool with having a dog in the house, too. Some people have allergies or they can't afford what a dog's food costs."

"So I can't have a puppy?" The little girl sounded as if she was going to cry.

Trey looked as if would do anything to change the world for this poverty-stricken child.

That look in his eyes was what Ella needed to be able to find her voice. "He's saying he can't promise you that, Annie," Ella said gently. "Your mom and dad would have to be okay with it."

Ella knew Annie, but she hadn't missed how Trey,

not knowing the child's family situation, had been careful not to use the words *mom* or *dad*.

Annie, looking less than happy but more hopeful, gave Fizz a quick pat. "Bye, doggie," she said. Fizz wagged his tail.

"It's how he says goodbye," Trey explained.

When Annie had gone, Trey took Ella by the hand and led her to a more private place. "When we're done here, we're going to talk."

"About...?"

But just then Santa returned, and Trey went back to making the children laugh and smile. Fizz worked more magic, and Ella helped the teachers ensure that everyone had enough juice and cookies, wiped mouths, cleaned up spills and shepherded four-year-olds to see Trey and Santa.

When the day was over, Trey looked beat.

"Tough stuff?" she asked.

"A little more demanding than my regular work."

"More demanding than saving the world from environmental destruction?"

He managed a small chuckle. "Engineers, designers and environmentalists don't whisper to me that their fish died and can I please find some way to bring him back. Or ask me to get their mommies and daddies back together again. Life can be harsh when you're only four and have no power."

That had been his life once. She knew that, so when they climbed in the car and Fizz was in his carrier, she reached across the seat and touched Trey's arm. "I wish you'd had a better childhood."

The look he gave her was deadly...or sinful.

"That does it. You and I and Fizz are going to get off

the pity train and the fix Trey train right now. For the record, I wasn't feeling sorry for myself for not having a perfect childhood. I'm fine. But some of those kids are living a really tough existence right now—and as for you, Eleanor Delancey…"

"What about me?"

"You're determined to make sure everyone else has a perfect existence, but what about *you*?"

"I'm fine."

"Hmm."

"What does that mean?"

He grinned. "It means…let's go make your life more perfect." He put the car in gear and began to drive.

"Where are we going?"

"You'll see." He was smiling.

"You're impossible. Isn't he, Fizz?" But Fizz had fallen asleep already. "Aw…he's so adorable when he sleeps," she couldn't help saying.

Trey laughed out loud. "He's snoring."

"But it's not loud snoring."

"Okay, you win. He's something special."

Ella turned around, a smile on her face, and Trey drove on. When he pulled up next to a tree lot, she gave him a look. "You're getting a tree when you're only going to be here two more days?"

"No. *You're* getting a tree."

"Trey, Fizz will knock it over."

"Not if we get a small one and put it up on a table. You said your parents always had one. You told me you like traditions. I'm pretty sure that in the perfect world of your imagination, every Christmas has a tree. Doesn't it?"

"That's an imaginary world."

"No. It's the world as you want it to be. It's the world you try to create for everyone else. That's why you want Stuart's festival to win everyone over, and it's why you don't want me to regret my past—why you're determined that Fizz will go to a home where he has company during the daytime and why you want Annie to have a dog. It's as if you don't believe that you can ever have your ideal world, so you live your life building perfect scenarios for everyone else. Well, this Christmas you're going to get as close to perfect as we can make it. That means a tree. Music, cocoa, lights, a fire and all the rest."

She studied him for a few seconds. "Is this payback?"

He blinked. "Explain."

"You still feel guilty that you called me bad names and made me cry when we were young?"

"I made you cry?"

Uh-oh, he clearly hadn't known that. How to backtrack?

She shrugged. "I was a seventeen-year-old girl. Everything makes you cry when you're a teenage girl."

He looked at her suspiciously. "This isn't about that. It's about some payback for all the selfless things you do for everyone. Restitution for making you cry is going to require a whole lot more than a three-foot Christmas tree."

And now they had stepped into dangerous territory. "I don't want—"

He looked at her.

She rushed on. "I don't want anything from you."

Trey frowned. "Well, you're at least getting a tree. It's Fizz's Christmas, too. His first Christmas. He darn well should have a tree to look at."

And that was the end of that. Ella shut her mouth. They marched off and found a sweet little Balsam fir. Trey tied the little tree to the top of the car and off they went.

When they reached Ella's house Trey waited until Ella had retrieved Fizz from the car, then he carried the tree inside. To someone who didn't know them, they might have looked like a real family.

But of course they would never be that. She knew she had wounded him when she'd said that she didn't want anything from him. No matter what had happened when they were younger, Trey was a man now. A generous man who cared about people. Being told that she didn't want anything must have stung…but she couldn't take anything from him. Even this tree was too much, because every gift, every gesture, everything he did for her sent out emotional threads that meant too much to her but were just the usual *modus operandi* for him. Like calling all the girls *love* in high school, kissing as many as he could. He was a man who spread himself around. It didn't mean anything important or lasting.

But little things like that could mean too much for a person like her. Those little things were like emotional vines, their slender tendrils twining around her heart, tugging at it. And she was afraid that her heart would never be free once he was gone if she allowed anything to happen that would create more tendrils. But she would accept the tree. For Fizz.

"Let's go make Christmas, Fizz," she said.

The sound of his name on her tongue was all it took. The puppy looked much happier than either she or Trey did.

CHAPTER TEN

TREY WASN'T SURE whether the tree had been a good idea or not. Ella obviously felt strongly about not accepting anything from him. For some reason that bothered him. A lot. It threw him into the ranks of people she didn't like well enough to accept gifts from.

Which was, of course, true. He'd been out of her life for years and hadn't been anything but trouble to her before that. His presence this Christmas had more or less been foisted on her by Stuart. Why should he expect her to actually want to spend time with him? Hadn't she made it clear that night with the cookies that she was only agreeing to come over to his house for Fizz's sake?

So after helping her with the tree last night, he had retreated back to his house, which had seemed a lot less cozy than it had the other day. Today was Christmas Eve: the day of the parade. By the day after tomorrow he would be back in warm, sunny San Diego, and Ella would just be someone from his past.

Wouldn't she?

He'd left a lot of people behind over the years. What was one more? Especially when she was looking for the perfect man and he was nowhere near perfect.

Still, she was all about duty, and she was convinced that her duty was to get him to the parade and make sure that he knew his part. So when the time was right, he strolled over to her house, pasting on his *I don't give a damn about anything* grin.

All he had to do was stop thinking about Ella and everything would be fine. He'd be right back where he'd been before he got the call from Stu. Should be easy. A piece of cake.

Ella stepped through her front door, carrying Fizz in a basket.

Trey's heart started booming around in his chest like some sort of weird electric drum stuck in the "on" position. She was wearing a red cloak with a hood, though she wasn't wearing the hood. Her hair was loose and flowing down her back. She was carrying Fizz in a basket lined with some sort of fleecy blue and white snowflake blanket, and he had a red collar with a bell and a bow around his neck. She was beautiful; he was adorable.

And I'm in big trouble, Trey thought. This was the woman who wanted perfection in a man and in a relationship; this was the puppy who was going back to the shelter the day after tomorrow and who was no doubt going to be snatched up immediately.

Breathe—breathe, Trey. This...distress is just because it's Christmas. Everyone gets wrapped up in very temporary sentiment at Christmas. But the day after Christmas arrives and all of that passes. Life returns to normal. By then you'll be on your way to putting Ella and Fizz behind you. And glad of it, too. Just be nonchalant. Distant.

"You look beautiful," he said.

She blinked. "You are a liar."

"No, I'm not. Your hair...have I told you how much I've always liked your hair?" It was true, even though he'd never consciously thought of it when they were young. "It's…" He reached out and curled a silky strand through his fingers, letting it slide against his skin. "It's very…soft." Like she was. He raised it to his face and breathed in. "And it smells like…" A smile lit his face. "Your hair smells like…Christmas!"

There was that pretty blush. "I used a Christmas-themed shampoo. It has a light balsam scent."

And he was embarrassing her. And doing the exact opposite of what he'd planned. Trey felt like kicking himself. What was wrong with him?

"We should go," he said out loud.

Ella nodded. "Stuart will be pacing if you're late. The float can't take off without you."

"Oh, yes. The float. Somehow when Stu asked me to do this I thought I would just be walking down the street."

"I know. I have to warn you there's a hideous Christmas tree dead center, made out of hundreds of tissue paper flowers. And a…a sort of a throne for you to sit on."

"A throne?"

"Well, it's really a very big chair, but they've painted it gold. And actually painted the words *Our Hero* on it. I'm so sorry. I hope that you're not regretting this too much. But they mean it in the very best way."

Her last words came out a bit soft and whispery. She sounded so apologetic, so embarrassed, and so…worried that he was going to rebel that Trey immediately put his distaste for the idea aside.

"Well, in that case…if it's gold…I'm all for it. What guy wouldn't be?"

Now those pretty eyes snapped. Did eyes really snap? Ella's seemed to. "Now you're just mocking me."

"Oh, no. I'm not, love. I never would. Right, Fizz?"

Fizz licked Trey's thumb.

"I'll take that as agreement," he said, and held out his hand. "Come on, Ella. Let's go win some points for Stu."

She slid her arm through his and they turned toward the center of town, walking together as a couple for one of the last times.

When he saw the actual float he must have reacted a bit, flinched slightly, his muscles tightening and signaling his reaction to Ella.

"I did try to tell them to go light on the hometown Christmas hero theme," she said.

Trey steeled himself to look at the gaudy float, decked out in Christmas red, white and green, with the gold throne and what looked to be a hundred banners that read, "Trey McFadden. Eagleton's Best."

"I'm going to have to do something about that," he said. "Who made the float?"

"Mostly the ladies of the Eagleton Improvement Committee. A lot of them are old, but they love the town, and they want to bring it back from the brink. They love Stu, and they love that an Eagleton boy owns a company that's been written about in the leading financial newspapers. None of them care that you were rebellious when you were young. They're just glad you made something of yourself."

Her voice was so soft and earnest. She had her hand on his arm and was looking up at him with those big, pleading eyes. He leaned down and kissed her on the lips. Just once.

"Don't worry. I'll try to do Eagleton and the ladies—and you—proud."

With that, Trey took his place on the garish throne. Someone gave the signal and the driver started the engine and moved the float toward its place in line. The strains of an instrumental version of "Deck the Halls" began to play.

Ella and Fizz began to disappear into the distance. Just as they would in actual fact much too soon.

CHAPTER ELEVEN

"DON'T FORGET TO WAVE," Ella called.

Fizz gave a little woof and then a whine.

"I know, Fizz. It feels symbolic, doesn't it? Watching him ride away from us?"

Fizz whimpered again, and Ella reminded herself that her time with the puppy was running short, too. She'd been a fool to let her heart flip over for these two males in her life, but there was nothing she could do about that.

Except paste on a phony smile and pretend she was okay with losing them.

That was just what she was going to do. No one, especially not Trey, was ever going to know how much she longed for him. She, who had always wanted the perfect love, had fallen for the worst man, the least perfect match for her, years ago, and she loved him still.

That little tidbit just appeared in her thoughts, and to her dismay she wasn't a bit surprised. But it wasn't the first time she'd shared a one-sided relationship with the most wanted man in Eagleton. Hopefully she still remembered how to play the part.

No, strike that thought. Hopefully she would play her part better this time. The last time she had messed up royally. Surely that couldn't happen again.

A short time later Ella almost felt that she was back

in control of her emotions. She was so busy running here and there, making sure that the bands and the floats fed in at the appropriate place in time, pinning costumes that had gotten ripped, and making sure that the cleanup committee was ready to sweep away any errant streamers, tinsel or glitter when the parade was over that she didn't have much time to even think.

Finally, however, things settled and she was able to line up along the parade route and enjoy the spectacle. In the distance she could see the Grand Marshall's float approaching. The crowds were strung out and, Eagleton being as small as it was, she still had a good view. Trey sat in the throne long enough to let the Eagleton Improvement Committee see that he had made use of it. Then he stood and started waving to the crowd.

People cheered and waved back.

Haley Snow, one of the women from the Eagleton Improvement Committee, settled in next to Ella. "What a handsome man, don't you think?"

Ella glanced at her. "Yes." What else could she say? There was no denying the truth. But, Ella thought, Haley looked entirely too interested in Trey. And not just as a hometown hero, either.

But then Haley noticed Fizz. "Oh, you brought that cute little puppy! Can I hold him?"

Ella hesitated. Fizz wasn't on a leash…and she liked holding him herself. She wouldn't get to do it for much longer. But Haley was looking at her eagerly, and the truth was that she *wouldn't* have Fizz much longer. There wasn't a good reason to be greedy.

Reluctantly, she took Fizz out of his basket and handed him over. She gave him a quick pat and a reassuring glance.

"Hey, Trey, lookin' good," someone called.

Ella looked up to see that Trey's float had moved much closer. She gazed up at him, hoping that no one could see the longing in her eyes.

"Trey, over here," someone else called.

Trey waved in the direction of the voice.

"Ella, this is a fantastic parade," someone yelled out. "But you should have put the pup up on the float with Trey. Nothing looks better than a big man like him holding a puppy, don't you think?"

"Well, how about Ella herself getting up on that float with Trey? After all, she planned the whole parade."

"Yes. Come on, Ella."

As a few other people took up the chant Ella looked helplessly up at Trey, who turned to look at her and almost lost his balance as the vehicle sped up slightly.

"What do you think, Trey?" someone asked.

"About what?"

That was all it took. Those two words. At the sound of Trey's voice Fizz started whining and bucking in Haley's arms.

"Fizz, hold still," Ella said, reaching for him. "We'll go see Trey."

But Fizz knew how to squirm with the best of them, and Haley lost her grip. He dove. Fortunately when he'd started squirming Haley had apparently anticipated disaster, and had lowered him enough so that his leap to the ground didn't hurt him. Instead he rolled, got to his legs, and started running toward Trey.

"Fizz! Trey!" Ella yelled, afraid that the little puppy would end up under the wheels of the vehicle.

She and Trey both started forward at the same time—

Trey running to the side of the swaying float and Ella running toward it.

With a leap, Trey jumped free of the float, whirled and scooped Fizz up—just as he was about to start dancing far too near one of the wheels. The float kept moving. Ella's heart was in her throat, and it must be in her eyes, too. No telling what she looked like. Trey looked…very pale.

When Ella and Trey had yelled, people down at the other end of the street had rushed down to see what was wrong. Now the crowd was all in one place, people were being pushed, and someone nearly got hit by a motorcycle in the parade. People were yelling.

"Fizz?" Ella whispered, looking toward the puppy as people pressed in on them.

"I've got him," Trey told her. "He's safe—aren't you, boy?"

Fizz's response was to try to lick Trey's face. Still shaky, Ella felt her heart break all over again, looking at the eager puppy and the man together. They looked so…right.

"That's enough." Stu's booming voice broke through the crowd as he walked among them. "Nothing to worry about. Just a puppy making a break for it. It's over now. Let's all get back to celebrating. Michael, you clear that motorcycle out of here. Alan, let's get everyone back to the curb. Margery, let's have some Christmas music, some singing. Let's get this parade rolling. You two okay?"

Ella nodded. "Thank you for that, Stu. I'm supposed to be doing that job."

"Well, no one's going to blame you for being otherwise occupied. You can't be everywhere at one time, Ella."

"Listen to Stu," Trey told her with a smile. "He's a wise man. Most of the time. Except when he gets some crazy idea in his head about bringing back relatives to ride in his parade."

Stu chuckled. "And I expect you to fulfill the rest of your duties. You *and* Ella."

"Oh, we will. Come on," Trey said, taking her hand.

"Where?"

He nodded toward the float that had stopped just up ahead. Order had been restored, but the entire parade had halted. "Still two blocks to go, and everyone, including Fizz here, seems to think we all belong up there together."

She shook her head. "I don't think so."

"I thought you were committed to making this the greatest Christmas Festival ever?"

"I am, but—"

"Tell her, Stu."

Stu laughed. "You think she listens to me? She orders *me* around. Ask them." He nodded toward the townspeople.

"An excellent idea. What do you say?" Trey called out to the crowd. "Should we talk Ella onto the float?"

A cheer went up. "Sure. She's been working her tail off behind the scenes. Put her up there, where we can all see her and give her a cheer!"

Trey handed Fizz to the nearest person. "Do *not* let him get away. I'll be right back," he said. Then he reached out for Ella, lifted her up onto the float and then, retrieving Fizz, joined her up there. The music started again. The float lurched. Trey wrapped one arm around Ella to keep her from falling. "Now, smile and wave, love," he whispered against her hair. "Enjoy the ride."

She didn't answer.

"Are you all right?" he asked.

She nodded slightly. With Trey's lips against her hair and his arm around her waist she was in heaven.

"Thanks, Fizz," he said.

She glanced up at him. "What are you thanking him for?"

He chuckled. "It was lonely up here alone. And a bit embarrassing. Sharing is so much nicer, don't you think?"

She did. She even allowed herself to lean into his touch. Was that a groan emanating from Trey? It must be her imagination or the gears of the car. It didn't matter. For the next block she was in Trey's arms.

WHEN THE PARADE was over, and the final festivities had ended, Trey dreaded taking Ella home. Time was flitting by too quickly. But it had to be done. They retrieved Fizz's basket and walked toward her house.

"Thank you for saving him," she said. "I can't believe I've let him escape twice in just a few days. A person like me shouldn't even be allowed near a puppy."

Trey chuckled.

"I mean it," she said. "A responsible owner would have had him on a leash."

"Then he would have gotten stepped on by the crowd, or been choked when he made his dive out of Haley's arms."

"You know what I mean. I wasn't paying attention. I was a bad—"

He stopped and turned to face her. He put one finger over her lips. "Shh. Don't say it."

Just the pad of his finger was against her soft lips, but even that slight contact made him want to sweep her into his arms and kiss her full-on. Hold her. Make love with her.

That did it. He retreated, continued walking. *Try for something light*, he ordered himself. Something that didn't involve touching her or wanting her.

"I have employees with toddlers," he said. "Several of them have told horror stories about their little ones slipping away unnoticed, or climbing on things when their parents' backs were turned. Some of them have had things like that happen several times. One of them even started a website where parents could share their horror stories and discuss solutions. They all feel as if they're terrible parents, but the truth, as I've been told by my older employees, is that you can make things as safe as is humanly possible and things like that will still happen."

Silence. They were walking up the path to her house. "Ella?"

She turned to him in the light of the porch. And she was smiling.

"What? Did I tell a joke? Did I convince you not to blame yourself for Fizz's brief foray as an escape artist?"

"You made me feel better," she confessed. "You don't know a thing about kids. And yet you made it sound as if you were an expert. I know you were just trying to soothe me. That's so sweet, Trey."

And with no warning she rose on her toes and planted a kiss on his cheek.

It was a friendly kiss, a nothing kiss. Maybe that made it worse. Because she was going to let it end here and now without any regrets, while he had regrets by the basketful.

"I'm leaving tomorrow," he said.

She blinked. "I thought… Tomorrow is Christmas Day. You can't be serious."

"Never more. I came here for Stu's festival. The festival is over."

"Where—what do you do on Christmas?"

"I have dinner with friends."

It was what he had done for the past few years and it had always been enough. Now it wasn't. He wanted to spend it with Ella. But that wasn't going to happen. Ella wanted a perfect marriage. She'd told him that she hadn't met the man who could be her perfect man. The fact that he was even bothered by that… It was time to go. All this Christmas festivity was making him think crazy thoughts. He needed to be gone.

"How about you?" he asked.

"Friends," she agreed. "And then home to bed and a good book."

The thought of Ella in bed made him think more crazy thoughts. He should leave right now.

"If this is goodbye," he said, "let me come inside. I have some things to tell you."

He wasn't even sure what those things were. He felt as if he had a thousand things to say to her, that he could keep talking with her forever and never want to be apart from her. That was ridiculous, wasn't it? It was just because she was pretty and because she cared about people. Because she'd once tried to defend him and he'd made her cry and he still hated the thought that it had taken him ten years to apologize. This time when he left he wanted to do it right.

Ella reached behind her and opened the door. They moved inside. Fizz immediately went to his basket, to make sure that no one had messed with it while he was gone. He turned around and sniffed every corner.

Trey smiled. His heart hurt at thinking about never seeing the little dog again. "Will they tell you who he goes to?" he asked.

"Probably not. I don't know, but I don't see why they would."

Her voice broke just a bit on the last word and he knew that she was probably already missing the little dog.

He caught her to him, touched his forehead to hers. "This time we're ending things right." He said the words he'd been thinking only seconds ago. "If it's at all possible, I want you to see if Fizz's new owners will let you visit him. Because…you'll miss him. I know you will. Don't be all noble and tell yourself and everyone else that it doesn't matter and that it's for the best if you don't see him again. Okay, Ella?"

She nodded tightly. "Okay, yes," she whispered, one hand reaching up to touch his face.

He leaned in to kiss her and she rose up at the same time. His kiss landed on the side of her mouth. It didn't matter. He was touching her. She was touching him. And then he was kissing her again. Deeper. Longer. Holding her so close there wasn't any room between them.

"I wanted that kiss to be perfect, but it wasn't. It still set me on fire," he told her. "Ella, you see what I'm saying? You want perfect, and you're going to deny yourself because you think it can't exist for you, that the perfect match isn't out there for you. Don't do that, all right? Don't wait for him to come along. Perfect is overrated."

She opened her mouth and then he was kissing her, kissing her, over and over.

"Do you see?"

"I can't see anything," she whispered. "I'm feeling too much."

"I know. I know. But I need to make my case. This afternoon, when Fizz ran and all hell broke loose, nothing was perfect—but look what came of that. Everyone got to see Stu handle a crisis situation. They got to see what a good, strong man he is. There were benefits to an imperfect situation. Okay?"

He was talking—talking too much when he wanted her in his arms, in his bed. But that was the old Trey, the cocky Trey. This was the Trey who wanted to make sure that Ella was happy down the road.

"Ella? Don't wait for perfect."

"I won't. I won't wait," she said. "Trey?"

He pulled back and looked at her.

"How did you get to be so wise?"

He groaned. "I'm not wise, Ella. I'm trying to talk so I won't do anything…unwise. Like touch you more."

"I see."

"You don't." It was hell holding her and not kissing her the way he wanted to, holding her the way he wanted to, making love with her.

"I see what you're doing, Trey, and it's useless. You can't win."

He shook his head, confused.

"It's our last night together. Ever," she whispered.

"And—" she looked at the clock "—Christmas will be here soon. We won't see each other tomorrow. We won't share the day or…anything. I guess what I'm saying is…kiss me more, Trey. Touch me. *More*."

It was too much. He couldn't resist her invitation. This was goodbye, the end of something that hadn't really ever had a chance to begin.

Ella led him to her room. The room whose window wasn't more than twenty feet from his own window.

Lying down with him braced above her, Ella stared into his eyes. She rested her palms on his shoulders. "You don't have to be gentle or worry about hurting me, Trey. It doesn't have to be perfect."

But it was.

As Trey left her just before dawn the next morning he didn't touch her for fear of waking her, even though he ached to kiss her goodbye. And when he passed Fizz curled up in his basket he placed one finger over his mouth and Fizz seemed to understand. He made no sound, simply looked up at Trey with big, sad brown eyes and licked his fingers when Trey gave him a goodbye stroke.

"Bye, buddy," he whispered. "You take care of her today, all right?"

He didn't say anything about tomorrow. There would be no tomorrow for any of them. The very thought made it difficult to move. Or think. And he knew that he needed to think. He'd told her that he didn't want her to wait for perfect because he didn't want her to be alone.

But in his heart of hearts he wanted her to have perfection. At least in some small way. He definitely needed to think about that.

CHAPTER TWELVE

ELLA HAD ALWAYS loved Christmas. Her parents had always made a big deal out of it and, even though they'd been so wrapped up in each other that they'd sometimes seemed to forget she was in the house after the initial present-opening ceremony, they'd always eventually remembered her and brought her into their circle of happiness. Since her parents had been gone, Christmas had been less fun, but someone always made sure she had an invitation, and no one ever made her feel like an unwelcome appendage.

This year, however, she couldn't find any Christmas joy. Trey had thought she hadn't known when he left, but she'd seen him from beneath her lashes. She'd felt him leave her, heard him say goodbye to Fizz. Last night had been wonderful, magical, as close to perfect as she could imagine and yet…very real. Practical person that she was, though, she knew that she couldn't live in that one moment, much as she wanted to. She couldn't have or hold Trey. And this was her last day with Fizz.

She thought about Trey's request that she not seek perfection in her life. He wanted her to marry. Maybe he felt guilty that he had loved her and left, but odds weren't good that she would marry. She wasn't really seeking perfection. She knew that now. Her parents hadn't been perfect people. Their love probably hadn't even been perfect, but it had been right for them. They had each been with the one they wanted. And she had always wanted Trey. She still did. Maybe she always would.

"Today it's just you and me, boy," she whispered to Fizz as they got ready to go to dinner with her friends.

And when they came home from their day out, and he settled himself into his basket with his little toys around him, he looked so sad.

"I miss him, too, Fizz. And you—I'm going to miss you like mad, too. But you're going to grow into a big dog. You need to have room to run and play during the day—not be cooped up in a tiny office building or here all by yourself while I'm at work. I want you to have better than that."

She heard Trey telling her not to ask for perfect, but this was different. This was Fizz, and no question lots of people would want to adopt him. People who would be able to give him exactly what he needed.

But when she petted him and he licked her hand he still looked sad. As if he knew what was coming.

Surely that was her imagination.

It was not her imagination, however, when she dropped him at the shelter the next day. He looked as forlorn as she felt. Somehow she made it back to her car before the tears began to stream down her face. She had lost both of her men in two days. How much heartbreak could a woman take?

She hoped, really hoped, that once the emotional rollercoaster of the season was over and she dove back into work she would be able to make something of her life and find some happiness. Even more than that, she hoped that Fizz would find a good and loving home with children, and that Trey…

But she couldn't think of Trey at all. She wasn't ready yet. Her heart howled with pain every time she got close to remembering all that she would never have with him.

TREY PACED HIS way around his office for what must have been the five hundredth time. It had been two days since he'd left Ella, and he was unable to concentrate. He was miserable. And he could no longer blame his emotions on the season. He was madly, irrefutably in love with Ella and he didn't know how to get past that.

The thing was…Ella had seen him at his worst— back in his cocky days, when he had been mad at the world and struggling to hide it behind a mask of *I don't give a damn.* She knew that he'd stolen, that he'd broken girls' hearts for no good reason, that he'd argued with his parents incessantly, that he could be tactless and mean when he was wounded. And for all that she excused him for those things, the truth was that he wasn't close to perfect. His love might not be anything like the kind she wanted. He'd seen all those guys flocking round her. He knew she must have dated a few of them. Or more. The woman kissed like a dream. Where else had she learned to kiss like that?

And none of those homeboys had measured up. Why should he be any different?

"You're going to make such a hole in the carpeting that we're going to have to replace it," his secretary told him.

"What?" He looked up.

"The rug. You're pacing again. You're agitated. Frankly, I've never seen you like this. Did you have a horrid Christmas? Did that trip to your hometown stir up bad memories?"

No. It had been the best week of his life.

"Bettina, I know you're mad about your husband. What does he do that makes you care so much?"

"Uh-oh, I should have known it was a woman. Or maybe not. You've never been like this before."

"Bettina…"

"Okay. He's funny."

"I'm not particularly funny."

"He's smart. You're smart," she coached.

"I'm not sure that's going to be enough."

"Well, the thing I love most about him is that he really cares about me. He wants me to be happy. Do you… love her like that?"

He gave Bettina as much of a smile as he could manage. "I love her like that."

"And you would want her to have whatever made her happy even if it wasn't you?"

Trey closed his eyes. Did he feel that way? "I want her to love me, but if she can't… Okay, you win. Her happiness is what's most important."

"And do you think she's happy now?"

"I don't know. I really don't." But he did know one thing. There was at least one area in her life where she probably wasn't happy.

"Bettina, book me a charter to Eagleton. Make it soon."

He hoped he wasn't too late. It was the second day after Christmas. A lot could happen in two days. Irreversible things.

"Bettina, make it now. I'm on my way to the airport." And a race against the clock. One he might have already lost. He wouldn't know that until he'd made a number of phone calls and arrived in Eagleton.

And even then it could still all end badly.

ELLA WAS SITTING at the kitchen table, listlessly tracing her fingertip around the edge of her teacup, when her doorbell rang. Who could that be? She didn't really want to see anyone right now. She was miserable, and after having had to smile all day long she didn't want to have to fake happiness or graciousness tonight.

Maybe if she sat here quietly, whoever it was would go away.

The doorbell rang again. With a sigh, she got up and pulled the door open.

And had to check the happy tears that threatened to fall.

"Trey! Trey, why are you here?" If he was here there must be something wrong. "You weren't ever coming back."

"No, I wasn't."

"So…" Her heartbeat was pounding. She could barely breathe. Talking was…difficult.

"So I forgot something. Or rather I remembered something."

She waited.

He seemed hesitant. "I remembered that you loved Fizz." He opened the zipper on his coat a few inches and she could see that Fizz was inside.

"Oh… Trey… Fizz…" Her eyes filled up with tears. "But I took him back to the shelter. Was there a problem?"

Trey frowned as he cuddled Fizz, and Fizz went wild

licking Trey's thumb. "The problem was that I didn't want you to go through life without him."

"But—"

"I know. You love him enough that you want what's best for him. So I'll hire a sitter for him."

"Trey, that's too much. You can't do that."

"I can. And I will. And if you won't accept that, then I'll keep him. I'll hire the sitter and you can visit with him all the time."

Trey had moved into her space, and he was so close that—

"You live all the way in San Diego," she said.

"That could change. I could live in Eagleton."

Fizz was so excited to see Ella that he was jumping around. Trey sat down on a chair and Ella took the puppy. She kissed him and let him down to run around as Trey pulled her in between his knees. Now he was very close.

"I don't understand, Trey." But, oh, she wanted to. She wanted him to be here in Eagleton.

"I missed you," he said.

She melted. "I was so…sad and lost…" Then she caught herself. "I missed *you*," she said, more primly.

"*I* was sad. *I* was lost," he said. "And I wanted to come tell you how you've changed my life. I've had such a terrible family life that I didn't even want to try that again. I didn't want to risk it. But, Ella, none of that matters with you. I know I was as much to blame for my situation as my parents were. I know I don't have all the answers. You make me want to be better, to be perfect, to be that one guy for you. But if I can't be that—and I don't expect you to say that I am—"

She placed her fingertips over his mouth. "Why would you say that?"

"You've been looking all your life and you haven't found what you're looking for. You've dated all those guys and not one of them seems to be the right one."

"Dated all those guys? Where did you get that idea?"

He kissed her then, softly. And then more deeply. "No one kisses like you do. Someone taught you that."

She could feel the heat climbing up her neck.

"Ella?"

"I've been kissed a few times, but I wouldn't say those men taught me anything about kissing."

He raised one dark brow and waited.

"When I was young, I wanted you to kiss me," she admitted. "I practiced on the mirror all the time. I watched every romantic movie, every sexy movie. I read books. I studied techniques. I figured that if I ever got lucky enough and you kissed me I might only have one shot at it. I didn't want to disappoint you. Or me. Or seem naive and inexperienced."

Trey was smiling now. Grinning, actually.

"Don't laugh," she said.

"I'm not. I'm just…entranced. I'm… Ella, I love you so much. I wish I'd kissed you when we were young. I wish you had invited me to practice with a mirror. We could have done that together."

"You would have ridiculed me."

"Maybe I would have back then. I'm not that person now. You freed me from my past and gave me hope that I might have love in my future. That I might have… more than I had ever aspired to. Maybe it started that day you told me that my father had taught me to be the opposite of him. Or maybe it was just you being you. I want you. I love you. But I don't know if I can give you that perfect love you—"

Ella grabbed his hand. She kissed it. She wrapped it around her waist and leaned close and gave him one of those kisses she'd practiced just for him. He kissed her, too, better than she'd ever imagined—and so much better than a mirror.

"Trey, I don't need perfect. I need you. Only you. I've always loved you. It's why I never met the perfect man. I already knew him, and he wasn't available."

Trey groaned. "He's available. He just didn't know it. Until you."

By now Fizz was getting upset that his two humans weren't giving him any attention. He was dancing around at their feet.

"Didn't anyone want you, sweetie?" she asked, picking him up. "I can't believe you weren't snapped up in an instant."

She looked at Trey, and realized he wasn't looking her straight in the eye the way he always did.

"Trey…?"

"He'd been adopted," he said quietly. "I had to think long and hard at that point. I didn't want to hurt a child. But he'd only been with them for half a day. So…I located two puppies and traded them two for one."

She looked suspicious. "It couldn't have been that easy. The shelter is very careful. Surely they wouldn't have simply let you trade. Or even told you who had Fizz. Unless… Trey, did you *bribe* the people at the shelter?"

"I didn't bribe them. I might have made a donation."

"A sizeable one, I'm sure."

"That might have happened. And I might have had

to sign my life away, give them more personal information than I'm sure most adoptive parents have to, and agreed to volunteer at the shelter twice a month."

"Trey, I love you so much." She kissed him again. "Thank you for bringing Fizz home."

"Merry Christmas, love."

"I'm afraid I don't have a present for you."

"Are you going to marry me?"

"You and no other."

"A man couldn't ask for a better present than that. This year has been the best Christmas ever, bar none. Thank you, Fizz."

Ella laughed. "I know what you're going to say. Fizz brought us together."

"And we didn't make it easy on him. Poor little guy. We've tired him out."

Sure enough, Fizz was snoozing away. He was home.

And so was Trey. As Ella gave him one of her special kisses, he was right where he wanted to be.

EPILOGUE

THREE years later, Trey stood in the yard and looked out over the changes they'd made to the property. "What do you think? Is the tree house too small?"

Ella laughed. They lived in her house now, but it had been built on so that the original house was merely an entranceway these days. Trey's family home had been torn down and the bricks reused to make a house for Fizz and a tree house for baby Sarah and the new baby on the way.

"I think it may be a few years until we're ready for any type of tree house, much less one this massive."

"Okay, I overdid things."

"It's okay. *You don't spoil Sarah too much.* More than most besotted dads do, I suppose. But you definitely spoil Fizz too much."

"Well, I owe you boy—don't I?" he asked the big golden dog at his side.

Fizz gave a little bark.

"He really does seem to talk to you," Ella said.

"He talks to you, too, but you two have a different language. Yours centers around hugs and food and back rubs. Fizz and I talk guy stuff. How to make sure our women are happy."

"Fizz doesn't have a woman."

"He does. He likes that little retriever two blocks over. She's still making up her mind about him, though."

"And saying that you're making sure your women are happy does sound a bit sexist, you know."

He grinned. "It isn't. Fizz just knows what you like, and if I'm on the verge of doing the wrong thing he gives me a signal. Like those earrings I bought you last week. I was totally going for a long, dangly pair, and Fizz barked to let me know they weren't your type," he teased.

"You know my type," she said, moving up close to him. "It's you. Always you."

"And I will be eternally grateful for that," he said. "You brought me a family. Right, Fizz?"

Fizz gave a little bark. Was he smiling? Maybe he was. He had come to them at Christmastime, after all. And miracles had happened that week.

* * * * *

For *Lycaon pictus*
and everyone who works to protect them

THE PATTER OF PAWS AT CHRISTMAS

Nikki Logan

Dear Reader,

"You had me at puppies...."

Those were my actual words to my editor when the opportunity to be involved in this fabulous anthology arose. I was supposed to be having some well-earned time off over the holidays but...well...*puppies!*

Writing it in the weeks leading up to Christmas was fabulous for getting in the festive mood and I finished editing it at 6:00 p.m. on New Year's Eve, just a few hours earlier than the story concludes. I really liked that synergy.

As soon as I said yes, I knew my pups would have to be superspecial, puppies-plus. And I knew, as soon as I said yes, who—or rather, what—my pups would be. Twice in my zoo working life I've spent fabulous hours waiting for the first gorgeous signs of the emergence of newborn African wild dogs. Once, I was the right person in the right place at the right time long after everyone else had gone home and got a glimpse of the first dark, inquisitive, sweet little pup that boldly climbed out of the den and into the dusk light.

That moment has never left me.

Now I share it with you, all wrapped up amid the love that emerges between two really compassionate and lovely people just as hesitantly as those pups emerged from the den. I hope you enjoy.

May love always find you,

Nikki Logan

CHAPTER ONE

Christmas Day

STARING AT A hole in the ground was as good a way as any to spend Christmas. Not the merriest of holiday spirits, but December the twenty-fifth hadn't been Ingrid's favourite time for several years. Although she did rather enjoy the double-time-and-a-half Christmas bonus. Plus overnight allowance.

She stretched her spine, resettled in the sling-back chair and let her eyes scan the four CCTV feeds showing the exhibit, the still-vacant den interior, and a close-up on the entrances of two dens: the one the zookeepers had had specially built for wild dog Mjawi—and then disguised an access hatch in—and the one the first-time mother had dug for herself, right next door.

No man-made elements. No sneaky human access. Smart dog.

There was still nothing on her observation report except the alpha pair coming and going for the past twelve hours. With long nap times in between.

Not a sign of the elusive pups.

'*Mon dieu...*'

She wouldn't have heard it normally—half whispered as it had been—but the bare concrete walls of the converted night-den did too good a job of amplifying the accented oath.

And the growl of disbelief that followed it.

She turned and glared at the tall shape silhouetted against the early-morning glow. 'Good to see you, too, Gabe.'

He didn't move from the doorway. But his head did drop just slightly. 'Sorry, I was expecting…'

Someone else? Anyone else? *I'll bet.* 'Cara wanted to be with her kids over the holidays. We swapped shifts.'

'Just today?'

Was he seriously not going to enter the room if she was in it? Wasn't that taking things a bit too far? 'All of them. Right through to New Year.'

He let his breath out slowly. 'Okay.'

But an okay from Gabriel Marque usually meant he was anything but. Which pretty much matched her feelings exactly.

'How about you?' she asked.

'Day shift. Through to New Year.'

Oh…joy. A whole week working parallel roster.

She pushed to her feet. 'Well, if you're here that means the night shift is officially over. I'll see you tomorrow.'

'What about handover?' he said, stepping in from the daylight into the low light of the monitoring room.

She didn't need full light to see him clearly. Hazel eyes, long straight nose, tanned skin. The tiny mole to the left of his amazing top lip. Perpetually mussed brown hair. The tattoo that reached up from his shoulder blade to rest its inky fingers on the pulse point just below his jaw. Her brain was perfectly accustomed to conjuring the tiniest details of his appearance with or without his presence. Usually at the most inconvenient times.

'Everything's on the observation report. Nothing, to be specific.'

'Still no sign?'

Amazing how civil things were between them in work mode. 'Nope. She's still in the B-den. No sign of the pups.'

'And no change to the den?'

'Not so far—though it's not the best-looking entrance I've ever seen.'

Gabe shook his head and Ingrid flushed. As if she'd seen more than one wild dog den—*ever*. He'd been working this round for sixteen months, and he'd worked with dogs in Zimbabwe three years before that. There was no one in the zoo who knew more about the captive husbandry of African wild dogs. Although that might have been different if she'd been successful in transferring from vet nurse to zookeeper a year ago.

If Gabe hadn't snaffled the vacancy of wild dog keeper out from under her.

If he and his hot accent and good looks hadn't swanned in and won more people over in three months than she'd been able to in six years. He'd taken one look at their zoo and the professional opportunities available and done everything he could to turn his short-term exchange into something more permanent.

Including undermining her.

She shot to her feet. 'Well, I'm going to get cleaned up before the staff Christmas lunch in the mess room.'

'That's not for four hours.'

Um... Nothing clever came to her. Her mind was the usual blank grey it was whenever Gabe was around.

'Ingrid…'

Did he *have* to say it like that—more like a purr than a word? She took a deep breath and looked up at him.

'Are you going to be able to do this? For a week?'

See him every day? Up close and personal and in the dark? Listen to that accent? The man who betrayed her?

Sure.

She smiled her most vacuous smile. 'I'm used to the night shift, Gabe. Who do you think does the nocturnal watches up at the hospital when we're hand-rearing something?'

His lips flattened in that way they always did when he was annoyed and he stared at her. 'That's not what I'm asking.'

Because he was on watch and not formally on duty he only had half his official zoo uniform on. A distinctly non-uniform black T-shirt was tucked into the work cargos that hung off his hips. It moulded to every curve of his defined torso and suddenly loomed hard and male in her vision.

She swallowed. 'Then what *are* you asking?'

His hazel eyes narrowed.

'Are you going to be able to get past the fact we slept together?'

INGRID'S DELICATE CHIN kicked up the moment the words left his lips and Gabe struggled not to respond to her courage. He'd always been drawn to strong women, and that quiet resilience was one of the things he'd admired about her when he'd first come to work here. Right after her pale blue eyes and spun-gold hair.

Slept together.

Such an understatement for what that night had

meant. And technically incorrect, too: there'd been no sleeping. A lot of touching. A lot of talking. A lot of heavy breathing. Neither of them had wasted a moment. Almost by agreement.

She crossed her slim arms hard across her chest, making herself into a human bullet. 'You think I lie awake at night wondering what went wrong between us?'

Strength had its down side. But he was a Marque, and well-practised at not reacting to sarcasm. 'I would be a fool to imagine that.' He smiled.

And clearly his father was right; he was *l'imbécile*.

Besides, they both knew what had gone wrong between them. The moment he became more than just a tourist Ingrid had lost all interest. The story of his life. *Gabriel Marque: for a good time but not a long time.* Even here, so far from home, so far from the lessons and influence of his family, women instinctively got out before they discovered how little he had to offer.

He was a zookeeper in a family of surgeons, lawyers and politicians.

But growing up with four Romeos for brothers had taught him a thing or two about women. 'So then it's no big deal,' he continued. 'Sit. Stay a while.'

She shrugged, but the flare in her eyes told him she knew she'd walked into that one. He placed a second seat carefully next to hers just as she sank back down into it.

For a chair so comfortable she made it look as if it was lined with spikes.

'I promised Cara,' she said tightly.

'I understand.'

'I can't go back on that. I won't.'

'I'm not asking you to. But we're going to have to work together.' *Believe me, cherie, I'm not looking forward to this any more than you are.* What man wanted a daily reminder of how out of his league he was?

Smart, passionate, intellectual types did not go for the runts of the litter. Not in the long-term.

On arrival he'd had his pick of the female zoo staff. Yet the only one who had snared his attention was the one paying him no attention at all. The serious one. The quiet one. The one who hid her sharp mind behind a very appropriate pair of reading glasses and her sweet body behind unisex surgical scrubs.

Not this morning. She'd thrown a pale blue cardigan over the white tank top that must have kept her cool in here over the hot Australian night, but its scoop neck showed off much more of her creamy throat and shoulders than she'd probably planned for anyone to see.

She would never have dressed so informally had she known it would be him walking in at eight a.m.

'It's fine,' she lied. 'We're working two totally separate parts of the day.'

Except that he hadn't told her the whole truth yet. That he was sticking around much longer than she knew. He steepled his fingers against his lips.

'I know that look.' She glared. 'What?'

'This litter is part of my captive management thesis. I'm going to need as much direct observation as I can get.'

She stared at him, not understanding. And then a flicker of outrage formed right at the back of the pale blue pools and rushed forward. 'You *have* to be kidding me! You're going to take my shifts as well?'

As well? 'Relax, Ingrid. I'm not taking anything. I'm

putting in some voluntary hours to make sure I fulfil my research quota.'

'But…if I leave I don't get paid.'

'So don't leave.'

'But *you're* here!'

'Although a moment longer in my presence is clearly *intolérable* to you—' he shoved the discomfort of that way down deep '—we'll be working. Just focus on that.'

She frowned. 'I'll be redundant.'

She couldn't have said anything more likely to resonate for him. Not that she knew that. No one did. 'I've got plenty of my own work to be getting on with. Besides, if Mjawi moves the pups into A-den it's going to be much faster to get them separated, chipped and vaccinated with two of us here.'

She turned and looked at the duffel bag that had slipped from his fingers when he'd spotted her sitting there. His very *full* duffel bag. Her outraged eyes came straight back to him.

'Just how long are you going to be here?'

All week. He didn't need to say it; his expression would say it for him.

Her eyes frosted over in response, then flicked to the tiny camp bed in the corner. 'Where are you planning on sleeping?'

'In my car—when I need to.'

Especially since she was on the night shift. The last thing he wanted was to give Ingrid Rose hours of time with nothing to do but watch him sleep and tally up the many ways he didn't measure up.

She stared at him, her sharp mind turning her options over. 'Fine.'

Was there a more dangerous word on the planet? His mother used 'fine' a lot. Only in French, of course.

He met her eyes. 'Okay.'

Gabe took twenty minutes to do what he could normally accomplish in ten, but he wanted to give her some space. A bit of time to accept the awkward inevitability of their situation. It had had to come up sooner or later. She'd done an admirable job of avoiding him since the day she'd walked out of his life but, for all the zoo's size it only had a small staff, and vet nurses and keepers interacted dozens of times a day on animal care issues.

He unpacked a few essentials, read her limited report through slowly—twice—and then finally turned back to her. 'How's her demeanour been overnight?'

On the job. Neutral territory. *Bon*.

'Hyper-vigilant.'

'Towards the pack?'

'Not targeted specifically, just generally watchful. Like she knows I'm here.'

'She can smell you. Your presence overnight is probably new enough to have her on edge.'

'Will she relax?'

'She's pretty adaptable. You have to be when you're alpha.'

They fell to silence until her soft Australian voice broke it. There was a vulnerable edge to her words, as if she was extending the courtesy despite herself. She cleared her throat.

'So…Merry Christmas, anyway.'

Christmas. Right. He'd nearly forgotten—again. 'And to you. I'm sorry you had to spend Christmas Eve alone.'

She shrugged but didn't elaborate.

He tried again. 'It was nice of you to swap with Cara.'

'She has kids.' Again with the shrugging.

'You don't have to have kids to do Christmas,' he pointed out.

She tipped her head up to him and threw him a look that was way too intuitive. 'I'm not the one working Christmas Day.'

No. *Pot—meet kettle*.

He tried again and wondered why he bothered. 'Are you doing something with your family later? After the staff lunch?'

'Which one?'

He slid into the seat right next to her and decided to take that sarcastic little snort literally. Opportunities to get to know her better came too rarely to pass up. 'How many families do you have?'

Her lips tightened. 'I'll do something with them later on.'

Funny how she made herself look at him. Almost like a challenge. Most people would look away when they were lying.

So... More than one family, but no one to spend Christmas with.

Intéressant.

'Gabe—'

She sat bolt upright as a dry black nose and a dark, scrappy snout slowly poked out of the entrance to B-den on the CCTV monitor. The keepers in the adjacent exhibit had started clanking and opening up for the day. B-den was barely more than a hole in the ground, dug into the compacted dirt mounded up high against the concrete night quarters, but every time the female or the male squeezed in or out of the opening the hole got marginally bigger.

And marginally less stable.

Their interest in encouraging Mjawi to move her litter back to A-den was because it was made of thick ply and wouldn't collapse in an earth tremor, let alone under the constant traffic of a litter of young dogs. As well as the fact it had an access hatch built in to it to let them check up on the pups.

His breath stilled as a golden head with dark satellite dish ears pushed out into the open and Mjawi's patched black, honey and white body followed, eager for breakfast. If she didn't eat, the pups didn't eat.

He and Ingrid both released their disappointment on a hiss as nothing but dust followed her out of the den.

Immediately after Mum went out another dog came and flopped down at the entrance to the den, guarding while she couldn't. Ingrid scribbled the time and the event on the observation report.

'How late are they emerging?' she asked carefully, as though it was some kind of reflection on him as senior keeper if his animals were tardy in developing.

'In captive terms, not that late. Plus whatever disturbed her out of A-den might have made her cautious enough to keep them in longer.'

'I suppose we do know they're in there at all?'

If he hadn't been a student of those guarded eyes and their many expressions for so long he might have taken that seriously. He reached over and plucked a disk from the pile stacked next to a spare monitor and player and tossed it to her. 'Watch this.'

Her laugh warmed him. A year was a long time to go without that feeling. 'Are you kidding? What do you think I entertained myself with all night? The birth was amazing.'

He shrugged. 'So they're in there.'

'Yeah, but how many? I couldn't even begin to count them. Between the low light, Mjawi's body blocking the view, and the solid colour of their birth coats they were just a writhing mass of black fluff.'

'That's why we're here.'

Numbers, genders, vaccines and microchips. As soon as humanly possible. Sooner, preferably.

'What's your research about?' she asked, when the silence weighed too heavy.

He stretched out a foot and jogged the edge of the mini-fridge set up under the monitoring gear. It opened with a jiggly clank, revealing the various vaccines every pup would need carefully housed in their ampoules. Ready to go as soon as they could get the pups separated from Mum for long enough. Every moment they went without immunisation was a moment longer that the virus could take hold.

'Captive management of a diseased population. Looking at methodology to eradicate viral strongholds over generations.'

Her eyes grew keen. As though he'd been speaking his native language until now and had just begun to speak hers.

'Is that why you came to our zoo? Because our collection had the virus present?'

Every muscle fibre tightened. It wasn't an unreasonable question, but it was unbearable coming from her. Someone looking to judge. Because it only highlighted all his deficiencies and all the reasons he judged himself.

But he wasn't going to start avoiding his responsibilities, either.

'No. The virus wasn't in the collection when I arrived.'

Ingrid's sharp mind worked it through and he saw the moment she arrived at the truth. Her eyes flared just slightly. 'Oh.'

'Hopefully my work can contribute to the solution.'

Since he'd contributed so directly to the problem.

Indecision clouded her usually clear eyes. She wanted to say more. He steeled himself for the inevitable criticisms.

'Well... Good luck with it—'

Vraiment? That was all she had to say? But it couldn't be. It never was. There was always a subtext.

'—let me know what I can do to help.'

And there it was... The patronising tone he'd grown up with. The unspoken implication that he wasn't up to the task without a support team. Why? Because it was medical in nature? He had the senior vet—her boss—overseeing the study. And he'd worked with infected populations in Africa. He didn't need seven years in medical school like his brothers in order to finalise a research project.

Instantly the faces of his family swam across his vision. He forced them away.

'Just do your job.' He frowned. 'That will help.'

The spark of professional interest in her eyes dissolved immediately, replaced by caution. Guilt nibbled at the edges of his mind, but he knew from experience that offers like that, no matter how nicely delivered, were always code for something else.

Something less nice.

Ingrid folded her arms again and turned her face back to the monitor to stare at the dog still guarding the entry to B-den, his white-tipped tail flicking regularly at the first flies of the day. A heartbeat later she pushed up and out of the chair.

'Technically my job doesn't start until tonight. So… I'll leave you to it.'

She scribbled her sign-off in the margin of the observation report, picked up her bag and crossed to the door. Offence saturated her posture but he didn't let himself be swayed.

If she didn't like to be snarled back across boundaries she should learn not to cross them.

Simple as that.

But it didn't feel simple as her soft words reached him from the door and wiggled their way straight down between his third and fourth ribs.

'Merry Christmas, Gabe.'

And then she was gone.

And he was alone.

And that was just a little bit too familiar.

CHAPTER TWO

Boxing Day

JERK.

He'd even managed to ruin the one bit of Christmas she actually enjoyed. Her turkey lunch with the other rostered staff would have sent her off into a much longer tryptophan-fuelled sleep without the residual pool of resentment bubbling in her gut.

Still, she'd had six good hours of sleep and was back for round two of night duty. And maybe round two with Gabe, since he was almost certainly still there and probably still itching for a fight.

She was the one hard done by here; he really had no reason to be griping.

It wasn't *her* building the career *he* wanted. It wasn't *she* who had swanned in at the eleventh hour and stolen the job *he'd* been inching his way towards all year. It wasn't she who had seduced him out of his senses and only then thought to mention he was staying.

And, by the way, I got the job you had your heart set on.

She'd seen no hint of that when he'd first arrived. A little arrogance—not surprising, given the rock-star treatment he'd got on arrival straight out of the field in Africa. A fair whack of drive and ambition—although she'd had no clue exactly how much until later. And a whole lot of good-looking. Enough to put him firmly out of her league and her right at the back of the long queue forming to the left.

So she'd forced her interest in the charismatic French-man way down deep and left him to his bevy of fans. Which didn't mean she hadn't liked to watch from afar and keep general tabs on what he was doing—and who with. It just meant she hadn't done anything about it.

At first.

'Hey.' That was as close to a greeting as he was get-ting from her. She stopped in the doorway.

'Good—you're here.'

He rushed straight towards her, his eyes intense, and she stumbled back and readied herself for unexpected contact. But at the very last moment he sidestepped and squeezed past her out into the daylight, into the refrigerated room across the yard behind the exhibits. Her heart played out the dreadful anticipation of just a moment before.

Idiot. Of course he wasn't going to hug her.

She took over observations at the monitors, glancing occasionally up to the door he'd disappeared through and then down again to scan the day's progress report. A lot of activity but none of it pup-related.

That would explain the frustrated gleam in his eyes when he'd shoved past her. He must have been count-ing down the minutes before she arrived.

He reappeared in the doorway, biceps bulging out from under his T-shirt because of the unwieldy sack in his arms.

'Sheep carcass,' he said, in clipped French tones.

Ridiculous that he could make even words like that sound sexy.

She reinforced her emotional barriers. 'Thanks, I've eaten.'

His grin nearly undid all her good work. She'd forgotten the impact it had when directed solely at her. He dumped the sack in the doorway. 'I have a good feeling about tonight.'

'Based on...?'

'Their behaviour. The pack has been extra active today. Something's up.'

His breathlessness reached out and infected her. 'Tonight? Really?'

'I have the carcass ready, just in case.'

'For the pups?' *The colostrum-and-milk-drinking pups?*

She deserved the disdain he threw her way. 'For the adults. To lure them into the night quarters so we can check the den.'

The wild dogs were one of several species that had the freedom to come and go between their zoo exhibit and their night quarters. Anyone wanting to break that routine and lock them in was going to have to come armed with some serious persuasion.

Like a fleshy, fresh sheep-half.

Tonight. That was exciting. 'You think Mjawi will leave them?'

He flopped down next to her in the seat he'd clearly spent a lot of time in today. 'Depends. Ordinarily one of the others would just regurgitate for her, but she's getting antsy. I saw her a lot today. She wants to be out. She might leave them long enough to get a good feed.'

And that's all they'd need. Just long enough to get

in there and do what they'd come to do. Anticipation stained his cheekbones near the corners of those hazel eyes and only defined his angular bone structure more. Another half-hour and they'd be back to a darkness only broken by the light the monitors were throwing off. And she wouldn't have to stare at that excited colour in his face and remember when she'd last seen it.

She cleared her throat. 'And if she doesn't?'

He threw her a look. 'If she doesn't then we'll move on to Plan B.'

'We have a plan B?'

He shrugged. 'That's what you're here for.'

'Right…' No pressure. But the glitter of anticipation in his eyes didn't ease up. 'This means a lot to you, doesn't it?' she risked.

His thick lashes dropped covertly, under the guise of checking the observation sheet. 'Sure.'

'Why is that?'

'Because I'm a perfectionist.'

Pedant. Obsessive. Same trait, different perspective. 'That goes without saying. But why is this so personal for you?' She took a breath. 'Did you bring the virus in on you? From Africa?'

It was possible. There were definitely cross-species viruses perfectly capable of hitchhiking in an unsuspecting human. And while they had strict quarantine regulations for their wildlife they had fewer for their staff. Even the ones straight out of the field.

His eyes flared and then grew wounded. 'Is that what you think? That I *gave* them this disease?'

'I have no idea what to think. I only realised there was any connection at all this morning.'

He stared at her.

'So what *is* the connection, Gabe? Why are you so hot to trot on developing a way to eradicate it?'

His gaze grew more thoughtful—a heap less comfortable—and the silence aged. But finally he spoke. 'One of the first things I did on joining this round was work with the species coordinator on finding two new members for the zoo's collection. He wanted to bring in two animals from New Zealand.'

'But aren't the latest arrivals from wild Zambian parents?'

'I won him over with their totally fresh genetic input. What neither of us realised was that one of them was carrying the virus. It didn't show up in quarantine.'

Because they hadn't screened for it. It was an unknown contagion. And by the time it had been picked up the pack was integrated and the virus had spread to the other dogs.

Viruses were nature's opportunists.

'So this is your *mea culpa*?' she said.

He lifted his eyes again. 'Partly. It's also my job.'

And it should have been mine. But fairness made her say instead, 'It was also the species coordinator's job. And my department's. A whole lot of people had a say in them coming.'

'But it was my recommendation originally.'

She stared. There was no arguing with guilt. 'So this matters?'

He nodded. 'It does.'

She could hate him for his values, but not for his dedication to these animals. 'Okay, then.'

Accord between them, after so long, didn't sit easily.

The first mosquito of dusk alighted on her skin and

she slapped it away. 'We should get that carcass in there before it's too dark to see anything.'

MJAWI WAS NOVICE enough that she betrayed her pups the moment the rest of the pack started running in increasingly agitated circles as they realised what was happening. Nine out of eleven of them were already in the night quarters, alternately squabbling, begging and stealing chunks of the carcass Gabe had sawn into more manageable pieces. Mjawi emerged hesitantly at first, but jogged over to join the other adults as soon as she realised what was on offer.

'Come on…come on…'

Ingrid stared at the monitor while Gabe stood by the external doors, ready to drop them the moment the last adult entered the safety of the night quarters area. With one eye constantly on the screen, she loaded up a box with the things they'd need to see to the pups.

Syringes. Vaccine. Scales. Microchips.

Dusk was the time most likely for the pups to emerge. By now the crazy Boxing Day crowds had been gone for a couple of hours and everything was quiet in the zoo, the temperature lower. Perfect pup weather. As she reached to place the chip scanner into the box a movement on the screen caught her eye. A black ball of fluff with two blackcurrant eyes poked its head from the entrance to B-den.

Gabe! She wanted to call out but didn't dare—not with the adults so close to coming in.

The first pup emerged, albeit hesitantly. It was either drawn by the excitement of its elders, looking for its mother, or just a little alpha-in-the-making, boldly going where its siblings hadn't gone before. At least not without Mum.

She glanced at the second image on the monitors—the one showing the whole exhibit—and saw Mjawi pacing uncertainly at the doorway to the night quarters. The door Ingrid knew Gabe was just *waiting* to slam shut behind her.

Come on...come on...

The shadow pup paused half out of the entrance hole, suddenly uncertain in the face of the big, wide, lonely world. It turned its head left. Then right. Then it lifted its tiny nose, sniffed the air, and then—

On the other screen Mjawi responded immediately to the uncertain yowl of one of her offspring. She abandoned her position by the door and sprinted straight back to the den, shoving her nose under the pup's belly and scooting it ahead of her and back into the den. Her big body squeezed in after it and both of them were gone.

She felt Gabe's frustration before she heard it.

'There was a pup, wasn't there?' He burst in from the doorway.

She nodded.

'How did it look?'

'Small. Healthy.' *Oh, good one—remind him of what's at stake.* That was sensitive.

Gabe played the CCTV footage back. 'Just the one.'

His despondency reached out to her. They'd already known there was at least one still alive in there. Mjawi wouldn't be guarding thin air. So they were really no further ahead than they had been this time last night.

'We have all week,' she reminded him gently.

But that didn't encourage him. At all. His eyes darkened dangerously.

'You're the best at what you do, Gabe. You'll get this.' It galled her to praise him, but his despondency spoke so clearly to her.

He snorted. 'Words.'

'No. Not just words…' They were, really. 'I hear what others say. I read your reports and recommendations. You know wild dogs. You *will* get this.'

He'd made something of the job he'd stolen from her. Small consolation. At least he wasn't wasting the opportunity. And somewhere down deep she knew that the job she would have made of it and the one he'd turned it into were vastly different.

That was an uncomfortable reality to swallow.

He sank into the sling-back chair and stared at the monitor before finally turning his eyes to her. They changed along with the topic of conversation. 'Did you see your family in the end today?'

That threw her composure enough for her not to guard herself completely. 'I… No, I thought sleep would be a better use of my time.'

One French eyebrow shot up.

'I can see them tomorrow…or…soon.' Heat surged up her neck. 'They knew I was working.'

Understanding dawned. 'You're avoiding them.'

'No.'

'You're avoiding them and telling them you had to work.'

She flicked her chin up. '*You're* working.'

'My family are all in France. What's your excuse?'

'It's Christmas lunch now in Paris. I don't see you rushing to get on the phone.'

He snorted. 'And you won't.'

She stared at him. 'So maybe we're both avoiding Christmas the politically correct way.'

His silence was almost an accusation.

'They'll have barely missed me,' she defended. 'The kids will be keeping them busy. Chewing the gift-wrapping and drawing on the wall with turkey stuffing.'

'Your parents have *petits enfants*?'

His surprise was reasonable, given she was twenty-five years old. That was a big gap between conceptions. 'Not together. But, yes.'

He frowned. 'They're divorced?'

'And remarried. Mum married a man only five years older than me. They have two kids under three. Dad inherited a new family with his new wife.'

'Another family,' he corrected.

Most of the time it definitely felt like his *new* family. 'So I figure I'm doing them a kindness in keeping Christmas simple. They don't need me to worry about.'

'You don't think they'd like to have you there to help with the finger-painting?'

'They'd both offer, of course. And then I'd have to choose. And choosing would only fuel a new *thing* between them. If I chose Mum I'd have to sit with Trevor's younger brother and endure him feeling me up under the table after he'd had a few drinks. And if I chose Dad then I'd make Elizabeth sick trying to over-please me.' She sighed. 'I think this was win-win for everyone, really.'

'Interesting family.'

She shot him a sideways glare. 'And yours is perfect, of course?'

'Far from it. But at least they're still all together. Way too together.'

She turned full-on to him. 'What do you mean?'

'Christmas at Château Marque is about showcasing. Wives. Cars. Gifts. Achievements. The whole family comes together before breakfast and then stays the night on the estate.'

'Ugh. That's a lot of Christmas. How many people?'

'I have four brothers. Each of them married. Two with children.'

She stared at him. Suddenly being felt up by your twenty-two-year-old step-uncle for an hour was looking pretty good.

'What sorts of achievements do they…showcase?'

'Career, mostly. Unique cases. Famous clients. Who got the newest to the front page in the newspapers and for what.'

'What do your family do?'

He shrugged. 'Two surgeons, a lawyer, a senior politician and an engineer.'

She blinked. 'Wow. Impressive genes.' To accompany the physical ones, apparently.

'Depends on your perspective.'

'You're not proud of their achievements?'

'They're proud enough of their own achievements without my assistance.'

'You don't like them?'

He held her gaze. 'They're my family. I love them. But I refuse to *be* like them.'

'Hence your travels?'

He shrugged. 'Africa's a hard place to Skype from on Christmas Day.'

Not at all what she had expected. In her mind Gabriel Marque came from a loving, provincial family who were heartbroken at his long absence.

'And Australia?'

He shrugged one shoulder. 'Busy working.'

She stared at him for a moment longer. Another bit of mortar was crumbling out of the walls she'd carefully mounded up around her.

She pushed to her feet. 'I have an idea.'

'For what?'

'Plan B.'

'YOU WANT TO tunnel between dens?'

'It worked for the new freeway. They tunnelled most of the way under the city and then just pushed the last bit through on the official opening day, with all the media there. We could do the same. When Mjawi's out of the den.'

'And if she unexpectedly returns?'

'Distraction is your job.' *You should find that no trouble.* 'But I can be out in seconds. And she'll find a new chamber leading to A-den. Maybe she'll use it.'

'Maybe she won't.'

'I bet she would if anything happened to her own den.'

Even he couldn't argue with the sense of an escape route. 'And what makes you think you'd be a better tunnel-digger than Mjawi?'

Her hands went to her hips. 'I was the sandcastle queen of my whole suburb. I've dug more moats and bridge arches and catacombs than you could imagine.'

'Catacombs?'

She glared at him. 'They were very detailed castles.' *Nerd!* The taunts of the kids at school came flitting back. As if her thick glasses and top grades hadn't been target enough.

His lips pursed as he tried to find a flaw with the plan. 'What if you disturb her?'

'I'll be doing it at night when she's asleep. It's probably only six feet. Cutting through A-den's wall will be the slowest part, and I'll use a hand saw so it's quiet.'

Gabe crossed to the hatch that opened from the monitoring area into the manmade den dug deep beneath the earth that was mounded up against the night quarters wall. He eased it open on its hinges.

'You won't fit,' she pre-empted. 'I barely will.' There was no way on this planet that the opening would accommodate those amazing shoulders.

He turned and glared at her. 'It's going to be hard work.'

'I'm not afraid of hard work.' She threw her hair back. 'Come on, Gabe, admit it. It's a good plan.'

'It's a crazy plan.'

'Because you didn't think of it?'

'Because if you make too much noise she could abandon the pups.'

She rolled her eyes and his glare intensified.

'And because you could be hurt.'

Oh. That was sweeter than she was comfortable with. 'If it all caves in on me then you can just pull me out by my feet.'

His snort was as good as a yes. 'Dignified.'

'You've seen worse.'

Whoops—straight from the place she kept all her secrets. But the eyes he lifted to her said he didn't misunderstand. And he hadn't forgotten. He'd been as clumsy and desperate as she had that night. As if they'd both known it was the only chance they were going to get.

The intensity didn't let up. 'You only dig while I'm in here monitoring.'

She would have baulked at the command if not for the fact there was a thread of genuine concern running under it. 'Who are you monitoring? Mjawi or me?'

He shrugged one shoulder. 'I'm responsible for you.'

'Actually, you're not,' she reminded him on an overly bright smile, 'because I'm the one rostered and you're a volunteer overnight. But I'm happy to have your back-up.'

He sighed and straightened. 'Okay. What are you going to need?'

CHAPTER THREE

December 27th

IT TOOK ALL of the next day for zoo management to sign off on the plan and get them what they needed for the dig. A hacksaw blade for the den material, a trowel, a metre and a half of large PVC pipe cut into segments, and some buckets to ferry the excavated earth. It seriously felt like something out of *The Great Escape*.

Or *Hogan's Heroes*. Depending on how it ended.

They hadn't been able to start until just before midnight to make sure the dogs were well asleep, and now Gabe tapped a thirty-second warning on her left ankle.

Ingrid quickly shored up the bit of tunnel she was working on with PVC pipe and then tucked her head down as he pulled on her feet and drew her and her bucket of dirt and tools swiftly out of the half-tunnel, back through the den and into the monitoring room. She slid to her feet in the circle of his arms.

He dropped them—extra quickly—then resecured the hatch cover. She did her best to stand gracefully. But several hours flat on your face in a burrow for one had a way of cramping your muscles into position. She winced as her aching arms dragged her protective mask off. It had been white once.

'You need to rest. It's dawn.'

'I'm fine.' He wasn't wrong, but she wasn't about to confess how tired and sore she was. 'How far do you think I got?'

'Two feet, maybe?'

She lifted gritty eyes and blew her dishevelled hair from her face. 'Two feet?'

'It's a good tunnel, though. You missed your calling.'

'Don't patronise me, Gabe.' Her tolerance for that had run out about three minutes into the hard dig.

'Here.'

He passed her a damp cloth and she pressed it gratefully to her dusty face.

'This was your idea,' he pointed out helpfully. She dropped the cloth and glared at him. He backed off, both hands in the air. 'You were just starting to relax around me, too.'

Her hands stilled. And here she'd thought she was doing such a good job of hiding her discomfort around him. 'I'll be fine. I just need a minute to breathe.' She arched her aching back and rotated her shoulders.

Suddenly two warm hands were on them, pushing her towards a chair. 'Sit, Ingrid.'

Before she could do more than suck in an objection, Gabe's strong fingers kneaded the muscles that were so close to cramping up, and the sheer bliss stopped her protest before it could take form on her lips.

The sound that came out of her throat belonged in one of the zoo's exhibits.

'Good?' he asked, though strangely his voice sounded as tight as her shoulders.

Her first attempt at speech was more of a gurgle. She cleared her throat and tried again. 'Amazing. Thank you.'

'Might as well make myself useful,' he muttered.

She cracked a single eye open. 'Are you always this bad with waiting?'

'I'm always bad with being redundant.'

Her head lolled back and then forward on her shoulders as he rubbed. 'As soon as the tunnel's dug I'll be the spare wheel.'

'It's frustrating, not being able to help.'

She opened her eyes fully, looked up to where he towered over her and spoke to the underside of his angular jaw. 'You're being serious?'

'Deadly.'

'Is it because I'm a woman?'

He dropped his chin until he was looking straight down on her. Funny how she'd never realised before how possible it was to laugh without a hint of smile or eye-crinkle. Or how very much his next answer mattered.

His gaze held hers. 'No, it is not.'

End of conversation. A polite person would take the hint. 'Then what is it?' she pushed. 'Why the burning need to—?'

Achieve.

As she almost said the word a lightbulb of awareness flickered into life above her head. 'Your family.'

'A Marque does not sit idle.'

Empathy washed through her. What kind of screwy life lesson was that to impose on a kid? 'You're not being idle. It's a practical necessity. I fit and you don't.'

He grunted.

Wow. 'Gabe, you just worked right through Christmas Day and you're into your twenty-second hour awake. Voluntarily.'

His hands resumed their heavenly squeeze-and-release on the back of her neck but he didn't speak.

Ingrid let the silence settle for minutes and focussed on the liquidating knots in her muscles. Her whole upper half tingled.

'Is that why you're such an over-achiever?' she finally asked. 'Because everyone in your family is, too?'

'Work ethic is a valuable commodity in my family.'

'How many of them are working over Christmas, do you think?'

His smile was reluctant. 'My brothers are probably on call.'

Ugh. Of course they were. 'Lord save me from principled men!'

His eyes dropped her way again and narrowed just slightly. 'You don't count integrity as a virtue in a man?'

She did. Right up there with compassion and honour. But she wasn't about to enumerate the reasons she'd first been drawn to Gabe *with* Gabe. 'It's a fine line between virtue and flaw.'

His hands stopped dead on her shoulders. His lips twisted for the first time. 'Why am I not surprised that you'd find a way to turn an asset into a liability?'

She frowned and coiled around to get a better look at his face. It effectively ended the heavenly massage. Probably not a moment too soon. 'What is that supposed to mean?'

The tension in his voice returned immediately, but he didn't shy away from her question. Valour? Another Marque trait?

'You can be a little judgemental, Ingrid. I can't be the first person to tell you that.'

Uh...yes, actually. The unfairness of that bit hard. 'How have I judged you?'

'Other than just now? For striving to achieve...?'

'That's not judgement, Gabe. It's empathy. I just think you should give yourself a break and let yourself be less than perfect now and again.'

'I get a lot of satisfaction out of doing something well.'

'Me too, but—' She shook away the confusion. 'Don't change the subject. How have I judged you when we've barely spoken in a year?'

He didn't answer, just lifted both eyebrows as if she'd just made his point for him.

She pushed out of the chair and spun on him. 'That wasn't judgement. It was—' *It was anger.* Just as unattractive, but a reality. 'It was thirteen months ago.'

His eyes were now carefully blank. 'As far as I'm concerned, it was the last time I spoke to you.'

'What has that got to do with me being judgemental?'

His eyes darkened. Then he turned away and collected up her tools. 'Forget it.'

'No. You brought it up. I want to know.' The little lightbulb flickered again. *No...* 'You can't possibly think I judged your—' heat rushed up her neck '—performance?'

Gabe turned and gave her the look that had first turned her knees to water. The one he'd fired at her that night at the party. Half-sardonic, half-seductive. Molten lava. It had exactly the same effect now. That night had been the most amazing of her life. And that fact only made what he'd done next hurt more.

'I'm glad something met with your satisfaction, then,' he purred, his accent heavy.

A sensual buzz tangled itself up amongst her confusion. She beat it away. 'You didn't exactly pound down my door the next day,' she said, at a loss as to how else she'd offended him in their five-second relationship. 'I'm pretty sure us being a one-off was mutual.'

It wasn't as if he'd fought for her. Or even responded to her when she'd done the talking for both of them and declared their night together a mistake. He'd just nodded—once—and then left. All very manly and stoic, but not very helpful in getting things between them back on a work footing.

'You're sure about a lot of things, Ingrid.'

That sounded like a criticism, too. She threw her hands into the air. 'Now who's being judgemental? I think I have more reason to be upset than you do.'

His eyes narrowed. 'Why?'

Because you stole my job! But it sounded as pathetic as ever, and they had to keep their voices down, so she kept the words constrained way down deep.

'Forget it,' she gritted. 'I'm going to wash my face and get a coffee. Will you watch the monitor for me?' She was still technically rostered for a few hours and he must be exhausted. 'You should get some sleep when I get back.'

Because the moment my shift is up, buddy, I'm out of here.

As SOON AS she was gone Gabe flopped down on the camp bed and made sure he had a good direct view of the CCTV feed. The canvas sling was as good as a mattress of clouds when you were as tired as he was. But as soon as she was back he would head to his car until morning.

He arched his neck. What in the name of all that was holy was he thinking—openly challenging Ingrid about the relationship that had fizzled before it began? That was the last thing he wanted to talk about, and she was the last one he wanted to talk about it with.

But done was done. He'd always had a fairly direct line from his heart to his mouth. It had used to drive his *maman* crazy. He'd worked hard as an adult to get a handle on it, but every sensory signal in his body had started short-circuiting the moment Ingrid began groaning in response to his touch—as if the chemicals in his synapses had turned to glue and the impulses that were supposed to make him step back…take his hands off her…keep his mouth shut…had just failed to get to their destination.

And then the words had come leaping off his tongue with long-repressed glee.

He tucked his hands behind his head and shifted more comfortably. She hadn't liked being reminded of the choice she'd made that night. The day after that night.

Or maybe he would have said anything to break through her carefully controlled exterior. To get a hint of the Ingrid he'd met that night when she was too re-laxed—or too immersed—to remember to be appro-priate.

Immersed in *him*. Exactly the way he'd been im-mersed in her.

They'd been at parties together before, but before he'd been perpetually surrounded by noise and clutter and people—women especially—and Ingrid had made a specialty of sitting away with an older group of staff. Talking. Laughing.

Watching.

As though she knew something he didn't.

She'd been easy to ignore at first—and he'd had plenty of eager distraction—but as the weeks had worn on the hairs on his neck had started to respond to her silent gaze. He'd been able to feel without looking when her blue eyes swung his way. And if he'd caught her in a stare they'd cloud with confusion before she dropped her lashes to screen herself from him.

It had driven him insane.

It hadn't been intentional. And it hadn't been rudeness—she hadn't ignored him if she'd found herself in a room with him. But she hadn't sought him out. Not the way everyone else had.

It was as if she'd simply been *tolerating* his presence. Just.

And then they'd found themselves in the same room at the same moment at that final party, and the crowds had parted like something biblical…and there she was. Nowhere to go but towards him, with no one to speak to but him.

Later, it had burned him to realise she probably would have slunk away if she'd had any choice, but at the time he'd thanked whatever angels looked over him for the opportunity, and he'd stepped up to her and started their first conversation.

Four hours later they'd been in each other's arms at the gate that led to his car.

And he'd been the happiest he could remember being. Something had clicked inside him that night, and he'd not managed to unclick it since. A kind of…rightness. Almost as though Ingrid Rose had come into his life to show him how *right* felt. What was possible.

In life.

But not with her, apparently.

He shook his head to stay awake and to rattle the uncomfortable sensation loose. The last thing he wanted was for Ingrid to return and find him asleep on the job. Wouldn't that just confirm for her everything she already suspected about his worth?

A woman like Ingrid set a high bar—personally and professionally. She might have made a concession that night because she'd thought he was just passing through, but she'd corrected it the moment he'd told her he was staying. Literally the moment.

Message received.

He'd done his best to push her rejection aside and focus on the opportunity the universe had provided. He'd get to stay in Australia—across the globe from the expectations of his easily disappointed family—to make his name in this job and make a difference to the conservation outcomes this zoo delivered.

Make the best of a bad situation, in other words.

Another Marque trait. He was the king of that one.

He'd taken a basic science degree and was turning it into something unique. Something he could be passionate about. Something that mattered. He'd worked multiple jobs and collectively they'd given him a breadth of experience he could never have gleaned from textbooks.

His parents might not be able to confess publicly what he did for a living, but what he did was making a difference. Slowly but surely.

Not bad for *l'imbécile*.

CHAPTER FOUR

December 28th

THE STROKING HANDS and breathless voice of his dreams resolved into Ingrid's gentle shake and whispered voice.

'Gabe...'

He pushed up onto his elbows—not easy in the tiny camp bed—and stared at her, still struggling to shake the images of his subconscious.

Light streamed in the open doorway.

'What time is it?'

'I'm getting ready to go.'

Go? But her shift had ended at... His watch told the shameful truth. 'Why didn't you wake me?'

She was trying hard not to smile. 'I am waking you.'

'Why did you let me sleep?'

'Because you were exhausted. I came back from my shower and you were practically unconscious.' She extended her hand to help him from the low-slung bed. 'I played back the CCTV. You didn't miss anything.'

Lucky, considering what a dumb thing falling asleep was. It pained him to take her hand, but it would gall him more to flail around in front of her trying to get out of what was effectively a hammock two feet off the ground. His cool fingers closed around her warm ones as she loaned him her strength until he found his feet.

He remembered that about her. She pumped off heat like a furnace.

'Thanks.' He righted himself and they stood toe to toe.

She stepped back. 'No problem.'

Well, weren't they being terribly *civil*? 'You're going home?'

'That's generally where I do my sleeping,' she breathed.

'Funny girl. What about the tunnel?'

'I'll finish it tonight.'

'What if the pups emerge?' Two seconds ago he'd been mortified that she'd watched him sleep. Now he was guilting her into staying.

'Then I'll miss it.'

He brought out his big gun. 'I could use your help.'

The earnest wide-eyed appeal. It always worked with his mother. His sisters-in-law. Pretty much every other female he'd ever known.

She stared at him. 'No, you couldn't. You'd love nothing more than to do this all by yourself and be the hero.'

Was she seeing completely through him or just partly? 'I'll need you if Mjawi moves the pups.'

'She can't move them. We've blocked the entrance to A-den until I'm done digging.'

Suddenly he had a blazing desire to play chess with this woman. Her brain and her insight would make her a formidable opponent.

She lifted her chin. 'You want me to sleep here? Why?'

'It's surprisingly comfortable.' He avoided the second part of her question entirely.

'I know. I've slept on one in the vet hospital.'

'I'll be quiet.'

'I'm sure you will.' Her hands slid to her hips. 'I'm still waiting for an answer.'

Why? The million-dollar question. He searched deep inside himself, then sighed. 'I don't want you to miss it.'

Her eyes narrowed, but the sudden appearance of several creases between her brows told him it was confusion, not suspicion. 'Isn't that my decision?' she said.

He took a deep breath and shoved his hands into his pockets. 'I don't want you to miss it…because of me.'

That startled her. Her blue eyes darted away.

'If I was anyone else,' he rushed on, 'would you be leaving? Or would you be staying to get this once-in-a-lifetime experience?'

Her answer took an age. 'You think she's going to let them out today?'

He had no idea. He only knew he didn't want to be responsible for Ingrid missing the best part of their job. '*C'est possible.* Do you want to take that chance?'

She chewed her lip. 'It would be typical. After I spent half the night digging.'

He smiled. 'Maybe she'll wait until you've dug the whole thing.'

She rubbed her eyes with the back of one hand. 'Ugh. She would, too.'

'Stay, Ingrid. You're tired. I'll wake you the moment there's something to see.'

The cogs in her mind practically groaned as they went around, weighing up her options.

'Okay. I'll stay. But the moment you turn into a chatty Cathy I'm out of here.'

Silence was good for him. He'd rather have peace with Ingrid than a dozen conversations with others. 'I'll just grab a shower and some breakfast before my shift starts. Give me fifteen minutes.'

She frowned. 'You have thirty before I clock off.'

If he only had a half-hour in her conscious company he wasn't about to waste more than half of it on himself. He reached for his bag.

'Fifteen.'

SLEEP WAS SIMPLE in theory but not so much in practice.

The time to force herself to nod off was when Gabe left for his shower, but Ingrid's body was too keyed-up to sleep yet. As far as it was concerned it had a few hours between work and sleep—regardless of the real time. Or all the good reasons it shouldn't stay awake.

So he'd walked back in, damp and freshly shaven from his shower, smelling like French soap and carrying an obscene amount of food for one person. As if he'd known he'd find her awake.

And they'd shared their first meal together. His breakfast, her dinner. Just breaking bread with Gabe—something she'd given up on ever achieving—had her feeling light-headed.

'Does your family approve of what you do?' Her subconscious thrust its curiosity up into the light.

He gave no sign of having heard her as he finished up the last bites of his meal and watched the monitor.

'They know,' he finally said.

Not what she'd asked. 'What do they think?'

He looked at her sideways. 'Is that a loaded question?'

It was certainly more personal than she had a right to ask, despite how much more personal they'd been once.

Once.

'My parents' kids are just getting old enough to think having a big sister who works at the zoo is pretty cool. I just wondered how yours felt.'

He stared at her for a long time before answering. 'My father tells people I work in a circus. Mother doesn't speak of it at all.'

The pain in that statement reached out to her. She paused with a bit of ham and cheese croissant halfway to her lips. 'A circus? Are you serious?'

'I am. So is he.'

Her brows lifted. 'He doesn't value what you do?'

'He does not.'

A circus? 'That's pretty harsh.'

'Welcome to the Marque family.'

'And your brothers?'

His dark brow dropped marginally. 'They are accepting. It suits them.'

'What do you mean?'

'My failings only make them look better.'

'What failings? When have you ever failed?'

He looked as if he wanted to say something, but had thought better of it. 'It matters little to my father if I achieve every objective I have if the goals are insufficient in his eyes.'

'Wow.' Suddenly her own parents—all four of them—were looking much less unbearable. 'You don't deserve that. I'm really sorry.'

'It's not your fault.'

'No. But I'm still sorry.'

He stared at her. 'Are you pitying me now?'

As if a man like Gabe needed anyone's pity. 'Understanding you better, maybe?'

He paused. 'Then, thank you.'

'You're welcome.'

Silence settled again. Then it was his turn with the questions.

'You really dislike Christmas so much?'

She licked a finger and tapped it into the flakes of croissant pastry still on her plate, then brought each one to her mouth in turn. He watched her closely, waiting for an answer.

'It's not Christmas. It's just…' she sighed '…awkward.'

'Awkward?'

'It seems ridiculous in light of what you just shared. But, yes.'

'Because of their divorce?'

'Because I'm not sure where I fit.' *Or* if *I fit.*

'You're their daughter.'

'One of several now.'

A knowing light blinked to life in his expression. 'Ah.'

She narrowed the eyes she lifted to him. 'What "ah"?'

'You were the only child.'

Just herself and her parents for twenty years. She nodded.

'And now you have to share.'

Tension pulled like a loose thread up her spine. Because it was true and not true at the same time. For her entire life her parents had focussed their love and attention on her, but it was only very recently she'd realised that had been symptomatic of a fatal flaw in their relationship. They'd both used her to avoid looking too closely at their changing feelings for each other. No surprises that they'd divorced almost the moment she left home.

'I'm twenty-five years old, Gabe. You make it sound so juvenile.'

'It's not about sharing?'

'It's about…' But her words evaporated just when she needed them. She stopped and tried again. 'It's about certainty, you know? Like my first twenty years were as invalid as their marriage.'

She glanced at her watch, glad of the excuse to change the subject. That was more than she'd ever imagined herself sharing with him. With anyone. 'It's eight o'clock. You're officially on. I'm going to try and get some sleep.'

And without waiting for an answer she rolled over and gave him her back, fairly sure there would be no sleep for a long time.

Gabe was as good as his word, and was silent for long, thoughtful minutes. But it couldn't last. His voice spoke softly from behind her.

'Why are you so angry with me, Ingrid? Is it about that night?'

She stared at the back wall of the converted night quarters and considered pretending to be asleep. Her breathing was regular enough to pull that off.

'No. It's not. It's not about you at all.' *It's about me.*

And it was—though she'd not even realised that until the words had trembled unspoken on her lips. There had been six other applicants for the zookeeping vacancy. Would she have been this bitter and twisted if one of them had been successful in Gabe's place?

Probably not.

Disappointed, certainly. She'd been raised to work

hard and expect the fruits of her efforts. But, no, this extra level of blame was solely for Gabe. It was personal.

Not that she had the vaguest clue as to why.

She wasn't brave enough to look him in the eye as she said it, so she just stared at the wall harder. 'I wanted this job,' she whispered.

'The dog-watch?'

'*This* job. Your job. I was an applicant.' The name right under his in the preferred candidates column.

She could practically feel him thinking through that day twelve months ago, when he'd tracked her down at work and broken the confidential news so excitedly. He had the job. He was staying. The flatness of her reaction.

'I didn't know I'd been unsuccessful until you told me you'd been offered the job,' she finished.

His breathing was the only sound in the room. 'Ingrid, I'm sorry. I had no idea.'

Of course he hadn't. She wouldn't have even been on his radar as a possible candidate. She was a vet nurse, not a zookeeper. She blinked at the wall.

'I just…' His voice dropped. 'I wanted you to know. I wanted you to be excited for me.'

Instead she'd broken off their twelve-hours-old romance. Suddenly she saw the whole incident from his perspective. And everything since. Discomfort curdled in her belly.

'I'm sorry if I've been rude, Gabe,' she said finally, and meant it. 'I'll try harder.'

Again a long, contemplative silence behind her.

'Maybe we both can.'

Maybe. The idea of a truce with Gabriel Marque

after all this time… It bothered and excited her in equal measures. Because her feelings of a year ago were only barely beneath her skin, and it wouldn't take much to have them pushing through and declaring themselves openly. They'd not gone away that day when he'd come to share his excitement with her. They'd only lain dormant.

And that was not something she was comfortable with.

At all.

SHE WOKE QUIETLY that evening and spent a few minutes watching Gabe without him knowing. He was halfway through a thick thriller, lit by a book-light and the glow from the monitors he glanced at repeatedly.

It was luxury time—just for her. As if it didn't really exist if he was unaware. As if she was still in some dream.

She found herself fixated on the tattoo that ran down the left side of his throat from just under his jaw to under the collar of his T-shirt and which—she knew from personal experience—splayed out over his left shoulder blade. It was an intriguing tattoo, tribal in nature, but in fact it spelled out a word if you looked at it just the right way.

Jamais.

Never.

She'd looked it up. And she'd never stopped wondering what it was he'd pledged in living ink never to do.

'When did you get the tattoo?'

If he was surprised she was awake he didn't show it at all. He slid a battered bookmark into place, closed his novel and turned to her. 'Just before Africa.'

Five years ago. He must have been only a bit younger than she was now. 'I think I expected it to be *in* Africa.'

He smiled. 'No. But it facilitated me going there.'

'What do you mean?'

'My parents were less than happy when they discovered it.'

And it would have taken all of one day, the way the ink reached out from the secrecy of his shirt and flexed its dark tendrils in full view on his neck.

Still, he didn't strike her as mindlessly rebellious. 'Why *"jamais"*?'

The smile flickered but his eyes remained steady. 'My father had arranged an internship for me.'

She frowned. 'But you were…what? Twenty-three?'

'Twenty-four. He didn't like the direction I was taking my life in. The firm was one of Paris's oldest financial institutions.'

'Why didn't you just say no?'

'Noncompliance is not an option in my family.' He turned more fully towards her. 'I learned early to be smart. I went to the interview in my best suit, with my hair cut short and banker-neat, and put my best foot forward. I did my family name justice.' His lips twitched. 'He had nothing to fault me on.'

Suddenly the decision to bring that tattoo out into the open made perfect sense. She could well imagine the gasped breath as the interviewer's eye fell on it, flexing out from under his stiff designer collar. 'They wouldn't take you?'

'No. They would not.'

'Did they tell him why?'

'No. They did not. But he knew. We all knew.'

She pushed up into a sitting position. 'Permanent

marking. That's quite a statement.' It was hard not to admire such dramatic resolve. And suddenly the choice of *never* made complete sense.

He returned her favour of just hours before and stepped over to the edge of the camp bed, lowering a large hand to her. 'But effective. He's never tried to manipulate me since.'

She slipped her fingers into his and pulled herself up, then lifted her eyes to his. His thick lashes swept his cheeks as he peered down at her. She stopped herself— barely—from bracing herself against the hard wall of his chest, and had to concentrate not to betray the pattering of her heart in the breathlessness of her speech.

'Well, their loss is our gain.'

His smile was worth her present discomfort.

She swallowed past the squirm of her stomach and glanced at her watch.

'I need to head home for an hour. Get some clothes, water the plants. You'll be okay until later?'

'You're going to stay.' It was more a sigh than a question.

She stared at him, right down deep into those fathomless eyes. 'I don't want to miss it.'

And with every moment that passed 'it' became more about the opportunity to spend some time with Gabe and not just about seeing the pups emerge. But she'd go on kidding herself as long as her subconscious would permit it.

This was about the dogs.

Sure it was.

CHAPTER FIVE

December 29th

'How MANY CHANGES of clothes did you bring with you?' Gabe asked slightly above a whisper as she wiggled backwards out of A-den's hatch the following night and felt around with her feet for the floor. She understood his question. She was filthy.

Again.

'Any further and I'll be in there with her,' she said, with no small amount of satisfaction.

It had been a tough dig, but the tunnel between dens was holding and it would only take a slight poke through to breach the remaining few inches of dirt. Curious Mjawi would do the rest. Or desperate Mjawi, to save her pups. Ingrid stood and steadied herself, then turned and smiled up at him. Bits of grit fell into her mouth.

'I think we're done,' she said past them.

Gabe shone his torch into the space she'd just been working in and nodded. 'Nice job, Ingrid.'

He reached his long arm up the den entrance and grabbed the inflated block they'd been sealing it with, let the air out through the popped valve, then quickly closed up the inspection hatch.

She shook her hair and loose dirt went flying. 'Remind me about this moment the next time I have a good idea that no one but me can carry out.'

Gabe chuckled and rattled the inspection hatch to make sure it was secure. 'I will.'

It was just something to say. It didn't imply any kind of future between them or any kind of intimacy. But it dried her mouth completely. Then he turned and inspected her.

'Hold still.'

Her breath grew even shallower as his large fingers slid behind her head and his thumbs wiped away the worst of whatever was on her face. She hated to think. She'd found more than just earthworms and the odd beetle while digging her way towards B-den. But this moment made those moments totally worth it. She stood, unusually compliant, and let him drag his flesh over hers.

It had been a long time between shivers.

'So now what?' she breathed, but didn't move away.

'Now we wait. Watch for signs of her den deteriorating.'

'You don't think she'll move them just because?'

'No. She'll only move them to keep them safe. But what you've just done... That will mean they have a safe bolthole if B-den caves in.'

It was an odd mix of pride and futility—she'd have been instrumental in saving their lives if their den collapsed, but if it didn't then all her work was purposeless. She decided to stick with pride.

He tipped his head. 'For someone who saves animal lives every day, you look pretty pleased about that.'

'I am. It's different. This is about prevention.'

'Is that why you wanted to change careers?'

'Partly. I like what I do, but I want to contribute to the long-term management of our animals, not just their occasional care.'

'Shovelling dung appeals that much, does it?'

She smiled, knowing that mundane tasks were the price they all paid for the more engaging, higher level tasks. Besides, she'd done her fair share of repetitive dirty jobs in the hospital.

'It's hard to form relationships with the animals there. The ones who are in long enough to bond with are the ones you can't afford to bond with.'

'Not sure zookeeping is the right choice, either, if it's bonding you're after. We can be transferred without notice, animals get transacted out to other zoos, there are management decisions. It's not exactly stable.'

'It couldn't possibly be a faster revolving door than at the hospital.'

'Is that what you're looking for—constancy?'

'I'd like to come to work every day and see the same faces. I'd like to get to know every dog out there by sight and have them be happy to see me.' *I'd really like not to come into work and find some animal I've spent two weeks nurturing back to health has declined and gone overnight.* 'I wouldn't mind working with them when they're healthy instead of only when they're sick.'

Maybe then she could get a bit of certainty back in her working life—if she couldn't get it in her personal one.

She stepped back a bit. 'Anyway, it's a moot point. I didn't get the job.'

'This time.'

True. It had been a year since the vacancy Gabe filled had opened up. That made the next one a whole year closer. Not everyone was wedded to the place as she was.

'Will you try again?'

'Maybe. Just don't *you* go for the next one.'

'I promise.'

His laugh was like fingers trailing up her skin. Seductive. Hypnotic. She let it coax a smile out of her.

'Careful. I'll start believing you're comfortable around me.'

It was testament to how he could winkle his way under her skin that she blurted, 'I'm *never* comfortable around you.'

Anyone else would have stepped back, offended. Gabe stepped forward and his eyes blazed into hers.

'Why?'

She could lie, she could mumble something with a passing resemblance to credibility. She could. But she didn't because he really wanted to know. 'You're always so intense.'

Although *always* wasn't strictly true. There'd been entire minutes the night they were together that he'd lain in languid half-sleep, his fingers tracing patterns on her skin, about as disarmed as a human being could be. But such moments had been as rare as some of the animals they cared for.

'I have a lot of passion,' he murmured.

Wasn't that the truth? In everything he did.

He frowned. 'I don't like that it makes you uncomfortable around me.'

'Uncomfortable doesn't necessarily mean unpleasant—' though this conversation certainly was leaning that way '—it just means I'm not…relaxed.'

'How can I change that?'

You can't. And there it was again. As many times in two days she'd realised her issue with Gabe was more about herself than him. She sighed. 'It's complicated.'

Something in his eyes shifted as he caught her drift. They gleamed. 'Good complicated or bad complicated?'

Really? You want me to spell it out? Fine.

'It's not getting any less…' She waved her hands as if that would help churn up words from the ether and fling them towards her struggling lips.

Gabe exhaled in the gaps between her speech, bringing their breathing into sync. An old zoo trick to help relax a stressed animal. It irritated her that it worked on her so immediately.

'Any less…?' he murmured.

But she wasn't that brave. 'You don't feel it?' she hedged.

'Depends on what you were about to say.' He shuffled closer and looked down on her. 'Are you talking about what happens to the air when we stand this close…?'

Sure enough the air around them seemed to thin and divest itself of its oxygen. She sucked in a pointless breath.

Okay. So he felt it.

'Or what happens to my blood when I touch you?' His thumb retraced its path across her cheek.

She just nodded.

His eyes darkened. 'That doesn't make me uncomfortable.'

You're not me. She turned away. 'It's not appropriate. We're at work.'

'I'm not working. Not till morning.'

'I am.'

'Yeah. You are.' He let the silence hang for a bit and lowered his hand. 'Until eight.'

She glanced back at him.

At the smile in his eyes.

At the badly disguised promise behind that.

He let her off the hook and returned to the monitor, hit rewind to view back what they'd missed while they'd been lost in each other.

Ingrid let her breath out slowly and quietly. She'd been foolish to go there at all. Just because she couldn't be mad at him any more for getting the job it didn't mean it was safe to let herself get close to him. Nothing else had changed for her.

One night was all well and good, but…longer? Trust was not something she gave easily these days.

They were colleagues, and maybe now they could be friends.

That was all.

CHAPTER SIX

December 30th

WATCHING GABE SLEEP was becoming a dangerous habit. Most people got less attractive when they were sleeping. They sagged and gaped and were somehow…diminished when unconscious. Gabe just got better with the relaxation of his muscles.

Softened.

But it hardly seemed fair to watch him, since she'd be mortified if he did the same thing to her when she was off shift.

She turned back to the monitor. Mjawi had emerged at first light from B-den for her morning salute to the dawn—squeezing, as always, out of the entrance hole and leaving the pups sleeping deep inside. A subordinate male immediately took the chance to crawl into the den and investigate. If it had been lion or hyena they were watching that would have been cause for alarm, but wild dogs were the closest thing to being caring that carnivores got, and every dog looked out for the future of the pack. Ingrid knew he'd nuzzle them to death before doing anything more sinister.

Mjawi thought a bit of puppy-sitting was just fine. She flopped down by the waterhole and enjoyed the fresh morning air. Ingrid zoomed one of the perimeter cameras in on her to check her condition.

It seemed hours and yet just moments until Gabe's raspy morning voice murmured from behind her.

'She looks good.'

Glossy coat, good clean muzzle, and as well fed as such a lean species could appear. 'She needed a break.'

'From a dozen pups? No doubt.'

Ingrid tipped her head back to look up at him. 'Are you truly expecting a dozen?'

Gabe shrugged. 'That's pretty common.'

Wow. From zero to twelve. That was some family. And here she was complaining about her shift from being one to one of five.

'Safety in numbers.' He shrugged. 'In the wild getting your pack size up is a priority if you want to survive. Family is all.'

Ingrid shifted against the uncomfortable thought that maybe that was what she was supposed to be doing. Her parents had done their job and got her to adulthood, and then they'd gone back again and brought more life into the world with the people they now loved—and they were working hard to get them to adulthood too. Her brothers and sisters were only babies—a mix of half and step-siblings—but they were family. And they might as well not have a big sister if she didn't get a handle on her unconventional family.

She glanced back at the empty entrance to B-den. That subordinate male wasn't complaining that he wasn't alpha, that he didn't get to have offspring of his own; he was just pitching in and doing what he could for the betterment of the pack.

Maybe the only person Ingrid was ultimately hurting was herself.

On screen, Mjawi jogged lightly back to the entrance to the den and squeezed her head and shoulders into the hole. Halfway in, her feet dug in and she started to retreat as the male emerged. The two of them met right at the entrance and a momentary battle for access broke out. As the male kicked and reared back the den entrance took quite a beating, and Ingrid suspended her breath and waited for it to cave in.

Gabe was up and out of the camp bed and halfway to unlocking the A-den hatch by the time the momentary flare-up settled.

'It's fine, Gabe,' Ingrid urged. 'He's out. She's gone back in.'

'How's the entrance tunnel?'

Ingrid stood aside so that he could get a good look on the monitor. 'Battered. But still holding.'

Though a clump of earth fell from its roof as they watched. She lifted her eyes to his.

'I think it's just a question of when, now,' he said, 'not if.'

'Should we break through?' Their estimations said there were just inches between Mjawi's tunnel and Ingrid's.

He thought about that long and hard. 'No. Not yet. But I think we're in for a long day.'

More earth sprinkled down across the entrance to the den. Ingrid pressed her lips together and tried to imagine a first-time mother—and a first-time tunnel-digger—knowing enough to get a dozen pups out in time.

Not likely.

'Just say the word.'

He turned and looked at her. 'Are you going to be okay if this doesn't end well?'

Occasional loss of life was a reality in being a vet nurse. And in running a zoo. 'Let's just do our best not to let that happen.'

Gabe nodded.

They watched the tunnel entrance until the earth found its natural stability again. Then Gabe left to shower and eat and be back in time for his shift. Ingrid splashed some milk from the drugs fridge into a wax-lined single-serve cereal packet that doubled as its own vessel and tucked into the crunchy flakes as she watched the other dogs investigating the morning. They frolicked until they flopped, exhausted, in the shade. But it would only take one to rouse the rest of the boisterous pack back into chaotic activity.

She smelled Gabe's return before hearing it. Soap and French aftershave were as good as a neon sign when you were working with the stinkiest species in the zoo. Her body half turned to him before she could temper its traitorous reaction.

At the last moment she turned her eagerness into a clumsy sort of update. 'No real change.'

Better that than have him see the flash of excitement she'd felt. He'd only been gone half an hour.

He strode from the bright morning light into the darkened room like some kind of archangel. Tall men had such a way of moving, and something about them being damp and smooth-shaven made that even harder to ignore.

She fought it—hard.

He stopped right up close to her, just behind her left shoulder. She could practically feel the amusement pumping off him. He knew what he was doing. He'd been standing extra close, whispering extra low, smiling extra sexy since she'd fumbled her way so badly out of the admission that she still responded to him physically.

Only it was more than physical—as her reaction of moments ago showed. It was *Gabe* she responded to, not just his body. It was *him* she wanted to talk to—for hours, to get deep under his skin, to see what made him tick and how he'd become the man he was. It was *his* mind that stimulated hers and his pain that hurt her.

'I'm going to grab some breakfast,' she lied, knowing her shift wasn't up for two hours yet, but knowing he would cover for her. 'See you later on.'

She was up and away from Gabe's *eau de gorgeous* and his high-frequency energy before he'd even acknowledged her words. She crossed the yard behind the night quarters and cut up an embankment on a set of stone steps that hadn't been used by the public for two decades.

A good hot shower would take her mind off Gabe. Or a good cold one. She just needed time away—a literal and emotional time-out. Working together so closely like this was bound to blur their usual boundaries. She just needed to get a better handle on her innermost thoughts and stop blurting them out.

Feeling them was one thing…

Indulging them was not an option.

A relationship was the last thing she wanted. Not when she was building herself a new career and future. Not when she was so determined to shore up her place in the organisation she'd worked at for so many years to bring her spinning world to a halt.

She'd allowed herself that one night with Gabe a year

ago because she'd believed it came parcelled up with its own expiry date. He was leaving. Except then he wasn't. The last-minute chance she'd thought she'd been exploiting had suddenly loomed long and open-ended in front of her, as unpredictable as the rest of her world.

She could forgive herself that one time because she hadn't known he was staying. This time she knew. This time there could be no forgiveness.

There could be no more 'times'.

Her job now was to push Gabriel Marque and his hard-jawed, purry-accented, broad-shouldered gorgeousness way back in her mind. Despite what her body thought was a good idea. Despite what her heart whispered.

Hearts were no way to run a life. They were way too capricious.

And when you were working hard to bring stability to your life inconstancy was not something to be encouraged.

All she wanted was a good job with a clear career path where she could build relationships with the people and animals she worked with. She didn't want complications. She didn't want tumult.

She didn't want Gabe.

Even if—very much—she did.

JUST FOR SOMETHING different she swung back, clean and emotionally shored up, via the visitors' side of the wild dog exhibit. Her path took her through the *Okavango Delta* exhibit, and passed lions, giraffe, rhino, zebra all resting in their enclosures. Meerkats. A serval. A mini-wetland dotted with flamingo and pygmy hippos.

Some lifted their heads, surprised to see a human up and about so early.

She rounded the thickly planted corner which opened out onto the viewing area for the African wild dogs. They were doing much what they had been when she'd left: lounging around with just one or two trying hard to goad the others back into play.

Two of them dashed back and forth, dodging and weaving in their version of a game of tag, splashing through the waterhole, skidding in the red earth and vocalising madly the whole time.

Ingrid's eyes lifted to the rear of the exhibit, where it backed onto the night quarters. She imagined Gabe in there, beyond the thick concrete wall, his intense eyes concentrating on the monitor. You could see the visitors' viewing bay on the camera that captured the whole exhibit, but she'd be a tiny khaki-coloured speck in the background. There was something dangerously appealing about imagining him hard at work while he didn't know she was watching. It was a little bit like watching him sleep.

It wasn't real if he didn't know.

One dog darted left to avoid its pack-mate and sprinted up the earth mounded against the night quarters. It spun to a halt right atop the dens and stood panting, waiting for the game to continue.

As she watched the dog lurched where it stood, braced its legs wide and looked sharply at the earth beneath its feet. It lurched again and leapt backwards, closer to the building.

Ingrid's stomach dropped the way the dog had and her feet started to move.

B-den was collapsing...

As she rounded the end of the exhibit pathway at full speed her mobile phone vibrated in her back pocket. She dragged it to her ear and uttered a breathless hello into the mouthpiece as she ran.

'Ingrid?' Gabe's deep, distressed voice barked. 'I need you.'

SHE FOUND HIM as she skidded around the corner of the night quarters. He tossed the last of several juicy carcass pieces into the holding area. 'We have to break through. Now.'

Oh, God...

'I've blocked the entrance to A-den. You get ready by the hatch. I'll get the pack in.'

Blocking the entrance was a risk. If Mjawi tried to move the pups using the entrance and found it blocked she might take them back into the collapsing den.

'What if she won't come in?' Ingrid couldn't safely break through to B-den with Mjawi still in it. She'd take her head off.

'I'll get her out.'

That sounded dangerously determined. 'Wait, Gabe...'

'I'll get her out,' he said, hard and certain.

It took only ten minutes to get the bulk of the pack into the night quarters. The very food-motivated wild dogs did everything as a pack, so once the first one caught wind of the carcass pieces it followed its nose into the holding area and fell on the sheep's leg. Its excited vocalisation immediately drew the others.

Ingrid had the hatch open and her digging tools in hand, ready to go the moment Mjawi was out of range. The monitors showed sprays of dirt being flung from the entrance to B-den as Mjawi tried to dig out some of the earth that had fallen.

Gabe swung around the doorway and leaned in. 'Everyone but Mjawi is in. I'm going to lure her out long enough for you to break through.'

'What? How?' Luring was a mile from approved protocol, and it would mean he was technically *in* the exhibit with uncontained dogs. Wild dogs. Her chest squeezed down into a tight fist.

'If we do our jobs right it'll be too fast to be dangerous. Mjawi will be distracted and the pups will be too startled to respond when you break through.'

If *we do our jobs right*...

Her uncertainty must have shown on her face. Gabe crossed straight over to her and curled one hand behind her neck. 'If we wait for other staff to arrive it could collapse.'

Concern mixed freely with the urgency in his eyes. He didn't want to do it, either. But her mind whizzed through every other option and there really were none that would mean the safety of the pups.

'You can't go in with her,' she whispered, staring up at him. He was strong, but not that strong, and a mother protecting her pups was capable of anything.

'I can't *not*. Besides, she likes me—remember?' He pulled her closer and pressed his lips to her clammy forehead. His brave smile died. 'Just be fast, *cherie*.'

If her speed reduced the danger for him, she'd dig like a demon.

Without thinking she reached up, pressed both her hands to his cheeks, and pulled him down to meet her lips halfway. If he was going to risk his life, she wasn't having him do it thinking she still hated him.

Because she didn't—and they both knew it.

Courage flowed from his lips into hers and warmed her enough to move again. 'Good luck.'

He smiled as he pulled away, hit redial on his phone, held it up and said, 'Put me on speaker.'

And then he was gone. Off to do something dangerous and against all rules. There was some hope that Mjawi's surprise at his unprecedented appearance inside the fence would stall her just long enough for him to stay safe.

She answered her ringing phone.

'Get in the tunnel.' Gabe's voice came through the tinny speaker. 'And get ready to break through. Don't make a sound. The moment you hear me call you, do it.'

He lowered the phone then, but she could hear him clanking and clanging as he opened the access door to the exhibit—intentionally loud, perhaps, to draw Mjawi's attention—and then he paused.

She paused, too, halfway through the hatch. Listening.

'Okay, I'm going in.'

A wave of anxiety washed through her that he was risking himself like this for them. For her. But being paralysed with fear wasn't going to help Gabe. Only her speed and accuracy would. She commando-crawled fully into A-den, and then beyond it into her hand-dug adjoining tunnel, and got herself positioned with her right arm tightly bent ahead of her.

And then she waited.

Through the speaker on her phone she could hear the sound of Gabe running—out into the exhibit, presumably—and then calling out to Mjawi in French.

'Viens ici, la chienne!'

She pressed her thumb over her phone's speaker to muffle it and the words became a tingle against her flesh. She thought she heard a scrabbling from beyond the thin sandy membrane between the dens, and then a moment later her phone cried out in Gabe's voice.

'*Now,* Ingrid!'

She dropped her mobile, punched forward with her trowel, and pushed her fist straight through what little dirt remained packed between the dens. High-pitched surprise greeted her, and a split-second glimpse of several pairs of blackcurrant eyes glinting back at her from a dark, stinky mass of furry bodies.

Ingrid pulled her fist back towards her and in the same moment started to reverse crawl out of the tunnel. She spidered backwards, breathing erratically, flung her legs through the hatch and used the point of the trowel to pierce the inflatable block sealing A-den entrance, then dragged that back with her out of the hatch.

She heard the repeat clanging of the exhibit gate as her feet hit the floor and she slammed the door shut.

Gabe was safe.

She was safe.

Now if only the pups could be safe.

'What happened?' He burst around the corner, pale and sweaty. 'Are you okay?'

'I'm fine. I'm fine.'

He pulled her hard against him and curled his arms around her head. She felt inelegant and uncomfortable with her face pressed into his armpit, but she wasn't moving for all the wine in France. He just stood there. Holding her hard.

As if he was never going to let go.

An odd noise finally drew both of them out of their adrenalin-fuelled embrace. A shoving. A rustling.

A snuffling.

They both looked at the phone held in Gabe's fist, still set to speaker phone. Ingrid looked at her empty left hand. Then at the hatch.

'I dropped my phone,' she mouthed.

The snuffling continued and resolved into a gentle mewling, some licking—the sounds of a mother comforting her babies. Together, Ingrid and Gabe sank into the chairs in front of the monitoring station and listened to the unexpected audio-feed while staring intently at the entrance to B-den on the monitors, which lost increasing amounts of earth clods with every minute that passed. The babies scrambled for Mjawi's reassurance. She gave it. Then they heard the sound of big paws scraping at the earth, heavy, doggy breath chuffing hard up against Ingrid's phone and experimenting with its taste.

At one stage Mjawi must have pushed it with her nose, because it seemed to slide away from them and land with a *thunk* on the floor of the slightly echoey, slightly lower A-den. They both looked straight at the hatch.

Silence.

Silence and then…a hint of something else. The snuffling resumed. Very small snuffling. Very inquisitive snuffling.

Ingrid opened her mouth to speak. Gabe pressed dirty fingers against her lips with one hand and set his phone to mute with the other. Then he lowered his fingers—but not far. He rested them on her cheek.

'A pup has moved over,' she whispered, excited.

He nodded and concentrated even harder on the sounds coming from her phone. More mewling. More pawing. And then the phone was muffled, as though someone had sat on it.

She's in A-den!

Gabe's wide eyes echoed her thought.

A flurry of rearrangement followed, and the high-pitched chatter from the pups continued. They rediscovered the phone and mouthed it and smothered it, generally explored the new toy.

And then—just when they'd begun to rely on it—something rolled on it and the signal was disconnected.

Ingrid stared at Gabe. 'They hung up on us.'

He laughed first, quiet and low now that the pups were just a few feet away, and that only made it all the funnier. Ingrid joined him, trying hard not to let it out. His hazel eyes sparkled with a mix of emotion as the adrenalin faded away, but he kept them locked on her.

They stared at each other for a dangerously long time.

'Five? Maybe six?' she whispered.

His dark brows folded.

She sat back. 'The number of pups I saw.'

His eyes widened. 'You *saw* them?'

'I saw fur and eyes. Just for a moment. It was hard to distinguish individual shapes, but I'm playing it back in my head and I'm sure there were five or six pairs of eyes.'

'How did they look?'

'Scared.'

He snorted. 'I think we all were. Mjawi looked terrified, but she ran me down anyway.'

There was something engagingly attractive about a

man who was perfectly willing to admit when he was frightened out of his skin. 'Show me?' she said.

They played the footage back and Ingrid mentally followed what was on screen with what she'd been doing and hearing underground. The moment Gabe entered the exhibit and started calling out Mjawi shot like a bullet out of the den, paused and crouched low as she spotted him, and then pelted straight for him.

Brave, given her pack was entirely absent, but determined to protect her babies. Ingrid could only imagine the pressing conflict of having a predator so close to her litter but knowing the den was crumbling around them, too. Wild animals were nothing if not outstanding prioritisers.

On screen, Gabe flung himself back into the night quarters and slammed the door shut. Mjawi skidded up against it bodily. Then she turned and jogged straight back to her litter.

'Just seconds,' Ingrid mused. 'It felt like eternity.'

Gabe snorted again. 'Tell me about it.'

'We're going to get in such trouble.'

He shook his head and locked eyes with her. 'I don't care. Do you?'

Did she? Breaching procedure like that and putting themselves at risk was technically a dismissible offence. She'd just poised the career—the organisation—that meant so much to her right on the edge of the toilet bowl and pressed flush. Everything she'd worked for. Everything she'd planned for.

Did she care?

'No.'

They'd done the right thing. They'd saved the pups.

If they got drummed out of the zoo for that it would be a pretty good way to go.

His smile just amplified the reward of what they'd done. 'Thought not.'

And then, before she could do more than take a hasty breath, he leaned in and breached the short distance between their seats and kissed her. Hard. Hot. All that nervous energy had to go somewhere, and Ingrid gladly let it flow straight into her. Deep down into that place that had been cold and empty ever since she'd last let it be filled with Gabe's energy.

His fingers forked up into her hair, closed gently around the strands and eased her head back so that their mouths could fit together better. Ingrid curled her fingers in the two halves of his shirt to pull herself closer to him. One of them was officially on shift, so one of them was being highly unprofessional, but she didn't know who and, as his lips moved over her skin, she really didn't care.

Her usual standards didn't stand a chance when Gabe was around.

'I've missed you,' he whispered when finally they had to breathe.

Sensual haze robbed her of speech. His words swam, lost, around her mind, looking for somewhere to connect and form meaning. He stroked the hair from her face and snared her gaze with his. She was as slow as a newborn babe to focus on him. When she did, she saw the uncertainty there, mingling with the desire.

'I didn't understand why you walked away,' he whispered.

She made herself find speech. 'The job…'

His eyes narrowed just slightly. 'That's all?'

A sudden tension washed through her. She nodded. 'It wasn't because I was staying?'

Thump, thump... Her heart got in on the conversation. 'Why would it be?'

His brows dipped. 'Just a pattern in my life. Women back home didn't last long once they realised I wasn't going to gild their future with Marque euros.'

She matched his frown. 'You thought that was what I was doing?'

A shadow flickered across his gaze. 'I thought it was similar. I've never had problems getting women—'

I'll bet...

'—just keeping them for more than a few weeks. One night, in your case. A personal best.'

She shook her head. 'That was—'

'The job. I know.' His eyes grew darker. 'It finally dawned on me that I was never going to find my kindred spirit amongst my family's world. And women of any kind were in short supply in the field in Africa. Then I came here.'

'Where you had no trouble sampling the local wares.'

His brows dipped again and he shrugged. 'I've had a couple of dates in Australia, but you won't find anyone in the zoo who can say they were one of them.'

Anyone else. 'Why?'

He thought about that. 'Because I wasn't looking for just anyone. I wasn't really looking at all.'

'Then what...?' Warmth flooded her cheeks.

'What happened that night?' He dropped his hand away from hers and sat back.

She felt the little loss to her core.

'You finally noticed me.'

It was all she could do not to gape at him. *Finally?*

She'd noticed him long before he'd even been introduced. And the fact he didn't know that made her inexplicably angry. 'False modesty doesn't sit well on you, Gabe.'

He straightened, and it put a few more necessary inches between them. 'Why do you think we ended up together?'

She shrugged. 'I assumed I was a challenge.'

He stared at her. 'No, you didn't. The woman I took home that night didn't have doubts about herself. You felt it as much as I did.'

Her skin shrank against her bones, constricting and limiting. Every part of her wanted to run. She couldn't let him know how deep her emotions ran. 'Felt what?'

'The thing that we had between us. That we still have.'

One by one Gabe had stripped back her layers, the barriers between them. But she wasn't going that easily. 'We just risked our lives together. That's a powerful aphrodisiac.'

'It has nothing to do with just now. I've wanted to kiss you since I walked in here on Christmas morning. And you twitch if I so much as brush against you.' He leaned back in, extra close, and breathed the challenge against her lips. 'You still feel it.'

She lifted her chin. 'Maybe I just don't like being touched.'

His eyes darkened, but this time it wasn't a mysterious shadow. 'Oh, *cherie*. Don't ask me to believe that.'

She *had* liked being touched. She'd practically bloomed in his hands.

'You kissed me back just now,' he pointed out.

She tossed her head. 'Maybe you're just a really good kisser.'

His smile said he knew exactly what she was doing. Exposure didn't sit comfortably on her. 'Let's take that as a given. So why are we wasting time? We could be kissing right now.'

They almost were. So she sat back. 'The moment's passed. I don't just kiss on command.'

He locked eyes again. 'What if I asked nicely? What if I begged?'

Breath escaped from her throat, leaving her speech tight and strained. 'You're too proud to beg. Besides, if it was just kisses you wanted you could walk into the staffroom and find a dozen willing participants.'

He shrugged. 'I only want *your* kisses.'

Her sigh physically hurt. 'Why?'

'Because they fit me.'

She stared at him.

'Because they haunt me.'

Every word he spoke cut her straight to the heart. They were words she'd always wanted to hear. And they were words she could not accept. But returning them like an unwanted gift…where did she even begin to do that?

'Are all the Marque boys this smooth?' she hedged.

'Smoother, generally speaking. I'm the rough-round-the-edges one, if you recall.' He stared. 'So, would you like me to beg?'

Not demeaning himself. Not for her. 'No, I would not. It's not going to happen, Gabe.'

Damn him and his height. He had so much further to lean and he gobbled up another few inches now.

'Why not? The job is no longer between us.' He

traced her jaw with a fingertip. 'You ignite under my touch. We were born to be together.'

Her skin tightened again. Any more and bones were going to start poking through. 'Because it's not just up to you.'

His snort was as good and every bit as challenging as a bull in an arena. 'Look me in the eye and tell me you don't want me.'

And there it was. Ingrid knew she couldn't stare into those all-knowing eyes and convince him she wasn't interested. And she couldn't hide behind the job any more. But anything else just wasn't possible.

'I don't want a relationship. With anyone.' Just saying it aloud was awful. Was she condemning herself to being alone for ever?

That stopped him cold. 'Why?'

'Because I don't. I know your monumental French ego will make this all about you, but it's not. It's about me. And *I* make the decisions about *me*.'

'I don't believe you,' he said, eyes narrow.

'Your loss.'

'You're pushing me away?'

'I'm trying to.'

'Why?'

'I'm not actually required to defend myself to you, Gabriel Marque.'

'No. But I'm asking you to tell me why you're rejecting me. Do me the courtesy.'

Rejecting me. The words came from way down deep, where child-like Gabe hid.

'I'm not…' She sighed. 'It's not rejection. It's choice. Free choice.'

'You're choosing to be alone rather than be with me?'

'I'm choosing—' *work, my career, the safe path* '—to decline.'

He slumped back in his chair. 'I see.'

No. He didn't. The wounded look at the back of his confused eyes confirmed that. But telling him the truth was just too messy. And too hard. 'Come on, Gabe. You're seriously going to pout because I choose to put my needs before yours? That's not you.'

And lying wasn't *her*, but it was coming more and more easily. Desperate times…

'It's not that I'm not attracted to you. I'm just choosing not to do anything about it.'

His lips pressed together, as if in trying to make it easier for him she'd said something horrible.

'You speak as though any of this is in our hands. As if there is a choice.' He pushed up onto his feet. 'The fact you can make that choice without blinking tells me everything I need to know.'

And with that he was gone, out into the bright morning light. She'd cover his duties until he was able to come back, but then she'd go. It was time to end the lazy make-believe world they'd created for themselves in their concrete bunker.

The pups were safe. Either of them could manage to vaccinate, chip and weigh them alone if Mjawi left the den. It would just take twice as long. She'd been foolish to let that be her excuse for staying.

She and Gabe would just go back to politely ignoring each other. Life would go on. The sun would keep rising.

It just wouldn't shine as brightly.

IT HAD TAKEN Gabe two furious circuits of the still-waking zoo to burn off the uncomfortable sensation of being

judged and found lacking. But then he'd walked back
in and found Ingrid with bag and keys in hand—just
waiting to get out of there—and that utterly innocent
gesture had undone all his good work.

Even the dogs had conspired to be utterly uninterest-
ing all day after she'd gone home, and they'd failed to
take his mind off the fact that, while he hadn't been able
to get her out of his head for the past twelve months,
Ingrid was entirely take-it-or-leave-it about him.

Not the greatest stroke for his ego.

Section staff had come to check on the pups' progress and gone again. His supervisor had hit the roof
when he'd heard how they'd managed to pull off the
den-swap, and then the director had got called in for a
departmental investigation. They'd talked it all through
and concluded that there had been no other viable option and that Gabe's actions were warranted. Just not
entirely desirable. He'd done his best to play down Ingrid's role and keep her from direct scrutiny. This place
was her whole world. She didn't need any black marks
against her name if she was hoping to get zookeeping
work in the future.

Her whole world.

The vulnerable part inside of him leapt on that. Was
she so focussed on her career that she didn't want anything getting in the way? But a zookeeper was the *perfect* person for her to form a relationship with. Who
better to understand the pressures of the unpredictable
rosters, the extra hours, the emotional attachment, the
highs of success and the devastating lows of the fail-
ures?

They were a great match professionally.

God knew they were physically suited, too. That instant *whoosh* when they touched; the perpetual hum that existed when they were in a room together; the simmering passion that she kept so buttoned-down most of the time…

He'd never wanted to conquer and cherish in such equal measure.

But obviously being good together wasn't enough to counter whatever it was he lacked. He'd managed much bigger disappointments in life, but always when he had some understanding and control of the situation. He didn't do powerless. It was infuriating not to measure up to a bar you couldn't see.

The beast in him paced in circles that grew tighter and tighter as the afternoon wore on.

'How are they doing?'

He spun around at the tentative words behind him. The tautness of his muscles was amplified in his voice. 'I wondered if you were coming back.' And just like that he understood his slowly growing tension.

Her brows lifted just slightly at his tone and her entire body stiffened. 'I'm not late.'

'You weren't here. What if something had happened?'

'Then I was only twenty minutes away.'

'Your mobile is probably inside a wild dog.'

'I left my home number on the observation sheet.'

She might as well have gouged it into the table; it stank of her desperation to be gone.

'You must really want the money. I thought for sure you'd swap shifts with someone else.'

'I want the experience, not the money.'

Right. That was why she'd stayed. He should have realised it was nothing to do with him. He swallowed the rest of his umbrage before he said something even more inappropriate.

'Are *you* staying?' she offered, to break the silence.

'We're too close now to bail.'

Her lips thinned. 'I didn't *bail*. I went home. And I came back for my shift. I'm doing my job.'

'*Oui*, I can always rely on you to do the minimum, Ingrid.'

Her gasp was overly loud in the concrete building. 'That's not fair. I work very hard.'

It wasn't fair. But he wasn't feeling fair. He was feeling hurt. And defensive. And a tiny bit curious. If he pressed the right button would he get the answers he was after?

He shrugged. 'At some things.'

'What's that supposed to mean?'

'It means that giving any part of yourself to someone else is hard work, and you're not up to it.'

'Are we back to this, Gabe?'

'Too hard to talk about?'

'I'm not enjoying hurting your feelings,' she hissed.

'My feelings are just fine. Thanks for the concern.'

'What do you want from me?'

'I want to know why you're backing away from this thing we have.'

'I'm not.'

'It started the day after you let yourself be with me.'

'I told you. I thought you'd—'

'Yeah, you told me. But I don't believe it was about the job. I think that's what you told yourself. What was really going on, Ingrid?'

Her face grew strained and distressed. 'Please don't make me say it again...'

She didn't want to hurt him. Even now her compassion moved him. And infuriated him. He pushed it down hard. He wanted to know. 'What is it, Ingrid? Holding out for something better?'

'Gabe—'

But the path to self-destruction felt too good. And any second now he'd have the truth. He'd know what it was that he was lacking for woman after woman after woman. 'I want to know, Ingrid. What kind of a man would it take to crack your hard exterior?'

That knocked her back physically in the doorway. He saw the impact of it in the slight curve of her body as it accommodated the pain. Like catching a football.

He was an ass.

'I'm not hard.' But the affirmation was quiet enough to be doubtful. And tight enough to be right on the edge of a deeper emotion. 'I'm just careful.'

'What have I done to deserve such caution? Am I a man who betrays trust? Who lies or sleeps around or steals?'

She spoke, but he didn't hear the mumbled words. She shook her hair across her downturned face.

'Huh?' His best French one-shoulder shrug. A classic Marque trait. It occurred to him that this emotional post-mortem was classic Marque, too. Sometimes he realised how much of his parents he had in him.

She cleared her throat. 'I said before. It's not about you.'

'Yeah, you did. But I don't believe you.'

'I can't help that. Your insecurities are your own to deal with.'

For seconds time stopped. How proud his father would have been of a son who flayed a woman alive rather than face his own inadequacies. Ingrid didn't want him—so be it. Why wasn't he able to take that like a man and walk away with his dignity intact? Why was he demeaning himself like this for a woman? For love?

In the same moment that word hit his consciousness a single tear hit the floor at Ingrid's feet.

He froze, breathless, and stared at the tiny glistening spot.

He'd never got over her. Despite a year of trying. And now he was foisting the blame for his own weakness onto his beautiful, bright Ingrid—punishing her for not sharing his feelings. For not loving him back sufficiently. Just because *he* wanted it.

And she was bowed before him, weeping.

His eyes fell shut. He was his father's son.

He tried to speak and failed. He swallowed and tried again.

'I'll sleep in my car,' he finally murmured, though it was more of a sigh. Apologies weren't going to help. Not right now. The kindest thing he could do for her was just get out of her face and leave her in peace. 'If you need me, call me from the feed shed phone.'

She nodded again. Still silent. Eyes still downcast.

He collected up a few things and squeezed past her in the doorway. He stopped halfway. Turned out he was too *not* like his father to walk out of there without apologising for his behaviour.

'I'm sorry, Ingrid,' he breathed, touching her shoulder. 'I accept your choice. I won't raise it again.'

He wouldn't. Though it would kill him always to wonder what it was that she wanted. What it was that he lacked.

He pressed his lips together even as he pressed past

her in the doorway. Then he was through and heading off into the growing darkness. The sounds of the zoo at night wafted all around him. The throaty rumbles of lion grumbling, the overhead clucking of roosting egrets, the sudden puffs of elephants settling for the night.

The half-choked sound of a woman's sob.

Gabe forced himself to keep walking. Though it was the hardest thing he'd ever had to do.

She didn't want him the way he wanted her.

Time to deal with it and move on.

CHAPTER SEVEN

December 31st

THE CCTV CAMERAS had infra-red light on them but Ingrid didn't need it. Not tonight. Tonight the fullness of the moon as it reached its zenith spilled soft light across the whole exhibit and bathed everything in beauty and silence.

Enjoy it while you can. Tomorrow night—tonight, really—the local council had a big New Year's Eve celebration on the shore of the river right next door to the zoo. There'd be thumping music and the cheering of families right up until midnight.

Great. Just what she and Gabe needed to highlight the awkwardness between them even more. The celebration of a new year. New beginnings. Resolutions. Letting go of the past.

Easier said than done.

She'd done the right thing; stepping back before anything further happened between them. Before she got more attached. More immersed.

If it hurt this much now, imagine leaving it a few more weeks.

She'd busied herself the moment he left. The moment she had the strength to peel herself off the doorframe holding her up. She'd set up everything they needed—workbench, scales, medical equipment, microchip scanner, hessian sacks—so if Mjawi emerged for long enough she wouldn't lose time scrabbling to get the gear assembled.

Lucky she worked with this sort of gear daily at the hospital, because it meant she could still function even while totally numb. Setting up the table, calibrating the equipment, estimating the dosages. Totally automatic. Why ripping Gabe permanently from her life—her future—should make her feel so dead inside...that was something she could look at another day. In the future, when she wasn't feeling so raw and didn't need to concentrate.

The distant future.

Now she stared, hypnotised, at the tranquil exhibit shown brightly on the monitor in the darkened room. Just as quiet but so much prettier than the ugly ache inside her. Like a ripple or an echo of the things they'd said to each other, softened and eased with distance.

On the outside, anyway.

Inside she was still churning—way down deep where her heart, not her head, ruled play. The part that was hoarse from shouting that she'd done the wrong thing in freeing herself from Gabe.

Her eyes lost focus on the screen.

She didn't want a relationship and she couldn't have anything less with Gabe. He wasn't a man you could walk away from easily. She'd found that out once already. At least back then she'd been able to kid herself it was all about the job. She'd taken her anger then and used it to mask the disturbing sense that something really important had just died.

Ingrid sighed and murmured aloud, 'We'll never know.'

As if roused by her soft words, a dark shadow emerged from the entrance to A-den. Her heart leapt just slightly but she didn't move from her seat. Another dog would swoop in the moment Mjawi left the pups unsupervised.

The shadow walked quietly down to her spot beside the waterhole and lay down.

Not sat.

Lay.

When she was just having a brief rest Mjawi dropped to her haunches, but when she was planning a long nap—Ingrid sat bolt upright, her pulse starting to thrum—she lay on her side.

Exactly like that.

Her eyes flicked back to the den entrance. No other dog was skulking about to assume puppy-sitting duties. They all slept soundly around the exhibit.

The pups were unsupervised.

Her heart lurched just as her mind cried out. *Gabe!*

Use the feed shed phone, he'd said. But that was across the compound; she could assess two pups in the time it would take to unlock the building and get to the phone. And every pup that was vaccinated tonight was one day further from being susceptible to the virus taking hold in the pack.

Her eyes snapped back to the hatch. To everything she needed all lined up near it, ready to go. It really wasn't a choice. She knew what Gabe would want her to do.

In a heartbeat she was up, muffling the sound of unlocking the padlocks on the hatch and carefully removing them from their catches. Then she fixed on a night-vision headlamp and slipped her hands into a pair of heavy-duty gardening gloves with the putrid waste the dogs left lying around the holding yards already ground in. She slipped on a medical gown, tossed the hessian sacks over her shoulder, glanced once more at the monitor to make sure Mjawi hadn't moved…then carefully opened the hatch.

Eight pairs of bright, inquisitive, fearless eyes stared back at her.

'Hey…' she murmured, low and non-threatening. They shifted—like a single writhing being—away from the hatch and the unfamiliar creature suddenly framed in it, scrabbling over her poor beleaguered mobile phone.

'It's okay. I won't hurt you.' They remained alarmed but didn't cry out. If they did she'd have just seconds to slam the door before Mjawi came skidding back into the den. 'Well, maybe just a tiny sting,' she whispered, 'but it's going to keep you safe and healthy.'

Her low voice seemed to soothe them. She wondered briefly if they'd grown accustomed to hearing her through the hatch. She glanced at the monitor for signs of any adult life. Still nothing.

'So who's coming first?' She bundled a folded sack into the den and quickly scooped three of the pups into it. Dark enough and snug enough to feel secure even as they were being handled by a human. She kept the monitor in her peripheral vision as she placed the writhing sack on the workbench. She stripped off one glove to prepare the vaccine, then loaded a microchip into a bigger syringe.

'Here we go…'

She lifted the first pup out of the sack and tucked it close to her gown with her gloved hand. She effortlessly delivered the vaccine into its rump with the other. With the baggy skin so typical of puppies, and the stoic nature so typical of its species, it barely blinked at the small sting. She examined its rear end to determine gender, and then sat the wide-eyed, blinking pup in the scales and got a start weight. Finally she caught up a scruff of neck skin and injected the tiny microchip in between the muscle and skin, then slipped the animal straight back into the bag with its litter-mates.

While the pups consoled each other, she scrawled a scientific kind of shorthand onto her notepad. Identification, gender, microchip number and identifying features.

Then it was on to pup number two.

'Gabe's going to be very sorry he missed this,' she said softly to the second pup. 'He really wants you guys to be strong and healthy. He's worked so hard to make sure you all make it to adulthood.' She flipped the surprised animal over and checked its genitals. A boy. 'You'll like Gabe. Everyone does. He's worked with all your wild cousins…' Jab with the vaccination. Quick physical check for condition, then onto the scales. 'You couldn't have someone more dedicated or determined to help save your species looking after you.'

She slipped the second pup back in with its siblings and went for the third, glancing at the monitor again in between.

'He's not always the easiest to understand,' she murmured, scanning number three with the chip-reader to make sure she hadn't already handled it. 'Maybe because he's French, or maybe just because he's a man.

We think very differently, human males and human females…' Vaccine. Weight. Microchip. And the whole time she kept up her gentle monologue. 'It's kind of our thing. But we all keep trying because we all want to find the right mate for us. Just like your mum and dad did…'

She returned the third pup to the sack, scribbled down its identifying features and then slid the stinky glove back on. 'Not that I'm saying he's meant to be *my* mate,' she said to the unconcerned pups as she lifted them carefully back into the den, 'and not because I believe love is for ever…'

She paused, frowned, and then reached for three new pups.

'Love doesn't last. I learned that the hard way,' she told the bag of puppies as she prepared three new vaccines and three sets of microchip injections. The bag wriggled and shifted on the table, but the pups stayed quiet in their warm, dark place. Good survival instincts. She checked the monitor again. Mjawi still slept.

'My parents split up after twenty years together. Turns out they only stayed together for me. All that unhappiness for me.' She carefully separated pup number four, and brought it out of the bag. 'Makes a girl wonder what else in my life they were faking.' She checked its underside. 'You get it; you're a girl. Imagine your whole life being based on a lie.' Both injections, and onto the scales.

'Is it any wonder I just want to do well here? Make a future for myself? To have something that's real and mine and won't change every five minutes. Huh?'

The tiny pup blinked its enormous black eyes at her, as though trying to empathise.

'Yeah, you get it.' She slid the female pup back into

the bag and separated the next one. 'Gabe thinks it's personal,' she confessed to it, 'but it's not. If I was going to let myself love someone it would totally be him. He's gorgeous, compassionate, bright, driven. I don't care what his family does, or who they are. I just like him for *him*.' Onto the scales. '*Seriously* like him.' Her thumb caressed the soft space between the pup's ears and she stared at the curious compassionate face tipped up at her. Its innocence made her heart squeeze. And it made her confess aloud what she'd not even let herself acknowledge internally. 'Love him, really.'

A ton of long-carried emotional pressure floated off her burdened back.

She loved Gabe.

Despite everything she believed, she'd gone and let herself actually fall in love with him. A year ago, probably. She'd just written the pain off as bitterness. And believed her own lies.

The little pup in her hands sighed, like a rotund little barometer of her mood.

'Not that it matters,' she said tightly, finishing it up and returning it to the sack, 'because I can't let anything happen between us. I can't risk that.'

Pup number six was already entranced by her voice and seemed entirely happy to pick up her monologue where the previous one had left it. She checked its gender first. 'You'll get to see him every day, and you're female so I know you'll be as much a sucker for those gorgeous eyes and French accent as I am. Let me give you a tip right now. He has tough standards for others— which I think is a good thing; it makes you want to do well to please him. But he has even tougher ones for himself. It's because of his family; seems like they're a bit heavy on expectation and light on acceptance.'

Something about finally admitting her true feelings for Gabe—even if only to a sack full of wild puppies—had opened up a tidal gate of awareness. She felt as if she was finally seeing him for the man he really was.

Too late.

Pup number six squeaked when she injected the microchip, and Ingrid's eyes flew to the monitor. Out in the exhibit Mjawi lifted her head for an eternity between heartbeats, but then flopped back down, relaxed. Ingrid's thumb stroked the pup back into silence.

'So,' she said, tumbling two of the three back into the den and collecting up the final two into the sack with their sibling. 'Gabe really needs someone to love him for exactly who he is—to convince him how amazing his dedication and determination are. And that can't be me,' she told pup number seven. He really seemed to empathise. 'So I have to hope it will be someone else. Even if that's hard to watch.' Gentle shot in the haunches. Quick weighing on the scales. 'And it will be.'

She treated the final pup. It sat happily in her hands, confident and unafraid, and she wondered if it was the same one she'd seen emerge briefly from the den before Mjawi shooed it back inside days earlier. It had the hallmarks of a leader.

'Well, there you go, little one,' she whispered, putting it back into the den with its siblings and feeling inexplicably sad. 'This has been the most amazing way to spend Christmas, and even though I won't see you again up close like this I want you to know that I'll remember it. For ever.'

And not just because of them.

She reached past them and retrieved her mangled mobile phone. Then she gave them one final look, turned off her head-lamp, swung the den door closed and locked it securely, and released a long, aching breath.

Discovering love and having an experience like that all in the same half-hour… She rested her forehead on the cold steel and let the cool of the hatch door soak into her warm cheeks.

'You rang?'

She spun at the deep, soft voice. Gabe stood leaning on the doorframe she'd used just hours ago to hold her up. How had he known to come? More importantly… how long had he been there?

'The pups—'

'I know,' he murmured, holding up his phone. 'You rang me.'

Confusion boiled in her mind, and though she heard the words it was moments before she could make sense of them.

'I didn't.'

'Someone did.'

She glanced down at the ruined phone in her hand. Its little screen glowed with half-life and displayed a number on its screen. Gabe's number.

The pups—had one of them sat on the recall button?

Her throat tightened horribly. 'Could you hear?'

His gaze was steady. 'Enough to know you needed me.'

She let her breath out carefully. Okay…so he'd only heard some of it.

But then he stepped into the little room. 'Enough to know you love me.'

Agony washed through her in a hot rush and her throat closed right over. He'd heard it all.

'I suppose it never occurred to you to stop listening?' she croaked.

He shook his head. 'No.'

'It was just…conversation. To keep the pups calm. I would have said anything.'

He stepped in again. 'But you didn't say just anything. You talked about me.'

'I…' But what could she say that wouldn't make it worse? 'Can we just discuss the pups, please?'

He nodded, but his eyes stayed locked on hers. 'I want to talk about the fact you love me first.'

Oh, God…

He stepped in again, and Ingrid stumbled backwards.

'You pushed me away to protect yourself,' he said.

She shook her head. 'I told you I didn't want a relationship.'

'You didn't tell me why. You didn't tell me how much your parents' divorce affected you.'

Old pain flared up. 'I'm an adult. I'm not supposed to be affected by it. I'm supposed to understand it.'

'You're their child first and an adult second.'

His empathy almost undid her. 'Did they think it was going to hurt me less if they waited until I left home?' she whispered.

'They probably did.'

'They have no idea how it hurt me.'

'Then tell them.'

Her pain morphed into a razor-sharp laugh. 'I can't *tell* them.'

'Why not?'

'Because they'll be devastated.'

'So instead you carry it alone—all that hurt and sorrow? Yours to bear?'

'They'll think I hate them.'

'Do you?'

Would it burn this much if she hated them? Or did it only ache because she didn't? Like with Gabe.

'Love hurts,' she blurted.

His eyes softened and he stepped right up to her, caressed her cheek. 'I'm sorry. It's not supposed to.'

'If they didn't love each other then how do I know they loved *me*? What if they were faking that, too?'

'You're their daughter. Of course they love you.'

She threw her hands up. 'I believed they loved each other.'

He stared at her long and hard. Nodded. 'From what you've told me they cared enough to let each other go with respect. Freeing them up to find true love.'

She stared at him, his handsome features shifting and welling through the tears in her eyes. 'How can they trust what they've found *is* love?'

'How can they?' He cocked his head. 'Or how can *you*?'

Her breath halted.

His murmur was lower. 'You *did* break it off with me a year ago because I was staying, didn't you?'

She pressed her lips together. Nothing she said now could be good.

'But not because I wasn't good enough, which is what I feared.' His fingers slid round to rest on her nape. 'You broke it off because I *was* good enough. And that scared you.'

'No…'

'Me leaving meant you could indulge the connection

between us and then weep as I headed for the airport a few weeks later.'

No...

'But me staying... That wasn't an option—because that would require you to take a risk.'

Realisation rushed through her.

'What if we made a mistake?' she breathed. 'Like my parents? Discovering five years into their relationship that they'd made the wrong choice and then sticking it out for another decade and a half because they had to.'

'Because they *chose* to. They wanted to protect you.'

'Then they should have stayed together!' The words burst out of some place way deep down inside. Confused anger rushed through her veins. She pulled away from Gabe's gentle touch. 'I just wanted them to love each other.'

'And I want my parents to love me differently. But we can't make it so. They're not perfect just because they're parents.'

'Love is supposed to be for ever,' she said, much softer now.

'*Oui.* It is.' He stroked her hair back from her face. 'But it's not faultless, and it's not easy. And staying together when the love has gone only destroys you, I think. Or those around you.'

She blinked up at him.

'My parents don't have the strength of character to release each other,' he said. 'To be free to find true happiness instead of slowly dying inside. It'll take them their whole lives to realise, and by then it will be too late. And my brothers might have gone with them.' He lifted his eyes back to her. 'So if anyone should question love, it's me.'

'But you don't?'

'I celebrate love. I believe in love.' His eyes darkened. 'I want love.'

Her breath grew choppy. 'Why?'

'Because what else is there—ultimately—when the money and the property and the air and water are all gone? What will we have to make us human if not love?'

Her laugh was watery. 'God, that's a dismal image. Is it supposed to make me feel better?'

He took her hands in his. 'It is. Because when we're old and grey and have spent every penny we have on living a life that enriches us, instead of hoarding it so we can feel rich, I will hold you in my arms and shield you from any more hurt or disappointment or loss, because that is what love is supposed to do.'

Her heart swelled up to constrict her air. She stared up at him. 'You love me?'

'Ingrid, you are more a part of me after our handful of hours together than the people I grew up with. I have a void inside me that is shaped just like you. I just didn't recognise the shape until I met you.'

Words simply would not come. But that was okay because Gabe was in full French romantic flight and he filled the silence for her.

'And every woman I dined with in the past year that wasn't you, every conversation I had that wasn't with you, every morning I woke up without you there, just made that void seem larger and more obvious.'

But naming her fear hadn't dispelled it. She took a tight breath. 'What if it doesn't work out?'

A dozen new creases appeared in his brow. 'How would we be any worse off?'

She shook her head. 'I used to be love's greatest

champion.' Back in the days of pink bedspreads and blissful ignorance and teen movies.

He scooped her hands into his. 'Let me champion it for you. You trusted me with your life in that tunnel. Won't you trust me with your heart?'

Trust.

Was that what this was all about? Trusting him? Trusting love? Was there anyone on this planet she had more faith in?

'Is it weird to be calling it love after just one week?' She threw up her final, desperate obstacle. After this there was nothing left.

Except potential so bright she dared not look at it.

He shrugged in that adorable French way of his. 'One year, one month and one week. I never stopped watching you, thinking about you. I never stopped loving you. Even if I didn't know that I'd started.'

'Never?'

He stepped closer. *'Jamais.'*

'What would have happened if I hadn't taken Cara's Christmas shifts?' she breathed.

He frowned. 'I'd like to think I would have come to you anyway. But I believed you'd walked away because I wasn't good enough. And until this week I concurred.'

'Oh, Gabe, you are *so* much better than me.'

He dipped his head. 'We'll have to agree to disagree.'

'Or you can let me spend the next twelve months proving you're wrong.' She pressed her lips against his fingers.

'I won't ever agree that you're anything but perfect.'

'Hardly.'

He chuckled. 'Look at that. Our first fight.' Then

he pulled her up hard against the warmth of his body. 'Some Christmas, *non*?'

She nodded and her cheek rubbed on his shirt. 'I missed it. But I was only hurting myself, really.' And probably her parents, without meaning to. 'Maybe we can do Christmas properly next year?'

'A tree? Gifts? Carols?'

She nodded. 'Family. Joy. Togetherness.'

He sighed. 'The Christmas holidays have always been a difficult time for me. Now they will always be the time that the woman I love came back to me.'

'I'll remind you of that every year.'

'I hope so. Until we're grey and old.'

She tipped her head up. 'And poor?'

'And rich,' he said, lowering his lips to hers again. 'With love.'

CHAPTER EIGHT

New Year's Eve

INGRID WENT HOME as soon as her shift was over, but this time it wasn't to avoid Gabe or to hide from him. It was to hurry back to him. Suddenly the best part of leaving was returning.

She knew she couldn't sit in front of the man she loved saturated with the rank smell of wild dog puppies and smeared with their dirt, and she feared she couldn't sit with him all through the day as their colleagues came and went and not be able to touch him again.

But while her shift should have started at eight p.m., her day—her new life—began instead. At a time when the last zoo staff had gone home and she could be alone with Gabe. She traded in her T-shirt and jeans for a soft skirt and blouse—casual enough to be appropriate, but feminine enough to be special. It had been a long, long time since she'd felt anything but beige.

Since she'd managed to check, vaccinate and micro-chip all eight pups the night before, Gabe had stayed on to finish voluntarily, going over her data and working on his study. But she wasn't about to let him leave that room without celebrating New Year's Eve since they'd both missed Christmas entirely.

She swung around the corner and nudged the door of the monitoring room with her basket.

Gabe tipped his head back in his seated position in front of the monitors, then tossed his notepad aside and swung to his feet as soon as he saw it was her. The concentration lines between his brows lifted and cleared, and the focus in his eyes was replaced with a different kind of interest.

Before she could speak he'd scooped her to him with one strong arm around her waist and pressed his hot lips to hers. The basket dangled from her suddenly weak fingers and nearly dropped—except he lowered her back to her feet just as it might have tumbled to the floor.

'I missed you,' he said.

'It was only a few hours.'

He shrugged. 'I miss you when I blink.'

Laughter bubbled up. 'Fool.'

As she said the word she remembered how sensitive he was to it, thanks to his father's careless wielding of it, and her stomach tightened with apology. But whatever it had meant to him before, it meant something new now.

His eyes blazed adoration. *Je suis stupide avec l'amour.*

'I'm going to have to learn more French,' she murmured between kisses, 'if you insist on whispering it to me.'

Non. He breathed on her neck. 'I like it that reciting a grocery list in my language can make you shiver.'

'Is that what you just did?'

'No.' His eyes grew serious. 'I said that I *am* a fool. For your love.'

Oh.

How was a girl supposed to focus on her picnic when

the man she adored said stuff like that? 'I thought we could have a picnic outside tonight. I unexpectedly find myself with no employment on New Year's Eve, and we'll be able to hear the concert from here.'

Ridiculous how nervous she felt. You'd think asking him on a quasi-date would be a no-brainer, given what had happened between them in the past.

But still her heart pounded as his eyes dropped to the basket. 'Is that what's in there? Food?'

'Multiple types. I didn't know what you might feel like.'

His lips twisted. 'How can I eat when my stomach can't settle when you're around?'

Her heart swelled stupidly. 'Oh, please. Does that work on French girls?'

'I wouldn't know. I've not said it before.' Then his hand slid down over hers to relieve her of the heavy basket. 'And that's because I've not felt it before.'

Okay, so it was getting harder and harder to doubt the whole love thing when he said things like that and while such sincerity bled from his eyes.

'Well, I have a basket full of French cheese already. I don't need more of it from you.'

His smile graduated into a full laugh. 'Let's go. I can pack up the monitoring gear later.'

Walking out together felt odd, and she realised that the last time they'd walked anywhere together had been that night thirteen months ago. She had the same breathless anticipation now.

'Where do you want to go? The picnic lawn?'

They could. It was what it was made for. Or they could go somewhere special.

Special to *them*.

'Would you mind if we went to the viewing bay?' There was a bench and a fold-down servery in the wild dog viewing bay that was used for private functions. No reason they couldn't have their own private party free of charge.

He smiled down at her. 'You still want to see it?'

They'd done ninety-five percent of their job but it didn't feel complete. The pups hadn't emerged from the den. She'd give the dogs one more chance before their watch officially ended. 'I really do.'

As they locked the night quarters behind them the band down by the river kicked into full amplified gear and Ingrid smiled at the popular dance song. Gabe swung the basket into his free hand and curled his fingers between hers.

Her smile broadened and her skin tingled just at that tiny innocent contact.

They walked around the long way, passing elephants and rhino and lion, rather than shortcutting through the staff accessways. The sounds of the riverside band merged with the snorts of the relaxed rhino, the throaty purr of the lions and the excited whoops of baboons. The recorded soundscape of an African wetland which played throughout the exhibit underpinned it all.

'I love this place at night,' she murmured. Especially this night. With Gabe. 'It's so beautiful.'

His lashes swept down over his high cheekbones as he dropped her an appreciative look. 'Doubly so this evening.'

She looked up at him as they entered the viewing bay. 'Are you flirting with me?'

'No need to flirt.' He chuckled. 'You already love me.'

So true, she thought as they unpacked their picnic

and spread the goodies out on a table. Motion sensors detected them and bathed the viewing bay in dim replicated moonlight.

There was more activity than usual from the pack—probably the result of the thumping bass line coming from outside the zoo. They raced each other around the exhibit and squabbled over prime sticks and old sacks. One kept racing around the front of A-den, making enticing play noises at its entrance, then dashing off, unrewarded, to the other side of the exhibit.

'I wanted to thank you, Ingrid,' Gabe said seriously, when the dogs' playing dropped off a little.

She turned to him, stretched out on the bench next to her. 'What for?'

'Officially for doing such a good job with the identification and vaccination. I couldn't have asked for a better watch partner.'

'And unofficially?'

He nudged her gently with his foot. 'Unofficially for reminding me of what's best about what we do. About why we do it.'

She tipped her head. 'You needed reminding?'

'I was starting to. My father's voice sometimes echoes extra loud in my consciousness.' He nodded out into the exhibit. 'That's why we do it. Every animal here is why we do it.'

'And you do it better than most.'

'I could say the same of you.'

'I hope you will when I put in for the primate vacancy.'

He sat up straighter. 'What vacancy?'

'It will be announced after New Year. I got a call

from the section supervisor this morning, encouraging me to apply.'

'You're going to?'

'Yes. I only missed out by a small margin before—to some French guy.' She wrinkled her nose at him. 'So I'm ready to give it another shot.'

'Two zookeepers in the family? We're going to have to get a pet.'

Her gasp was partly disguised under the dogs' roughhousing, which had moved to the part of the exhibit closest to them. 'In the *family?*'

A hint of colour bled up his throat. 'In our future family.'

She kept her eyes on his. 'We have a family in our future?'

His eyes grew cautious. 'Don't we?'

Did they? She'd only just found her way back to him. 'I'm not sure I'm ready to share you yet.'

'Not yet. But the day will come when one of me is just not enough.'

Suddenly she had a vision of a miniature version of Gabe, running around a big backyard, chattering in a mix of English and French. It was as close to a picket fence as she'd ever let herself imagine. And she didn't hate it.

At all.

The tightness in her chest was hope, not dread.

'I'd be willing to consider a dog in a few months. As practice. I find myself strangely drawn to them all of a sudden.'

He scooted up behind her on the long bench and pulled her back into him. 'Based on your performance last night, I think you've more than earned the opportunity,' he breathed into her hair.

They sat like that for long silent moments, both absorbing the import of what they'd just said. *A family in their future...*

The thoughtful silence descended again.

In the exhibit, two dogs took their rough-housing to the den entrance and paid an unnatural amount of attention to it—then unexpectedly one disappeared down the hole entirely. Barely a moment passed until it scrabbled back out, with Mjawi in close pursuit. She stepped aside at the entrance and looked over to where Gabe and Ingrid sat, instantly identifying the scent of both predator and food. She moved to the top of the den and flopped down there to keep an eye on them.

The smaller of the playing adults stuck its front half in the den entrance again, its tail wagging furiously. Then it began to back out, and a tiny shadow appeared.

Ingrid sat up straight. 'Gabe!'

The shadow sat right on the edge of the hole, catching its breath from the climb up the tunnel, then disappeared back into the den.

Ingrid's heart sank.

Gabe wrapped his arms around her and tucked her closer in to him. 'Keep watching.'

Sure enough it was back just a moment later, with another tiny shadow in tow. A second pup! Ingrid swallowed her cry and held her breath.

Two, then three, then five.

Suddenly the whole slope leading to the den entrance was alive with tiny, tubby black shapes, finding their feet and blinking up into the moonlight as their older cousins enticed them into play. All eight of them had emerged.

The alpha male sauntered over and nosed each pup roughly, as if making sure they knew who was boss, and then he, too, flopped down to keep guard on his suddenly vulnerable offspring.

Their milk-round bellies were fuller now than when Ingrid had weighed them, and practically dragged on the ground between their stumpy, dark little legs, but they made do and wobbled around in the dirt, sniffing and exploring and romping with each other, and briefly with the bigger members of the pack.

'Won't they hurt them?' Ingrid asked, worried by the unevenly matched playmates.

'They'll protect them with their lives. Literally, if necessary. That's the beauty of wild dogs.'

She shook the gathering tears free. 'That's the beauty of family.'

He pressed his lips to her hair.

'I'd really like you to meet my parents,' she blurted into the night. 'All four of them.'

She'd almost let fear drive a wedge between her two families. And she was that wedge. But she was also the only one who could hold the two together. She felt his nod in the subtle move of the torso pressed into her back.

'And I'd really like you *not* to meet mine.'

Her snort wasn't very gracious. 'And I was so looking forward to explaining the difference between zoos and circuses to your father.'

'One day, perhaps.' The chuckle vibrated against her scalp. 'With me at your back.'

She threaded her fingers more tightly through his

and felt a surge of protectiveness as powerful as Mjawi had shown for her pups. 'Or with me at yours.'

'Really?' His voice grew grave. 'You'd come with me?'

She tipped her head back and met the gaze directed down on her. 'Always, Gabe. And anywhere.'

His Adam's apple lurched twice before he tipped his face down and found her lips. Their kiss lasted an age, and when he lifted his face again his eyes were narrow. 'Or do you just want to meet my handsome brothers?'

As she laughed, the sky exploded in fireworks from the direction of the river and all eight pups dived straight back into the den, causing a tubby puppy-jam at the entrance. Mjawi got to her feet, as did the alpha male, but the other dogs carried on romping as the crackle and hiss of the overhead light show went on and bright colours showered down over the river.

Ingrid stretched up her arms to hook them around Gabe's neck and drag his mouth down to hers. He resisted at the very last moment.

'Happy New Year, *mon amour*,' he whispered.

The face she adored above all others blocked out the light from the spectacular light show happening just outside of the zoo's gates, and within moments her pulse thrumming past her eardrums blocked out even the dull cracks and pops overhead.

She smiled and pulled harder on his neck until their mouths touched, so that he could feel her words against the lips she was coming to love so very much.

'Merry Christmas, Gabe.'

* * * * *

REQUEST YOUR
FREE BOOKS!

2 FREE NOVELS
FROM THE ROMANCE COLLECTION
PLUS 2 FREE GIFTS!

YES! Please send me 2 FREE novels from the Romance Collection and my 2 FREE gifts (gifts are worth about $10). After receiving them, if I don't wish to receive any more books, I can return the shipping statement marked "cancel." If I don't cancel, I will receive 4 brand-new novels every month and be billed just $6.24 per book in the U.S. or $6.74 per book in Canada. That's a savings of at least 22% off the cover price. It's quite a bargain! Shipping and handling is just 50¢ per book in the U.S. and 75¢ per book in Canada.* I understand that accepting the 2 free books and gifts places me under no obligation to buy anything. I can always return a shipment and cancel at any time. Even if I never buy another book, the two free books and gifts are mine to keep forever.

194/394 MDN F4XY

Name _____

(PLEASE PRINT)

Address _____ Apt. # _____

City _____ State/Prov. _____ Zip/Postal Code _____

Signature (if under 18, a parent or guardian must sign)

Mail to the Harlequin® Reader Service:
IN U.S.A.: P.O. Box 1867, Buffalo, NY 14240-1867
IN CANADA: P.O. Box 609, Fort Erie, Ontario L2A 5X3

Want to try two free books from another line?
Call 1-800-873-8635 or visit www.ReaderService.com.

* Terms and prices subject to change without notice. Prices do not include applicable taxes. Sales tax applicable in N.Y. Canadian residents will be charged applicable taxes. Offer not valid in Quebec. This offer is limited to one order per household. Not valid for current subscribers to the Romance Collection or the Romance/Suspense Collection. All orders subject to credit approval. Credit or debit balances in a customer's account(s) may be offset by any other outstanding balance owed by or to the customer. Please allow 4 to 6 weeks for delivery. Offer available while quantities last.

Your Privacy—The Harlequin® Reader Service is committed to protecting your privacy. Our Privacy Policy is available online at www.ReaderService.com or upon request from the Harlequin Reader Service.

We make a portion of our mailing list available to reputable third parties that offer products we believe may interest you. If you prefer that we not exchange your name with third parties, or if you wish to clarify or modify your communication preferences, please visit us at www.ReaderService.com/consumerschoice or write to us at Harlequin Reader Service Preference Service, P.O. Box 9062, Buffalo, NY 14269. Include your complete name and address.

ROM13R

HARLEQUIN®
Romance

Next month, Harlequin Romance bestselling
author **Susan Meier** brings you her
heartwarming romance

Single Dad's Christmas Miracle

Recently widowed Clark Beaumont is trying
to make it through the holidays for the sake of
his kids. But with his son failing at school and
his little girl talking only in whispers, he needs
nothing short of a miracle…. Is Althea Johnson
the miracle he's been hoping for?

Look for

Single Dad's Christmas Miracle,
coming next month from Harlequin Romance!

Available wherever books and ebooks are sold.

HARLEQUIN®

SPECIAL EDITION

Life, Love and Family

New! From *New York Times* bestselling author
Rachel Lee

THANKSGIVING DADDY—the next installment in
the *Conard County* miniseries

An Unexpected Family...

Pilot Edie Clapton saves navy SEAL Seth Hardin's
life—and they celebrate with a passionate encounter.
Little does Edie know she has a bundle of joy on the
way...and possibly the love of a lifetime.

Look for THANKSGIVING DADDY next month, from
New York Times bestselling author Rachel Lee.

*Available in November
from Harlequin® Special Edition® ,
wherever books are sold.*

HSE65777

Don't miss the first book in The Legend of Bailey's Cove trilogy!

In the sleepy, picturesque town of Bailey's Cove, Maine, restaurateur Mia Parker and anthropologist Daniel MacCarey discover each other while dealing with a two-hundred-year-old skeleton found in her wall. The attraction between Mia and Daniel is immediate and irresistible, but an unyielding darkness from his past stands between them and love.

Better Than Gold
by **Mary Brady**

AVAILABLE IN NOVEMBER

HARLEQUIN®

A *Romance* FOR EVERY MOOD™

Love the Harlequin book you just read?

Your opinion matters.

Review this book on your favorite book site, review site, blog or your own social media properties and share your opinion with other readers!

Be sure to connect with us at:
Harlequin.com/Newsletters
Facebook.com/HarlequinBooks
Twitter.com/HarlequinBooks

HARLEQUIN®

A *Romance* FOR EVERY MOOD™

Stay up-to-date on all your romance-reading news with the *Harlequin Shopping Guide*, featuring bestselling authors, exciting new miniseries, books to watch and more!

The newest issue will be delivered right to you with our compliments! There are 4 each year.

Signing up is easy.

EMAIL

ShoppingGuide@Harlequin.ca

WRITE TO US

HARLEQUIN BOOKS
Attention: Customer Service Department
P.O. Box 9057, Buffalo, NY 14269-9057

OR PHONE

1-800-873-8635 in the United States
1-888-343-9777 in Canada

Please allow 4-6 weeks for delivery of the first issue by mail.